A *LIBRARY JOURNAL* BEST BOOK OF THE YEAR

Praise for Jennifer Close's

$\mathcal{G}$irls in White Dresses

"Close's witty voice . . . charts the romantic shenanigans of a bevy of New York women in their twenties, before career success or Botoxed foreheads. Dating is a phenomenon to be analyzed in improvised group therapy over cocktails."
—*The New York Times*

"The one book that I will be recommending over and over again to all of my friends. I laughed, I cried, I nodded knowingly. . . . I can't remember the last time I loved a book as much as this one." —Allison Winn Scotch,
New York Times-bestselling author
of *The One That I Want*

"Close straddles the line between melancholy and breeziness as she chronicles the exploits of recent college grads trying to make it in New York City. . . . Hints at something deeper and truer: not just the adventure of being young, but the unmooring of it, too." —*Entertainment Weekly*

"[An] irresistible, pitch-perfect first novel." —*Marie Claire*

JENNIFER CLOSE

Girls in White Dresses

Jennifer Close was born and raised on the North Shore of Chicago. She is a graduate of Boston College and received her MFA in Fiction Writing from the New School in 2005. She worked in New York in magazines for many years and then in Washington, D.C., as a bookseller. *Girls in White Dresses* is her first book.

Girls in White Dresses

JENNIFER CLOSE

ANCHOR CANADA

Library and Archives Canada Cataloguing in Publication

Close, Jennifer
    Girls in white dresses / Jennifer Close.

ISBN 978-0-385-67644-1

    I. Title.

PS3603.L67G57 2012   813'.6   C2011-908568-2

Cover art: Mayer George Vladimirovich/Shutterstock
Cover design: Abby Weintraub

Printed and bound in the USA

Published in Canada by Anchor Canada,
a division of Random House of Canada Limited

Visit Random House of Canada Limited's website: www.randomhouse.ca

10   9   8   7   6   5   4   3   2   1

TO M & D

with love

Contents

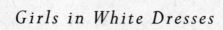

Girls in White Dresses

The Rules of Life

Isabella's sister, Molly, was married with ten bridesmaids in matching tea-length, blue floral Laura Ashley dresses. It was, Isabella believed, the most beautiful wedding anyone would ever have. She was twelve.

"More beautiful than Princess Diana," her mother told Molly that morning as she helped her get dressed.

"I need more bobby pins," her sister replied.

Isabella sat on the bed with her hair in a tight French braid. Early that morning, the hairdresser had teased and twisted her hair back, stuck baby's breath in it, and sprayed it with an entire can of hairspray. From the side, it looked like a plant was growing out of her head. She kept touching it lightly to make sure the braid was still there, and every time she did, she was surprised at the crispiness of her hair.

"Isabella," Molly said. "If you keep touching your hair, you're going to ruin it." Isabella put her hand in her lap and watched Molly fluff her own crispy hair. Molly stared at herself in the mirror until her face got white. "I feel funny," she said. "A little sick."

Isabella walked downstairs, where she saw her mom running around like a crazy person and her dad walking briskly and trying to look busy so he wouldn't get yelled at. "Molly thinks she's going to throw up," she announced. Her mom took the stairs two at a time to get to Molly. Her dad gave her a little smile with no teeth, and continued his pacing.

The Mack family had been getting ready for this wedding for over a year. It was all they talked about, all they thought about. It was getting tiresome. Isabella's parents wanted everything to be perfect. They'd had the trim on the house repainted and the garden redone. "What's the point?" Isabella asked. "No one's going to see the house." Her parents just shook their heads at her and Molly rolled her eyes.

Isabella's mother and father went on a diet. They walked every morning and ate fish for dinner. When Isabella's dad ordered a steak or put butter on his bread, her mom would shake her head and say, "Oh, Frank."

"What's the difference?" Isabella asked. "No one's going to be looking at you guys." As soon as she said it, Isabella felt bad. She hadn't realized how mean the words sounded until they were out of her mouth, which had been happening a lot recently. It surprised Isabella, how nasty she could be without even trying.

Isabella's mother hung the wedding picture in the front hall. It was the first thing people saw when they walked into the Mack house. If you looked at it quickly, it was just a blur of blue dresses and big hair. As the years went by, it began to look like something you would see in a magazine, in an article titled "Fashion Mistakes of the Early '90s." Even the faces in the picture seemed to change. The bridesmaids began to look embarrassed to be caught in such blue dresses. But there was nothing they could do about it. They were trapped there, framed for the whole world to see.

"Whoa," Isabella's friends would say when they saw it.

"I know," Isabella would say. "It's horrendous."

Before Isabella moved to New York, her mom made her clean out her closet. "There are things in there that you haven't worn in years," she said. "Let's get it all cleaned out and I'll give it to the Salvation Army." She said it in an upbeat voice like it would be a fun thing to do. "You'll feel so much better when it's done," her mother added.

"I really doubt that," Isabella said.

Isabella sorted through old notebooks and shoes. She threw out T-shirts from high school sports teams and collages she'd made in junior high. In the back of her closet she found the blue floral beast. It was even worse in person. Isabella thought the color would have faded over the years, but it was just as vivid as ever. She held it up for a moment and then brought it to the dress-up chest in the playroom. Maybe her nieces would like to play with it. She shoved it in with the pirate costumes and princess dresses and forgot about it.

New York in September was busy, like everyone was in a hurry to get back to real life after the lazy summer. Isabella liked the feeling of it, the rushing around, and she let herself get swept along the sidewalks. She walked quickly, trotting beside the crowds of people, like she had somewhere important to be, too, like she was part of the productivity of the city, when really she was just going to Bed Bath & Beyond to get a shower curtain.

Isabella had decided to move to New York because she didn't have a plan, and New York seemed like a good one. Her friend Mary was moving there to go to Columbia Law. When Mary announced this, Isabella was floored. "You got into Columbia?" she asked. "How?"

"Thanks a lot," Mary said. But Isabella knew she didn't really care. It wasn't that she thought Mary was dumb. She just didn't know when Mary had found the time to make a life plan, study for the LSATs, and apply to schools. Isabella had barely finished her final photography project senior year.

"That's not what I meant," Isabella told her. She thought for a moment, and then she said, "Maybe I'll move to New York too." Isabella hadn't considered this before, but as soon as she said it, she knew it was a good idea. She had a roommate and a city all picked out, and that was something.

Isabella told her parents that she was moving to New York. She expected them to ask more questions, to want to know the details of what she planned to do there. But Isabella was the youngest of six, and her parents were not nostalgic about their children moving out of the house. Each time one of their children left, another one returned, and they had started to think they would never be alone again. "New York sounds great," they told her. "We'll help you pay rent until you find a job."

Isabella was almost insulted, but she understood. They wanted her out of the house and on her own, so that she didn't end up like her brother Brett, who graduated from college and then moved back home for two years, where he spent most of his time playing video games in his pajamas. During those two years, her parents had many whispered conversations where her dad said things like, "Five years to graduate from that college, and the kid's just going to sit around here and pick his nose? Not on my watch."

The apartment that Isabella and Mary found was barely bigger than Isabella's bedroom at home, but the broker told them this was as good as it would get. "For this neighborhood," she said, "with a doorman, this is the size you can expect." She sounded bored, like she'd given this speech to thousands of girls just like them, who were shocked at the amount they would have to pay to get their own shabby little corner in the city. The broker didn't really care if they took it or not, because she knew there was a long list of girls just like them, fresh to the city and desperate for a place to live. If they didn't take it, surely one of the others would.

Isabella and Mary signed the lease and moved into the apartment, which had gray walls that were supposed to be white and a crack in the ceiling that ran from the front door all the way to the back windows. When Isabella stood in the bathroom, she could hear the upstairs neighbors brushing their teeth and talking about their day. They were from somewhere in the South, and their accents made everything more amusing. Isabella often found herself sitting on the side of the tub, her own toothbrush in hand, task forgotten, listening to one of the girls talk about a date she'd been on. Sometimes the neighbors smoked cigarettes in their bathroom, and the smoke traveled down the vent, seeping into Isabella's bathroom and making the air hazy.

They hung mirrors on the walls to make the apartment seem bigger, and put up bright yellow curtains to distract from the grayness. They put up a fake wall to make Mary's bedroom, a slim rectangle that held her bed and desk and not much else. The wall was thin and Isabella could hear when Mary sneezed or turned a page. Mary was always shut up in her room working, which drove Isabella crazy.

"What are you doing?" she'd ask through the wall.

"Studying," Mary always replied.

"Again?" Isabella would ask. Mary would sigh.

"Yep. Again."

After the first month, Mary started to go to the library more. "I'm too easily distracted," she told Isabella. It was quieter in the apartment with Mary gone so much, but Isabella never really felt lonely. And if she did, she'd go to the bathroom and listen to her neighbors chat, breathing in their smoke and laughing along with them as they said things like "Y'all knew he was a bump on a log" and "Back that train up!"

Isabella got a job as an assistant, working for two high-level executives at a mailing-list company. She wasn't sure what they did exactly, but she did know that they called her their "executive assistant" and that her main job every morning was to get Bill a corn muffin with raspberry jelly and to get Sharon a chocolate chip muffin. Bill asked for his muffin, and Sharon did not. This was part of the game. Each morning, when Isabella placed the muffin on Sharon's desk, she said, "Oh, I shouldn't!" but she still ate it. "I was just getting Bill's muffin and I thought maybe you'd want one?" Isabella would say in response. As long as she did this, they seemed happy.

Isabella's days and weeks fell into a routine, but she always felt like there was something else she should be doing, something better that was waiting for her. Sometimes on Saturday afternoons, she and Mary went to the park across the street and ate hot dogs in the sun. Mary always brought her textbooks with her, and took notes and read. Isabella just stared at people.

"This is the first fall that I haven't gone to school," Isabella said to her once.

"Mmm-hmmm," Mary said. She turned a page and uncapped a highlighter.

"Maybe that's why I feel so weird all the time," Isabella said.

"Maybe," Mary said. She filled the whole page with yellow smudges and Isabella was jealous of her. She didn't want to go to law school, but Mary had purpose and assignments and for that Isabella envied her. All Isabella had was two bosses who just wanted muffins. And sometimes jelly.

Their friends from college, Kristi and Abby, lived in the same building as they did. Kristi was the one who'd recommended it to them. "You have to live in a doorman building," she'd said to Isabella, as though it was something everyone already knew. "It's not safe otherwise." Sometimes Isabella went out with them, but they exhausted her. Kristi and Abby always wanted to get dressed up and go out for sushi or go to a party where you had to have your name on a list to get in. They both worked in PR and all they talked about was events and RSVPs, which Kristi pronounced "Risvips" for some reason. "I can get you on the list," Kristi would often say to Isabella. Isabella didn't want a list. She just wanted to get a drink.

Sometimes, if she was lucky, Isabella could convince Mary to go out. They usually just went to Gamekeepers, the bar right down the street. "Come on," Isabella would say. "It's so close! We can be there in two minutes and have a drink and be home in an hour." She always hoped, of course, that once they got there Mary would stay out later, but getting her out was the first step.

Gamekeepers was a brightly lit bar, with neon signs on the walls and a black-and-white tiled floor. In the back room, there was a whole wall of bookshelves crammed full of every board game ever made. The first night that Isabella and Mary went there, they stood in front of the wall and stared at all of the games. The bar had all of the big hits—Scrabble, Trivial Pursuit, Monopoly—and some older games too, like Operation, Boggle, Life, and Sorry!

"Whoa," Mary said, as they stared at the shelves. "This is crazy." All around them, people were playing games on long wooden tables, rolling dice and slapping cards.

"Oh my God," Isabella said. She pulled a box off the shelf. "Look, they have Pig Mania. I can't believe it."

"What is that?" Mary asked. She looked at the box.

"It's this game, from the seventies, I think. You roll pig dice and get scores for different things."

"Weird," Mary said.

"The seventies were weird," Isabella said. "Come on, let's play."

They rolled the pigs, but Isabella could tell that Mary wasn't into it. Two guys came over to join them, which was encouraging at first, but then they started snorting and squealing when the pigs rolled into any position that looked dirty. "I got Makin' Bacon!" Isabella screamed, and they just snorted louder. One of them was so drunk that he kept swaying and bumping into the table, causing their drinks to spill and the pigs to topple.

"I think we should go," Mary said. She stared at one of the snorters. "I have to get up early to study anyway."

"Fine," Isabella said. She surrendered the pigs to the boys so that they could roll them alone.

"You're leaving?" the drunk one said. He closed his eyes and Isabella wondered if he had fallen asleep, and then he opened them and repeated his question. "You're leaving?"

"Yeah," Isabella said. Mary was waiting for her by the door. "I have a lot of things to do tomorrow," she said. "Just a really busy day."

Isabella met a boy named Ben and went on a date. She wanted something to fill her empty weekend days when Mary was studying and Kristi and Abby did things that Isabella had no interest in, like going to the gym or shopping in SoHo. Isabella went to the gym with them once, and Kristi wore earrings and a necklace while she ran on the treadmill, which bothered Isabella so much that she couldn't ever bring herself to go back again.

"I've never been on a date before," Isabella said to Mary as she got ready that night.

"You've been on plenty of dates," Mary said.

"No," Isabella said. "I've been out to eat with boys who were my boyfriend, but that's not dating. That's just parallel eating."

Mary looked up from her books and tilted her head. "Parallel eating," she said. "Huh. Sometimes I think you should have been a lawyer."

Isabella and Ben starting spending a lot of time together, but he never really wanted to do anything. He was fine sitting on the couch in their apartment. "Maybe we should go out?" Isabella would suggest. "To a museum or the zoo or something?" Ben just laughed at her and patted her knee.

She and Ben went to bars with flip-cup tables and jukeboxes that played Neil Diamond. They danced on floors covered with sawdust and drank shots with clever names like Baby Guinnesses and Buttery Nipples. On the weekdays, they'd drag themselves out of bed, get bagels at the corner, and head off to work on different subways. On the weekends, they'd stay in bed for most of the day, getting up in the late afternoon to get brunch.

They mostly stayed at Isabella's apartment, because Ben's

place smelled like ramen and feet and had a sign over the door that said "Beware Pickpockets and Loose Women." He had two roommates, large looming boys who sat on the couch in their boxers and were always eating huge bowls of cereal and watching ESPN. They didn't seem to mind Isabella's presence, but they didn't really notice her either. Any conversation she tried to start with them usually ended in a grunt, and so she was happy that Ben preferred her apartment.

Ben slept easily in her bed, his mouth open, covers kicked off. Sometimes Isabella woke up with a headache and hated him for being able to sleep. Sometimes she crept into Mary's room and got into bed with her. "He's snoring," she'd whisper. And Mary would grunt and roll over.

The more Ben stayed there, though, the more time Mary spent at the library. Their apartment, which was cramped with two of them, could barely hold three. Isabella got the sense that Mary was getting more and more annoyed at her, pointing out that the garbage was full, saying things like "I guess I'll go get more toilet paper, again," and shutting her door extra hard when she came home. Once, in the middle of the night, Ben left the toilet seat up and Mary fell in as she sat down. Isabella tried to make it up to her, cleaning the bathroom and buying candy. She could tell that Mary appreciated her efforts, but the apartment remained crowded, and still sometimes caused Mary to sigh loudly or snap about the dishes, depending on the day.

Isabella was surprised to find that she could do her job in a constantly hungover state. She wasn't sure if this was a wonderful discovery or a sign that she should run. Either way, her performance reviews were superb.

"Stick with me for one year and you'll go places," Bill always said to her. He had a big stomach and ate Greek salad for lunch every day, which made him smell like onions, always. Isabella knew that he thought the Greek salad was super healthy, and for that she pitied him. She also wished he didn't smell like he did.

Sharon was less direct. "I got a run in my panty hose," she would announce. Then she would stand and stare at Isabella, making a face that said, *What should we do about the pickle we're in?* until Isabella offered to go get her new ones.

Standing in Duane Reade, picking out someone else's panty hose, Isabella thought, "This is really happening." She chose a control-top package and went to the counter to pay.

In late October, Isabella's sister, Molly, brought her two girls to the city for the day. They came on the train from Philadelphia, wearing matching plaid jumpers and clutching American Girl dolls. Molly insisted that they come to Isabella's apartment so that she could see where she was living. They all stood in the TV room and looked around. Missy and Caroline used the bathroom and sat on Isabella's bed.

"It's very efficient," Molly said, and gathered up her things to go.

As they walked down the street, Missy, the older one, told Isabella about their trip in. "There was a man sleeping outside the train station," she said. "He made some bad choices in life."

"Really?" Isabella asked. She looked at Molly out of the corners of her eyes.

"Yeah," Missy said. She grabbed Caroline's arm and started offering advice. "Watch out for dog poop on the sidewalk," she said. "Don't look at anyone, or they'll take you."

"Missy, no one is going to take you guys," Isabella said. Missy, who was nine, shook her head like Isabella was stupid. "They told us about it in class, Auntie Iz. There are kidnappers everywhere, but especially in New York."

All of Isabella's nieces and nephews called her Auntie Iz, a ridiculous nickname given to her by her oldest brother when he had his first baby. It made her sound like some wicked aunt in a fairy tale, like a forgotten character from *The Wizard of Oz*.

Missy stood there with pursed lips and wide eyes, as though she wanted to warn Isabella of the dangers of New York. Missy was a clone of Molly, and sometimes, even though she was only nine, it was hard to like her. Isabella bent down to Caroline. "No one's going to take you," she whispered in her ear. Caroline smiled.

They trekked around American Girl Place, watched a movie, bought some new outfits, and had tea with the dolls. Caroline's doll had a Mohawk in the front, where she had tried to cut the bangs. "I wanted her bangs to be gone," Caroline explained. She touched her forehead. "Like mine."

"That's why she's not allowed to get another doll for at least a year," Missy said. She fed her doll some tea. "Because five-year-olds don't really know how to take care of them."

After tea, Ben met them in Central Park and chased the girls around like a monster, while Molly and Isabella sat on a bench. "He looks like a keeper," Molly said. She elbowed Isabella. "Maybe this is the one?"

Isabella sighed. Molly had been trying to marry her off since she was in seventh grade.

"You know, Isabella, you need to make sure that he still respects you. The only thing a girl has is her reputation."

"Oh my God," Isabella said. "Molly, please stop."

"You can listen to me now or learn it on your own later," Molly said.

"If you talk about the cows and the milk, I'm done," Isabella said. "You sound just like Mom."

Missy came running up to them, her hair escaping from her ponytail and her cheeks flushed. She looked adorable, and for a moment, Isabella wanted to grab her in a big hug. Then Missy said, "Ben is so funny." She turned and smiled at Isabella. "I hope you marry him."

Missy leaned in close to Molly and whispered something. She looked concerned, but Molly told her not to worry. Missy ran back to Ben, who raised his arms and started stomping toward her. She squealed and ran.

Molly said, "Missy just asked me if you were poor. She asked if you needed to move in with us. She said she's never seen a place to live that's so small." Then Molly tilted her head back and laughed and laughed with her mouth open so wide that Isabella could see her fillings.

ॐ

Isabella had always thought that New York would be devoid of animals, but that wasn't true. They were everywhere. They were just the kind of animals you didn't want to see. "I read somewhere that in New York you're never more than five feet away from vermin," Mary said. This knowledge haunted Isabella. The building posted a sign-up sheet once a month for exterminators, and each time the list went up, it was immediately filled with capitalized, underlined descriptions of what people needed to get rid of. "MICE!!!" the list read. "ROACHES AGAIN!!!" it said.

Isabella and Mary could hear scratching between their walls, and they were sure it was a mouse, although they'd never seen him. "I hear it," Isabella would say. They named him Brad and pretended he was the only mouse in the place. When he scratched at night, it made Isabella squirm in her bed. If she heard him, she wouldn't get up until it was morning, afraid that she'd run into him on her way to the bathroom. Even if she had to pee, she'd wait. The mouse was probably giving her a bladder infection.

Because their apartment was approximately a hundred degrees on any given day, the sliding windows had to be left open. They had no screens, so very often Isabella woke up to the butt of a pigeon facing her. They called the pigeon Pete, and tried to figure out why he only came to Isabella's window. Pete perched there almost every morning and cooed and pooped on her windowsill. It was possibly the grossest thing she could imagine.

"Pete, get out of here!" she would scream.

"Don't yell at him," Mary would say. "You're going to scare him and he'll fly into the apartment."

Isabella thought she was overreacting, until one morning when she screamed at Pete and he flew backward into her room. She ran to get Mary, who grabbed a broom and slammed Isabella's door shut. She was always good in these types of situations.

"Okay," she said. "When we open the door, you run to the window and open it as far as it will go. I'll shoo him out."

"You're so brave," Isabella told her.

It took almost an hour and a lot of screaming, but Pete found his way back outside. They stood sweating and panting, shaking their heads at each other. "I never thought there'd be so much wildlife in New York," Isabella said.

"Me neither," Mary said.

ß

Ben took the train to Philadelphia with her for Thanksgiving. He ate turkey and played with the kids and was charming in a way she hadn't known he could be. Isabella's mom insisted on wrapping up loads of leftover pie for Ben. They took the train back together and he rested his hand on her thigh the whole way. The week after, she didn't hear from him once, and she wondered if she'd imagined the whole holiday.

ß

It got colder, but their apartment still hovered around a hundred degrees. In Rockefeller Center, families of five came to see the tree, and walked around holding hands in a line, forcing Isabella to dart around them on her way to work. It was like one big game of Red Rover, and Isabella felt sure that she was losing.

Isabella went home for Christmas alone, with two bags of dirty laundry. The night before she left, she and Ben went out to get drinks. They laughed and had fun, and as they stopped for pizza on the way home from the bar, Isabella began to think she was wrong to imagine that there was any trouble between them.

Later that night, as Ben played with her hair in bed, she let out a happy sigh and he said, "My ex-girlfriend used to make me play with her hair before she fell asleep." Isabella pulled away from him, but his fingers were tangled in her hair and he ended up pulling out a few strands.

"What?" Ben asked.

"Nothing," Isabella said. How could she explain what he did to her? She let him lie there, holding the hair he'd torn out of her head, and think about it.

Christmas at the Mack house was loud and busy. Stuffed reindeer peeked out from the corners, and Scotch tape and snickerdoodles were everywhere. All of the grown-ups played board games while the kids ran around upstairs. It was safer that way, Isabella knew. Mack board-game nights weren't for children.

The night before Christmas Eve, they played Scattegories, and things were already getting messy. Her brother John was mad because he'd brought Cranium to play but had been overruled. "I don't think we should play anything that involves clay," Brett said.

"Yeah," Isabella said. "It might get physical."

There were twelve players, so it was impossible to tell if anyone was cheating. Isabella's partner, her sister-in-law Meg, chugged appletinis all night and taunted the other teams. "Whooo!" she kept squealing. "Wooohoo! We are going to kick your asses." Then she held up her hand and made Isabella give her a high five.

Isabella's mother had banned all premade pitchers of drinks

after the pomegranate martini incident of Thanksgiving 1998, but someone must have forgotten. When Isabella had walked into the kitchen that night, she'd seen a big pitcher of unnaturally green liquid. "Appletinis," Meg had said brightly. "Do you want one?" It was the last complete sentence she said that night. Isabella's brother Joseph quietly ignored his appletini-loving wife, leaving Isabella to high-five her alone.

Brett had barely spoken since he'd tried to submit "whore" in the category of "things that are sticky." Isabella's mother had exclaimed, "Sweet Jesus" and closed her eyes in horror. Never mind that the letter for that round was *H,* and Isabella's mother should have been concerned that her twenty-seven-year-old son couldn't spell.

Molly talked about Ben, and Isabella regretted ever introducing him to her family. "He was so cute with the girls," Molly was saying. "Just really adorable."

Isabella saw Caroline run by in a flash of blue, and soon all of the kids were rumbling downstairs from the playroom. Most of them were in costumes, and carrying plastic teacups for reasons they never explained. Scattegories was forgotten. Molly suggested that all of the kids could sleep in Isabella's room, as a treat, but only if Isabella agreed, of course.

"Can we, Auntie Iz?" they asked her. "Can we sleep in your room?"

Isabella looked at Molly, who didn't look back. "Sure," Isabella said. "You can sleep in my room."

Caroline cheered, then tripped herself on the long blue dress she was wearing and started crying. Isabella picked her up and held her in her lap. Caroline had always been her favorite. When she tried to whisper, she talked right into people's mouths. Last Thanksgiving, when she'd dropped a drumstick on the floor, she'd said, "Fuck it." And when Molly had asked her where she'd learned that word, she shrugged and said, "Grandma Kathy."

"Did you get me a present, Iz?" Caroline asked.

"Caroline, that's rude," Missy said. She patted Isabella's arm. "Auntie Iz doesn't need to get us presents." Missy, still worried about Isabella's possible poverty, treated her like a homeless person that the family had taken in.

Molly looked over at her girls, and her eyes narrowed at Caroline's costume. "Is that my bridesmaid dress?" Molly asked.

"No," Isabella said. "That's my bridesmaid dress."

Molly rolled her eyes up at the ceiling. "You know what I mean. Caroline, where did you get that?"

"In the dress-up chest," Caroline said.

Molly turned to Isabella. "How did that get in there?"

"What else was I supposed to do with it?" Isabella asked. "Goodwill wouldn't take it." Brett laughed from across the room and Molly narrowed her eyes.

"They were very in at the time," Molly said. "You don't remember, but those dresses were the thing to wear."

"I'm sure they were," Isabella said. "That dress has been in the dress-up chest forever, by the way." Caroline watched Isabella and Molly talk, turning her head as each one spoke.

Isabella could tell that Molly wanted to say more, but she turned away and took a sip of her wine. Isabella took the kids upstairs to get them settled in her room, and she heard Molly talking in the kitchen. "So, Missy thought that Izzy was poor," she said. She laughed loudly. "I know! Do you believe it?"

ॐ

There were so many bodies in Isabella's bed that she was afraid it would break. Little kid limbs were everywhere. Four of her nieces were shoved into the bed, and Isabella kept waking up to feet and hands flying through the air. When she finally fell asleep, she woke up less than an hour later to screaming. Her nephew Connor had been locked in the closet. "You guys," Isabella said, but she couldn't get enough energy to really yell at them. Her nephews were blobs of shadows on the floor, and after she rescued Connor, she told them all to be quiet and go to sleep.

In the morning, all of the kids were gone except for Caroline, who sat on the bed talking to her orange teddy bear, explaining how Santa got into the house. Isabella smiled at her. "Where is everyone?" she asked.

"They went downstairs," she said. "I didn't want you to be alone." Caroline touched the top of Isabella's head with her chubby baby hand, and Isabella wondered how Molly had been able to produce such a sweet child when she was such a horrid person.

There was a missed call on her phone from Ben, but he hadn't left a message. Isabella had thought it would feel better to be home, away from him. But it didn't. She called him back and he didn't answer. She didn't leave a message.

ॐ

On Christmas Eve the whole family went to St. Anthony's to watch the pageant. Caroline was a nervous-looking cow, and waved her hoof as her mother snapped pictures like a spazzy paparazzo. The church was noisy, full of chattering and shuffling, until a pint-sized Jesus and a mini Mary walked out to the manger, and then the whole place became quiet.

Isabella still remembered being chosen to play Mary in fourth grade. Her teacher asked her to bring a doll for the baby Jesus, and she took the job very seriously. She went home and, after careful consideration, picked her Cabbage Patch Kid Rosco. She apologized to the others, and explained that Rosco was little and bald and right for the part. He would make a great Jesus.

Every night, Isabella would wash Rosco's head in the sink and then carefully dry it. She would dress him in his blue terry-cloth pajamas and tuck him into bed next to her. "You're going to play Jesus," she would whisper to him. "Don't be nervous," she would say. "You're going to be great."

The night she played Mary, she felt holy, as though she were a saint of some kind. "It was my holiest Christmas," she wrote in her diary.

On the altar, mini Mary said something to Caroline and then petted her as though she were a real cow. Caroline stared at the doll in the manger and Isabella felt something like jealousy. After the pageant, they all walked out into the cold air, their breath making white clouds as they wished everyone they saw a Merry Christmas, and Isabella thought that it didn't feel like Christmas at all. All the kids went to their own houses to wait for Santa, and in her bed that night, Isabella missed the sound of other people's breathing.

Back in New York, everything was cold and slushy. "At least the snow was pretty for a minute or two, right?" Isabella asked

Mary. Mary just shook her head and closed her door. She had a head cold and new classes to deal with.

Ben was around less and less, and when they were together they seemed to squabble. "Don't put all your chickens in one pot," Kristi advised her. "That boy wasn't for you anyway." She said it with such authority that Isabella almost believed her.

Isabella got knee-high rubber boots to wear on her walk to work. When she'd first seen people wearing these, she'd thought they were just trying to be cute, but now she realized they were necessary for the three-foot-wide puddles of dirty, cold water that surrounded the curbs and gathered in the streets.

Sharon had decided to go on a diet for New Year's, and so the muffin game got more complicated. "Are you sure?" Isabella would have to say. "I can't believe you're on a diet," she would sometimes add. The one morning she didn't get a chocolate chip muffin, Sharon made her file clients by their Social Security numbers. Isabella never made that mistake again.

Even with her boots, Isabella's feet always felt wet and cold. The heat in their apartment was on full blast, and there was nothing they could do to turn it down. They had to keep the windows open to avoid suffocating, and Isabella was always afraid that the pigeon would come back. At night, she woke up in the apartment sweaty and dehydrated, flapping her arms to protect herself from imaginary birds.

It seemed like spring would never come, but it did. And mysteriously, Ben started appearing more and more. He offered no explanation of where he had been all those nights when she'd tried to call him. He just showed up all the time again, wearing his white baseball hat, smiling and laughing, buying her drinks, dancing, and waking up in her bed.

"What do you think happened?" Isabella asked.

Mary shrugged. "Maybe he was hibernating," she suggested.

Isabella was promoted at work, and a new assistant was hired to get muffins for Bill and Sharon. When Isabella was training the new girl, Bill said to her, "You have some big shoes to fill. This one here was a dynamo." He put his hand on Isabella's shoulder, and she could smell onions. She hoped the odor wouldn't stay on her sweater. Sharon wished her luck, shook her hand, and gave her a card that had an office full of monkeys on it. On the inside of the card it said, "We'll miss you at this zoo!" Isabella moved to the floor above and didn't see any of them much. Sometimes she found herself at the bakery downstairs about to buy muffins before she realized she didn't have to do that anymore. She thought of Sharon saying, "Oh, I couldn't," as Isabella placed the muffin on her desk, and she hoped the new girl understood the rules and remembered what to do.

Mary started her summer internship at a law firm downtown, but at least she was more willing to go out at night. At Gamekeepers, over a game of Scrabble, she told Isabella that she'd be moving out in the fall.

"I need my own place," she said. "I love living with you, but I have to study all the time. Plus, I should live closer to campus. And you don't want to live all the way up there."

"I know," Isabella said. "I'm distracting."

Isabella found a one-bedroom apartment on the West Side. She was sad not to be living with Mary anymore, but the new apartment had screens, so that was something.

The last night in the apartment, Isabella and Mary went to Gamekeepers with Ben and his roommate Mike. They played Connect Four and Sorry!, and then Ben pulled Life off the shelf. "How about this one?" he said. "A good old-fashioned game of Life."

They spun the spinner and gathered jobs and paychecks and children. Isabella hadn't played in a long time, and she found it sort of boring. Mary and Mike lost interest and got up to order new drinks at the bar.

"You know," Isabella said to Ben, "when I was little and my family played Life, we had this rule. If any of the pegs fell out of your car, then you lost them. It was considered a car accident and the plastic peg was dead. You had to give it back."

"Really?" Ben sounded bored.

"Yeah," Isabella said. She'd told that story before, and usually people at least laughed a little. Ben just looked around the bar.

"Don't you think that's kind of a mean rule?" Isabella asked him.

"I guess," he said. He rattled the ice in his glass. "I have to go to the bodega to get smokes."

"Okay," Isabella said. When he left, she pulled one of his pegs out and laid it down right next to his car.

The dead-peg rule had always made Isabella cry. Somehow, her little pegs never seemed to stay put, and they always popped out. "That's the rule, Izzy," her brother Marshall always said to her when she tried to protest. It was so rotten, Isabella thought, the way that everyone squealed and laughed when someone's peg fell out, the way they all clapped at that person's misery and misfortune. Molly would always pat Isabella's back when this happened and say, "If you can't follow the rules, then maybe you shouldn't play."

Ben came back inside, but he didn't notice his dead peg.

Isabella went to the bar and ordered shots for herself and Mary. "Here," she said, handing it to her. "No excuses. This is a time of mourning. We're never going to live together again."

"Don't say that," Mary said.

"It's true," Isabella said. She could feel herself getting sentimental, which she always was. Sometimes she missed people before they even left her, got depressed about a vacation being over before it started.

"Well then, cheers," Mary said. They clinked the glasses, touched them to the counter, and drank.

"You're going to miss me," Isabella said. "There won't be anyone to blame for the dirty dishes in the sink."

"I don't leave dirty dishes in the sink," Mary said.

"Exactly," Isabella said.

Ben and Mike came over and suggested another bar. "This place is beat," Ben said. He leaned back and stretched his arms.

"We can't go anywhere," Isabella told him. "We still have to finish packing. The movers are coming early."

"Okay," Ben said. "Talk to you tomorrow." Isabella noticed that he didn't offer to help her move, but she didn't say anything. She and Mary had another drink and headed back to the apartment, which was full of boxes and still had stuff all over the floor.

"What is this stuff?" Mary asked.

"Crap," Isabella said. "It's just all crap." She kicked at a pink hand weight. "When have either of us ever lifted weights?" she asked.

"I think I bought those thinking I'd lift weights in my room," Mary said.

"How did that go?" Isabella asked.

"Not great," Mary said. "I think that's why they were underneath the couch."

"Here," Isabella said. She reached into her pocket and took something out. "I stole these for us." She opened her palm and showed Mary two pink peg people from Life and two pigs from Pig Mania. She handed Mary a peg person and a pig. "They're us," she said. "Roommates always."

Mary laughed. "Who's the pig?" she asked.

In her new apartment, Isabella glued the pig and the peg person on a piece of cardboard and hung it in a frame by the door. People always commented on it when they walked in. "Hey, look," they'd say. Sometimes they recognized the peg from Life, and some people even knew where the pig was from, which usually made them laugh. When the glue wore out and the peg person or the pig fell down, she didn't throw them out. Instead, she glued them right back on and said a silent prayer that they were the only critters in her home.

Summer Sausage

*O*ur friend Ellen dates ugly boys," Lauren used
to say. She said it all through college. She
said it to warn attractive boys who were interested
in Ellen. "You're not her type," she'd try to explain.
"It's weird, I know, but you're far too good-looking
for her." Most of the time, these boys didn't listen.
They'd just nod and keep staring at Ellen, thinking
about how they were going to approach her, as Lauren insisted in the background, "Our friend Ellen
dates ugly boys."

All of Ellen's friends accepted this. They weren't
surprised when she introduced them to boys with
receding hairlines and mild cases of rosacea. They
didn't laugh when she picked out the one guy in the
bar with braces and said, "Look at him!" When she
got breathy and excited about someone new, they
all mentally prepared themselves to meet a guy with
a creepy carnival mustache and a mean case of dan-

druff. Even in first grade, when the only acceptable boys to like were Jon Armstrong and Chris Angelo, Ellen announced that she liked scabby Matthew Handler. It was just who she was. Ellen dated ugly boys.

It was surprising, mostly because Ellen was pretty—and not just your average, well-groomed and well-dressed kind of pretty. She was the kind of pretty that people noticed, the kind of pretty that made people watch her walk by. She had long eyelashes and skin that didn't seem to have any pores. There was a glow about her, something that always drew boys to her side. If she'd been anyone else, Lauren might have been too jealous to be her friend. But it never mattered, because Ellen would look at all of her admirers gathered round, and point to Mr. Fatty and say, "I choose you." Lauren got to keep the rest of them.

Some friends are gossips and some are sloppy drunks. If you like them well enough, you ignore this trait and continue to be their friend. And that's what they did with Ellen—they tolerated her taste in men.

Once, in college, Ellen kissed a guy who lived down the hall from them. They called him the Wildebeest because he was portly with wild curly hair and he snorted when he laughed. He was the guy who got drunk at parties, stripped naked, and did the worm on the floor in a pool of keg beer. They all knew him. They all liked him well enough. And they were all shocked when Ellen announced that she'd kissed him the night before when he'd walked her to her door.

"Hold on," Isabella said. "Please back up. You made out with the Wildebeest?"

Ellen shrugged. "I didn't plan it," she said. "He offered to walk me home and he's so funny."

"Of course he's funny," Lauren said. "He's a Wildebeest. Wildebeests are supposed to be funny. But Wildebeests are not for making out with."

Ellen was unashamed. She just smiled and shrugged and went back to her room. All the girls stared at each other and shook their heads. "Making out with a Wildebeest," they whispered to one another. "What will be next?"

For the most part, Ellen's boys were harmless. That's not to say that they all had sparkling personalities or quick wit to make up for their appearance. No, some of them were truly blessed with nothing. But still, the girls never really objected to Ellen's choices. "Different strokes for different folks," their friend Mary always said whenever Ellen brought home another one. And they all laughed and let her be. "What harm could it do?" they asked each other. And so they let Ellen have her ugly little fun.

But then she met Louis. And Louis was awful.

Louis weighed about ninety pounds, had soft, wispy blond hair, and wore the same pair of rust-colored corduroys their entire junior year. He was pretentious and socially awkward and Ellen was crazy about him. Louis sat in their apartment and chain-smoked cigarettes while he ignored all of them. Once, when Lauren asked Ellen for an opinion on which shirt she should wear out that night, Louis weighed in. "It can be dangerous to care too much about clothes. It makes you shallow," he said. Then he reached into his pants pocket, took out a paper-back copy of *Why I Am So Wise* by Nietzsche, and started reading.

"I hate that guy," Lauren said later that night. "He's such a dick."

"Relax," Isabella said. "It won't last. They never do."

The first time Louis dumped Ellen, they silently cheered. But a week later, the couple was back together, and Louis showed up again in their apartment, smoking cigarettes and making comments about how silly girls were in general. Louis broke up with Ellen over and over again, and she kept going back to him. None of them understood it.

"He looks like Ichabod Crane," Lauren said once. "I mean, what I think Ichabod Crane would look like if he wore the same pants for a year, you know?"

"I just don't understand when he has time to wash those pants," Mary said. "He wears them every day. That's just so gross." They all agreed.

After graduation, Louis broke up with Ellen again. He told her that he couldn't be tied down, that he was going to travel through Europe alone and needed his freedom. "Please let this one stick," they said to one another. Sure, Ellen was devastated now, but she'd meet someone else, someone who would make her happier. They were sure of that. It was all for the best.

They all spent a year after graduation living with their parents in their respective suburbs, saving money and looking for jobs. It was miserable, sleeping in twin beds in their childhood rooms, sending out millions of résumés, and trying not to get annoyed when their parents said things like "What time will you be home?" and "No drinks upstairs."

Lauren, Ellen, and their friend Shannon all moved to Chicago that summer. Ellen had gotten a job offer in Boston but had turned it down, claiming that she had always wanted to live in Chicago. "It's such a fun city," she said. "The lake is so great." Lauren and Shannon rolled their eyes at each other. They knew she was lying about the lake. Louis was from Chicago and Ellen was just hoping he'd come back there soon. It was sad, really. Even a little pathetic, they thought.

But they didn't really care that much. One year after graduating, they were finally on their own. They rented an apartment on Armitage with two and a half bedrooms, one tiny bathroom, no air-conditioning, and a giant deck. It was almost like college, except they had to get up and go to work every morning.

It was so hot that summer that no one could stay inside. They tried (for the sake of being grown ups) not to go out every night. They sat on the deck in ponytails and shorts, reading magazines and painting their nails, trying to imagine a breeze from Lake Michigan. Eventually, someone would suggest having a beer or a glass of wine. They'd sit awhile, and someone would suggest going to the bar below them, just for one drink, just to sit in air-conditioning for a while. And before they knew it, it was two in the morning and they were listening to Karen, the crazy bartender with missing teeth at Shoes Pub, tell them about Craig, the asshole who broke her heart.

Lauren blamed the weather for a lot of what happened that summer. It drove them out of their apartment, to bars and street fairs and concerts. It made them restless and irritable while they waited for something to start. They all knew they ought to feel different in their new lives, but they felt the same and it put them on edge. Hot and impatient, they fidgeted in the heat, grumbling and asking each other, "What next? What next?"

Ellen was at a loss without Louis. She hadn't so much as flirted with an ugly boy since he'd left for Europe. He sent her postcards from Paris and Florence that said things like *Be yourself or be nothing* and *Live humbly but live true.*

Lauren and Shannon snatched these cards from the pile to read them before Ellen did. It was one of their greatest sources of entertainment.

"Live humbly?" Shannon said. "Uh, yeah. I'm pretty sure his parents are paying for his humble trip around Europe."

They always put the cards back in the mail so that Ellen could take them to her room and read them over and over again. They knew she was pining over him in there.

"We've got to get her over this," Lauren said. So they dragged her to bars and scouted for unattractive men. A few times she even met some homely boys, let them buy her a drink, and talked to them for a while. But when the girls got close, they heard what Ellen was saying to these guys. "He really broke my heart," she'd say. "I just really miss him."

"What can we do?" they asked each other. They shook their heads in disappointment. Why couldn't she just let it go?

They all got tickets to a concert at the old steel factory down the street, to see a young, handsome singer who wrote tortured love songs and whined about the troubles of being twenty-five. Their friend Isabella was visiting from New York, and she came over before the concert to drink beers on the porch, but all she did was wander around and say, "This place is huge. Your apartment is huge."

"Yeah, we like it," Lauren said.

"No," Isabella said. "You have no idea. You should see my apartment in New York. It's teeny. And expensive. This place is a mansion."

"Then move here," Lauren told her. "Move to Chicago!" Isabella just smiled and continued to look around in wonder.

Lauren and Shannon were in a fight that started when Shannon called Lauren a slob. "Isabella, don't you think it's disgusting when someone leaves Q-tips on the sink?" Shannon asked. Isabella shook her head and kept quiet.

"You're the one who sits in that bathroom for an hour and plucks your hairy eyebrows," Lauren said. "If anyone's a pig, it's you."

Isabella just smiled and looked happy that she didn't have to weigh in. Now Lauren and Shannon were sitting on the porch, sighing and scoffing to let everyone know that they weren't speaking to each other.

Ellen was in the kitchen pouring wine when Isabella asked her, "So, have you seen Louis since he's been back?"

It was like a movie: Ellen spilled her wine, Isabella jumped, and Lauren and Shannon forgot they were ignoring each other and looked at each other with wide eyes.

"Louis is back?" Ellen asked.

"Yeah." Isabella made a face. "Sorry, Ellen. I thought you knew."

Ellen shook her head and swallowed some wine. "No," she said. "I didn't know."

"Sorry," Isabella said again. "I just assumed he would have called you. I saw Phil last weekend and told him I was coming here for the weekend and he mentioned it. He just got back a couple weeks ago. I'm sure he was going to call you."

They all looked at Ellen, who was now calmly drinking her wine. Lauren could tell that she wasn't upset. Surprised, yes. But not upset. They'd known Ellen long enough to be able to read her mood by the way she held herself, and right then, she was as straight as a pole, alert, and excited.

"Fuck," Shannon said softly.

"Yeah," Lauren answered. "I know."

They went to the concert, where Lauren and Shannon made up, then got in a fight again when Shannon forgot to watch the Porta-Potty Lauren was in, and let a man open the door, which had a broken lock. "Everyone in line saw me with my pants down," Lauren screamed.

"So what's new?" Shannon asked.

They went to a bar called Life's Too Short near the old Cabrini-Green buildings. The whole area was under construction and the streets were lined with half-built condos and shells of townhouses. Because nothing was around it, the bar paid no attention to the city's rules about shutting down by four a.m.

The bartenders let everyone stay in the bar's outdoor area. Nothing good ever came of this, but they kept going back.

They sat in a corner of the patio where they could see everyone that walked in. They were fascinated with watching Margaret Applebee, a girl they knew from college. She'd always been kind of fat, but had dropped about forty pounds that year and was, according to Shannon, "whoring it up all over town." She was talking to their friend Mitch McCormick, pressing herself against his arm, and they were all waiting for him to tell her to go away.

"Who does she think she is?" Shannon asked. "Like Mitch would ever be interested in her. It's so embarrassing."

"She's persistent, though," Lauren said. "You gotta give her that."

"I don't even recognize her," Isabella said. "She lost forty pounds? She's a whole different person."

None of them saw Louis walk in. They were all so focused on the Margaret Applebee fiasco that they didn't notice him until he was standing at their table saying, "Hey, Ellen." Ellen tried to smile and then immediately burst into tears.

"She's really drunk," Lauren said to Louis.

He took her by the arm and led her away from them. Now they watched the two of them, heads bent together, talking quietly to each other.

"Oh shit," Shannon said. "Margaret Applebee is gone. We missed it. Where's Mitch?"

Ellen came back over to the table, crying harder now. She couldn't really talk, but they could guess what had happened.

"He's a jackass," Lauren said.

"He's not worth it." Isabella rubbed Ellen's back.

"You should just forget him," Lauren said.

"I think Mitch went home with Margaret Applebee," Shannon said.

Ellen was up and out before any of them the next morning, and she came back to the apartment with Bloody Mary ingredients, a large block of cheddar cheese, and a log of summer sausage.

"I'm sorry, you guys," she said. "For how I freaked out last night."

"No worries," Shannon said. She'd already made herself a Bloody Mary and was now cutting off hunks of cheese and sausage to shove in her mouth. Isabella lay on the couch, listening to the conversation. She was too hungover to move, but made a noise and motioned for some cheese and sausage. Lauren cut some off and brought it over to her.

"I called Louis this morning to apologize to him too," Ellen told them.

"Why?" Shannon asked.

"Because I want to be friends," Ellen said. "I at least want to be friends with him."

"Do you think that will work?" Lauren asked.

"I think it's my only choice," she said. They were quiet for a few moments.

"There's something weird about summer sausage," Shannon said.

"There's a lot of things weird about summer sausage," Ellen said.

"It should be disgusting," Lauren said. "I mean, you leave it wrapped up and unrefrigerated forever, but when you open it, it's still delicious. It's one of the great world wonders."

"I think it's curing my headache," Isabella said. She tried to sit up and then lay right back down. "Never mind," she said.

"I think you guys might still be a little drunk," Ellen said.

Later, they all agreed that she was a disaster waiting to happen.

Lauren met Tripp at a bar in Bucktown that had maps all over the walls and pool tables in the corner. He wasn't much, but she kept seeing him. For her birthday, he gave her gift certificates to the bar downstairs and a dirty romance novel that you buy at a grocery store. "I know you like to read," he told her. The card read *Dear Lorin, Happy Birthday. Sincerely Tripp.*

"Do you think he knows he spelled your name wrong?" Ellen asked.

"He didn't even put an exclamation point after 'Happy Birthday,' " Shannon said. She frowned at the card. "So serious. Happy Birthday—period."

"I'm just calling because I'm bored," Lauren explained to her friends when she dialed his number.

"You must be," they answered.

Chicago was small that summer. No matter where they went, they ran into people they knew: Tripp, Louis, and even Margaret Applebee were always around. If they didn't see them at

Shoes or Kincade's, then they saw them at Big John's or Marquee Lounge. And if they didn't see them at any of those places, they always found them at Life's Too Short.

Every once in a while, Ellen would announce that she wanted to meet someone. She'd talk to the first boy who offered to buy her a drink. They would smile, encouraging her from across the bar. Then Louis would show up and Ellen would stop talking to the boy and come back to them. "Ignore him," they'd tell her, and she would nod. About thirty minutes later, she'd decide to just say hello to Louis. "I have to be civil," she would say. She would cry a little and tell him that it was hard to just be friends with him. Some nights he would enjoy the attention, pulling her aside and talking closely to her. Other nights he would get angry and tell her that he couldn't deal with her, then storm out of the bar. Almost always, she'd cry back at the apartment, while they drank beer and ate late-night macaroni and cheese.

"You can find someone else," Shannon would tell her as she chewed the bright orange noodles.

"This whole thing is getting really predictable," Lauren would say.

They could have changed their patterns, Lauren thought later. They could have tried to go someplace new so that they wouldn't see the same people over and over again. It just never really occurred to them at the time.

Their new favorite thing to do on Sundays was to sit on the back porch, drink Bloody Marys, eat summer sausage, and talk about the weekend. Shannon was mildly obsessed with Margaret Applebee, and wanted to talk about her all the time.

"Just because she's not fat anymore, she's a huge slut? I mean, come on," Shannon said.

"Maybe she wants a boyfriend," Ellen suggested. "I don't think she's ever really had a boyfriend before." She didn't like it when they talked about Margaret Applebee.

"Well, she certainly doesn't have a boyfriend now," Lauren said. "She probably just has herpes."

"Oh, Lauren." Ellen looked at her like a disappointed mother and shook her head a little. "What's going on with Tripp?" she asked, to change the subject.

Lauren shrugged. "Not much. We see each other when we see each other."

Tripp and Lauren sometimes went days without speaking. She kept thinking they would either decide to start really dat- ing or stop seeing each other altogether. But things just kept going like they had been. Most of the time, she saw no reason to change this. Once, she saw him go home with another girl from Life's Too Short and it felt like someone slapped her. It was over, she decided. But then a week or so later, she saw him and made no mention of it. She would ignore it, she decided. After all, it's not like they were exclusive or anything. He was just a good way to pass the time until something better came along.

At the end of July, their friend Sallie called to tell them that she was engaged and getting married in a month. And also, one more thing: She was pregnant. They weren't sure what to say, so they told her congratulations. They couldn't believe it. Sallie and Max had dated in college, where Max was known for doing keg stands until he vomited and Sallie sometimes forgot she had a boyfriend and kissed other boys at the party. They were getting married? They were having a baby?

"I think it's exciting," Ellen said.

"You think it's exciting that their lives are over?" Lauren asked her. She was appalled.

"But you know them," Ellen said. "They're in love."

Lauren snorted. "They'll be divorced in five years," she said.

"I hate to say it," Shannon said, "but I kind of agree."

⏀

Lauren learned something important at Sallie and Max's wedding: You never want to be the first one of your friends to get married. If you are, just resign yourself to the fact that your wedding will be a shit show. Most people are still single, open bars are a novelty, and no matter how elegant the wedding was planned to be, it will wind up looking like a scene out of *Girls Gone Wild*.

They almost didn't make it to the actual ceremony, because Lauren was throwing up all morning. "Please wait for me, you guys," she kept saying before she ran back to the bathroom. "I'll be ready in just a minute."

They had five friends in town for the wedding, camped out all over the apartment on couches and air mattresses. When their guests had arrived the night before, they'd done their best to be good hostesses and show them a fun night, but had ended up staying out way too late. It was all they could do to shower and put on clean dresses.

"Is this going to be a long mass?" their friend Mary asked. She had gotten ready and then lain down on the couch to take a nap in her dress.

"You're going to get wrinkled," Ellen told her.

"I really don't care," Mary said. She kept her eyes closed.

Ellen was the only one who seemed to be excited about the wedding. She hadn't stayed out too late the night before, and she was ready on time, looking fresh and ironed. She sat on the edge of one of the couches with her ankles crossed and watched as the rest of them scrambled to get ready.

ᛒ

The wedding was a mess. Everyone stampeded the bar and ordered tequila shots until the bride's father demanded that the bartenders stop serving them. Their friend Isabella was one of the bridesmaids, and she informed them that the bride's mother had been crying all morning. "She kept saying, 'I can't believe this is how it's happening,'" Isabella said. "It was awful."

Their friend Joe threw up on the dance floor and it had to be cleared and cleaned before anyone could continue dancing. One of the bridesmaids was found passed out in the bridal suite and had to be sent home. People made out in corners, girls fell down and ripped their dresses, and finally the band stopped playing and everyone was kicked out and decided to go to Life's Too Short. Shannon kept slurring, "Their lives are ruined, you know. Their lives are ruined."

Louis was at the wedding and they all knew this meant Ellen

would cry. Louis and Ellen danced together at the reception and then sat alone at a table in the bar. They were sure that Louis would stand up at any moment and storm out, but every time they looked over, Ellen and Louis were laughing and he was touching her knee.

Tripp was at the bar and when he saw Lauren he said, "Oh, you're here?"

"See?" Lauren said to Shannon. "Chivalry is not dead."

Tripp didn't say anything, and Lauren had a feeling that he didn't know what "chivalry" meant. It was becoming clear that he was stupid. She would have to end it. But before she could say anything else, he walked away.

"What a loser," Lauren said. Shannon nodded.

The night ended when Tripp and Margaret Applebee left together. Lauren started crying, and Shannon and Isabella decided they should go to the diner and eat. Lauren ordered eggs and corned beef hash, poured ketchup all over her plate, and didn't eat anything.

"He's not worth it," they said to her. She went home, left her dress in a pile on the floor, crawled into bed, and cried until she fell asleep.

By the time Lauren woke up the next morning, most of their guests were gone. Only Isabella remained, sitting on the couch with Shannon. They both looked like hell.

"Where's Ellen?" Lauren asked.

Isabella shrugged. "She didn't come home. We think she stayed at Louis's."

"I can't believe she went home with him," Shannon said.

"Who? Ellen or Margaret Applebee?" Isabella asked.

"Both, I guess. But I was talking about Ellen," Shannon said.

"Can we please not talk about Margaret fucking Applebee?" Lauren said. She could feel Shannon and Isabella exchange a look behind her back.

ఎ౨

Ellen came home later that afternoon, carrying all of their usual supplies for a Bloody Mary—and—summer sausage picnic. She hummed as she mixed together a pitcher of drinks, and bounced around the kitchen getting glasses and knives.

"You seem happy," Shannon said.

"I am," Ellen said. She smiled. "You guys, I had a really good night. Louis and I decided to get back together."

"Oh," Lauren said. She waited for someone else to be supportive.

"You can't date him," Shannon finally said. "He's awful. He's awful to you, and he's awful to us, and he's just awful."

"He does seem to make you really unhappy most of the time," Isabella said.

"Do you really think that?" Ellen asked. She looked straight at Lauren. "Lauren," she said. "Do you think that?"

Lauren had no idea why she said what she said next. Sometimes she thinks back to that moment and imagines that she could take it back. She blamed it on being hungover, on the wedding, on Margaret Applebee, but really she had no excuse. Because what she said was "He's just so ugly."

Ellen was cutting the summer sausage when Lauren said this,

and they all watched the knife slice right through her finger. Her hand was completely covered in blood before she even looked down.

"Holy shit," Shannon screamed. Isabella ran inside to get a towel, and Shannon called 911. When they answered, she apologized and then spent five minutes on the phone explaining why they didn't need an ambulance.

"Come on," Lauren said. "We'll take a cab to the hospital."

Ellen's face was white and she refused to take the towel off to look at her finger. "I think I cut it off," she kept saying. "I think I cut off my whole finger."

Lauren assured her that her finger was still attached. "Don't worry," she said. "You'll just need a few stitches."

They had to wait over two hours in the emergency room. A man sat across from them with his head leaning against the wall. When he was called to go in, he left a bloody headprint behind.

Lauren and Ellen didn't talk much while they waited. Ellen looked like she was going to pass out any second, and Lauren didn't think it seemed like the right time to continue their conversation. Maybe Ellen hadn't even heard her when she'd called Louis ugly. It was possible, she thought. They sat in silence until the doctor called them in. Lauren walked back to the examination room even though Ellen hadn't asked her to.

The doctor looked at Ellen's finger quickly and started numbing it for stitches. "That's a nasty cut," she said. "How did this happen?"

"A knife," Ellen said. "It was summer sausage."

"Summer sausage bites back," Lauren said. Ellen looked at

her with her eyebrows wrinkled together while the doctor stitched up her finger.

Lauren apologized later, but they both knew it was too late. "I don't know what's best for you," Lauren said. "You're the only one who knows that."

Ellen said she understood. "Lauren," she said. "I get it. You were just being a good friend. Don't worry. I'll be fine."

᠍ ᠍

When Ellen and Louis got engaged, Shannon screamed. "Well," she said, after she stopped screaming, "I guess some people just want to be miserable." They all went to the wedding and tried not to be somber. After all, she was their friend and they wanted her to be happy.

They lost touch with Ellen. Not all at once, but little by little, so that they didn't even notice until it had already happened. Maybe it was hard for Ellen to be around them, since she knew they didn't approve of her marriage. Maybe their lives just went different ways—Lauren and Shannon both moved to New York and Ellen moved to a house in the suburbs. Sometimes they thought that Louis was behind it, that he had forbidden Ellen to see them. In the end, Lauren thought it was probably a combination of everything, but she knew they would never really know.

᠍ ᠍

Lauren talks about that summer a lot. It has a point, a moral of some kind, but she's not quite sure what it is yet. When people tell her that their friend is marrying a guy they hate, she says,

"Have I got a story for you." When she gets a Christmas card from Sallie and Max with a picture of their two little boys on it, she shows it to people and says, "You've got to hear about this wedding." And whenever she's at a party and someone serves summer sausage, she says, "Did I ever tell you about my friend Ellen?" and if the person she's talking to shakes their head no, she says, "Well, let me tell you. We had this friend. And our friend Ellen, well, Ellen dated ugly boys."

JonBenét and Other Tragedies

Isabella didn't want to go to the wedding. They were Ben's friends. She had never met the bride or the groom, and besides, she was fairly certain that she and Ben were going to break up any day. While she was getting ready that morning, she sat down on the bed and said, "My head hurts."

"You don't have to go if you don't want to," Ben said. He was tying his tie and not looking at her. She knew he really wouldn't care if she didn't go and that pissed her off.

"Your tie is crooked," she said, and stood up to finish getting ready.

⁂

They were early to the church, which never happened with them. Ben hated weddings. During the ceremony, he'd roll his eyes or sometimes say, "Oh *God*," if the couple read their own vows or started to cry.

They sat in the pew and Isabella paged through the program. "You know who's going to be here?" Ben asked. "Mike's girl-friend. You know, the one that looks like JonBenét."

Isabella had been hearing about this girl for months but had never met her. A while back, Ben caught her lying on the couch watching *E! True Hollywood Story: JonBenét*. "Why are you watching this?" he asked.

"There's nothing on," Isabella said. Little girls marched across the stage with their faces full of makeup. JonBenét stood in the middle of them, twirling an umbrella and smiling.

"This is really creepy," Ben said.

"I know." Isabella couldn't take her eyes off the screen. They were such little girls, but their hair was so big.

"I know a girl who looks just like her," Ben said.

"Like who?"

"JonBenét," he said.

Isabella turned to him. "You know a *little* girl who looks like her?" she asked, and Ben shook his head.

"No," he said. "You know my buddy Mike? His girlfriend looks just like her. It's fucking creepy."

Isabella didn't believe him. "Ask my friends," he said. "I swear, she looks just like her."

All of his girlfriends confirmed the story. "She's a dead ringer for JonBenét," they said, and then they laughed. "Plus," they told Isabella, "she's crazy. She's obsessed with getting married and talks about it all the time. She introduces herself to people as 'Mike's girlfriend and future fiancée.' She sends him pictures of engagement rings constantly. She buys bridal magazines and carries them around with her!"

Isabella wasn't sure she believed all of it, but she still couldn't wait to meet her.

She looked around the church for someone who fit the description. "Is that her?" she whispered to Ben, and pointed to a small blond girl sliding into a pew in front of them.

He shook his head and smiled. "No," he said. "When you see her, you'll know. And you'll die."

Ben hadn't officially moved in, but he was in between apartments and his stuff was overtaking Isabella's place. When the lease was up on his old apartment, she'd told him he could stay with her until he found a new place. They hadn't talked about it since. That was three months ago.

"I can't believe he's still staying with you," Lauren said one night. "You only let me stay with you for two weeks."

"I never kicked you out," Isabella said.

"Yeah, but you made me sleep on the couch after the first two days," Lauren said.

"That's because you licked me in your sleep," Isabella said.

"I told you, I was having a dream," Lauren said.

"That doesn't make it okay," Isabella said. "Anyway, I'm sure Ben will find a place soon."

"Maybe you should ask him," Lauren said. But Isabella didn't want to, which she knew probably meant that she really should. Instead, she decided she wouldn't worry about it for a while.

Ben sold medical supplies for a small company based in Tennessee. Isabella wasn't sure what it was he actually did. He didn't go to an office. He worked from his computer at home, and then drove around in his car, delivering products and doing presentations. His workday lasted from about eleven a.m. to three p.m., when he returned home to watch *The Simpsons* and smoke a joint.

Isabella was home sick when she discovered this. "Why are you home so early?" she asked. For a second she thought he'd come back to take care of her. Maybe he'd brought her soup or ginger ale.

"I'm usually done around this time," Ben said. He settled himself on the couch and Isabella sniffled into a tissue. She stood there waiting for him to ask her if she needed anything. "What?" he asked her.

She shook her head. "Nothing." She took a NyQuil and went back to bed. She had fuzzy dreams until Ben turned on the television in the bedroom and woke her up. Isabella stared at Ben that night while he slept and tried to figure out how he'd gotten there.

Isabella and Ben fought all the time. They even fought the first night they met, when he cut in front of her to go to the bathroom at a bar. She yelled after him and continued to yell at him through the door. "Sorry," he said when he came out. "It was an emergency." Ben was tan with messy hair and a white smile. Isabella forgave him and went back to his apartment that night. He had black lights and a gravity bong. He reminded her of the boys she'd been in love with in high school, relaxed and impossibly sure of himself.

The fights they had now were much worse. Isabella had never fought like this with anyone before. With Ben, she had all-out, drunken marathon fights that lasted for hours. She was sure the neighbors thought they were crazy.

Isabella woke up the morning after these fights with a sore throat from yelling and swollen eyes from crying, sure that she had done damage to her insides. Ben was an asshole, a jackass, a dick. But just when Isabella thought the end was near, she felt a little hole of panic open. He was also funny, and could be sweet. Was she really ready to let that go? Wasn't she partly to blame for the fight?

The ceremony was a full mass and Ben shuffled his feet and breathed loudly through most of it. Isabella kept turning to give him a look. She gave him these looks often, the kind that you give to small children to let them know their behavior is inappropriate. Usually he just ignored her.

After the wedding, they all stood outside the church waiting for the bride and groom to make their exit. Ben smoked a cigarette and talked to some friends, and Isabella watched the clouds and tried to calculate how much longer it would be before they were at the reception and she could get a glass of wine. She was interrupted from her dreaming by Ben's voice. "Hey!" he said. "Look who it is."

Isabella saw Ben slapping the hand of his friend Mike, giving him a half hug–handshake–pat on the back. "Mike, you remember Isabella?" Ben smiled at her and she smiled back. Ben almost never remembered to introduce her. He was just excited for her to meet JonBenét.

"Yeah, definitely. How's it going?" Mike nodded to her. "And this is my girlfriend. You guys have met, right?"

Isabella watched the tiny girl emerge from behind Mike. She was a pixie! Isabella hadn't even noticed her standing there. All of her features were teeny; her hands and fingers were almost childlike. Isabella stared at her. She couldn't help it. It was Jon-Benét, and no one had been exaggerating about the resemblance. If anything, they hadn't prepared her for this. Isabella got goose bumps just being near her.

"Hi, Ben." JonBenét had a raspy, breathy voice that made her sound like she'd just been running. "Wasn't the wedding beautiful? I told Mike in the middle of it that if one more person from his fraternity gets engaged before us, I'm done!" She laughed and turned to Mike. "Right, baby?"

Mike ignored her. "You guys want to get over to the reception? It's not supposed to start for another hour, but maybe we can convince the bartender to get us some drinks."

"Yeah, sure," Ben said. "You guys want to ride with us?"

☙

Isabella gave Mike shotgun so she could sit in the back with Jon-Benét. "Mike just got a new car," she said to Isabella. "And I said to him, What's that? I can't wear that on my finger." She laughed and waved her left ring finger in the air.

Isabella laughed and caught Ben's eye in the rearview mirror. They smiled at each other.

The reception was at a country club in some New Jersey suburb. Isabella felt like she'd been to a million of these weddings. By now, they all blended together in a blur of fabric-covered chairs, pink napkins, and crab cakes. Isabella looked around. The centerpieces made her sad.

"Isn't this beautiful?" JonBenét said to them. She sounded dreamy, like she couldn't believe her eyes. Mike put his hand on her back and she smiled up at him. He didn't look at her. Isabella had once seen a TV show called *Tarnished Tiaras* that exposed the truth behind child pageants. It focused on one mother who offered spray tans to the little girls to make some money. She stared at JonBenét and wanted to ask her if she ever got a spray tan. But she stopped herself.

The bartenders were still setting up. They looked up warily when they saw the four of them approaching. "Hey, man," Ben said to one. He lifted his chin in a nod and the bartender did the same back. Isabella was always amazed at how people just liked Ben immediately. Strangers in bars and people on the street treated him like an old friend. They welcomed him wherever he went. Isabella didn't even think he noticed. It was just the way things always were for him.

"You got any Red Bull?" Ben asked. The bartender shook his head.

"Ben," Isabella said. "You can't order that."

"Why?"

"What are you, fifteen? We're at a wedding."

Ben rolled his eyes. "Relax," he said. "They don't have it anyway."

"But you can't drink that at a wedding," Isabella explained.

"You have a lot of rules," Ben said. "I'm going out for a cigarette."

Isabella ordered a white wine and stood by herself on the side of the room. She watched the bride and groom arrive and hoped that they wouldn't come anywhere near her. They had no idea who she was.

When Ben finally came back, about ten minutes later, he was carrying a brown paper bag and smiling a proud smile. "What?" Isabella asked.

"Red Bull," he said. "I got it at a convenience store down the street. Now I can just order vodka on the rocks. Pretty smart, huh?"

Somewhere after the dinner was served and before the cake was cut, Isabella lost Ben. Everyone at their table was up dancing and mingling. Isabella sat there and drank wine. She felt like a fool.

JonBenét smiled at her from across the room and then walked over to the table. "Hey, Isabella."

"Hey," Isabella said. She was happy not to be sitting alone.

"Where did your date go?" JonBenét asked, smiling.

"Oh, I don't . . . I don't know. I haven't seen him in a while."

"He's probably off somewhere with Mike getting into trouble. Boys can be such shits sometimes, right?"

Isabella laughed. JonBenét was being very kind, but Isabella found it hard to look at her straight on for too long. It made the hair on her arms stand up. She thought about the JonBenét footage that showed her in the swimsuit competition of the beauty pageant. She wished she had never seen that part of the documentary. It haunted her.

"So, how did you and Ben meet?" JonBenét asked.

"In a bar," Isabella said. Sometimes she tried to make the story a little better, to embellish it with details. But she didn't feel like it right then.

"Mike and I met at a wedding," she said.

"Really?"

"Yeah, his cousin married one of my friends from college. It's funny, isn't it? The way things happen?"

Isabella nodded. "Yeah, it is."

How she met Ben could have been a cute story, Isabella realized. If they ended up together, she could tell people, "That Ben! So impatient, so impish!" But for that to happen, Ben would have to be a different person. And he wasn't. He was just a cocky boy who didn't want to wait his turn. That was all. He had to go to the bathroom. That was their story. The next time someone asked, "How did you meet?" Isabella could say, "Ben had to pee."

JonBenét chattered on about the different people at the wedding. She talked about her friend's wedding that she was in next month. "The bridesmaid dresses are beautiful," JonBenét assured her. Isabella had never met someone so in love with weddings. She tried to picture JonBenét as a bride, but she kept seeing the real JonBenét, overly made up in a poofy dress.

Ben came back about twenty minutes later, and JonBenét stood up. "I should go find my prince."

"Where have you been?" Isabella asked. "I've been sitting here by myself for almost an hour."

"Whadya mean, by yourself? There's people all around."

"These aren't my friends, Ben. You just left me alone. Everyone's been staring at me. I was sitting all by myself before she came over here."

"So what? Are you mad because you had to hang out with crazy JonBenét?"

"She's not that bad, Ben."

"She's crazy," Ben said, like it was a fact. Like it was something everyone knew.

Isabella felt bad for JonBenét, the way that everyone at the wedding was talking about her, like she was some kind of freak show. No one knew what went on in her relationship with Mike. No one even really knew her. Maybe she loved Mike more than he liked her. And wasn't that horrible? Wasn't that sad? But people forgot about that. They didn't see a tragedy, just a good story. To them, it was just some girl they could point to and say, "Well, at least my life isn't as fucked up as that."

"So what if she wants to get married?" Isabella asked. "Why is that the worst thing in the world? It's not such a crazy thought. She and Mike have been dating for a while. Isn't it weirder that Mike is avoiding it?"

Ben shrugged. He took the straw out of his drink and downed the rest of it. "Why do you care?" he asked.

"I just think it's mean the way that you and your friends treat her. I mean, what about Mike? If he doesn't want to marry her, then why doesn't he just break up with her?"

"Not everyone is dying to get married, Isabella."

"I'm not saying that everyone is. But she clearly wants to. And if he doesn't want the same thing, then shouldn't they just break up?"

"Why are you fighting with me?" Ben asked. She hated when he did this, when he turned things on her. He could act however and say whatever he wanted, and if she called him on it, then she was the bad person who'd instigated the fight.

"I'm not fighting with you," Isabella said. She knew that the night was already gone. It was ruined. They should just leave now instead of indulging in an evening of arguments and accusations.

"Really, well, that's what it feels like. I need a new drink," Ben said, and walked away.

Ben loved this stupid game show called *Deal or No Deal*. He loved the part when people had the chance to walk away with a ton of money and then made the wrong choice and left with nothing. It made him laugh out loud.

"Don't you feel bad for them?" Isabella would ask.

"No," he always said. "They're stupid. They deserve it."

When Isabella watched him laughing at those people, she felt like she was sitting next to the cruelest person in the world.

Less than a week after the wedding, Ben moved out. They had finally broken up, and it was just as awful as Isabella thought it would be. She couldn't sleep and so she stared into the darkness every night. She was alone, and she felt the aloneness in everything she did. But that was just at first. It went away after a while, or maybe she just stopped noticing it.

She never ran into Ben, although she always thought she saw

him in a crowded bar or walking down the street. Her eyes played tricks on her everywhere she went. But that, too, went away and then the only time she really thought about him was when she smelled pot.

The weird thing was that long after she got over Ben, Isabella thought about JonBenét. She couldn't even recall the girl's real name, and still she entered her mind with alarming frequency. Isabella remembered how she had laughed at JonBenét without really knowing her and how kind the girl had been to her that night. She thought about how everyone gossiped about her behind her back and wondered if she knew. And mostly, Isabella wondered if JonBenét was finally engaged or even married by now. She almost e-mailed Ben once, just to ask. Isabella wished for JonBenét when she threw pennies into fountains, when she blew on eyelashes, and when the clock read 5:55. She wished for her that she was married. She wished for her that she had a beautiful wedding. She hoped she was happy.

The Peahens

Abby's family was weird. She had, on some level, always known this, but as she got older it became much more clear. When Abby was four, her dad's uncle died and left them all of his money—and there was a lot of it. Instead of using it to buy a house or a boat, like normal people, her parents bought a farm in Vermont and spent their days smoking pot and refurbishing antique furniture. Sometimes her dad called her mom Lil' Bit, and sometimes they let their friend Patches park his trailer on their property and live there. Yes, Abby's parents were weird, her sister was even stranger, and the whole lot of them together was sometimes too much to bear.

Abby didn't try to hide this information. In fact, it was usually the first thing she told people. "My parents are weird," she'd say, as soon as the topic of family came up. "They're hippies," she'd add. A lot of times, the people she was talking to would nod their heads like they understood and say, "I know, my parents are total freaks too." If this happened, Abby had to explain further. "My parents grow pot," she'd say. "My mom raises chickens for us to eat." If this didn't get a rise out of them, she'd say, "My dad once kidnapped the neighbor's peacocks." That usually shut them up.

Abby wasn't complaining when she told people this. She just wanted it out there. It was better, she'd learned, to tell people right up front, instead of waiting for them to ask questions like "What line of work is your dad in?" and having it all come out like that.

When Abby was thirteen, her parents sent her to boarding school. They talked about sending her to the local high school, they even entertained the idea of enrolling her in the hippie high school that took place on a VW bus and drove around the country, to teach kids through real-life experience. But in the end, her parents decided on Chattick, a really well-known and snobby boarding school in Connecticut, where all the kids had parents who were lawyers or bankers, and everyone bought their chicken in grocery stores.

At boarding school, Abby learned to study. When she arrived that first year with a canvas bag of clothes and a homemade patchwork quilt for her bed, she knew she had her work cut out for her. She studied hard, taking notes on the silver link brace-lets all the girls wore and the bright patterned duffel bags they carried home at the holidays. She made lists and bought these things for herself, quickly and quietly, so that no one remem-bered that she hadn't had them before, no one knew that she looked any different than when she'd first gotten there. Some-times she thought she should have been a spy.

By the time she was a freshman in college, she had it down. When she met her freshman roommate, Kristi, she appeared totally normal. But still, she told Kristi about her family as soon as it was acceptable. Abby had perfected her five-minute rant about her parents, and she performed it well. Kristi laughed in all the right places, and Abby was sure that they would be friends.

And still, Abby tried to keep her friends at a distance. She was quieter than the rest of them, always listening, always watching to see if there was something she was supposed to be doing. It was exhausting, but she knew the alternative was worse. By senior year, she had been to stay with the families of all of her college roommates. She'd been to Chicago and Philadelphia and even California, but she'd never invited anyone to Vermont. She also discouraged her parents from coming up for Parents' Weekend. "It's no big deal," she always said. "No one is really coming." This was a lie, of course, and she felt bad about that, but she didn't have a choice. It was one thing to hear about her family. It was another thing to see them.

Kristi was the one who brought it up one weekend when most of their friends were out of town for one reason or another. "I'm so bored I could die," Kristi said. She rolled over onto her back and sighed. "I could literally die."

Their friend Isabella laughed. "Don't be dramatic or anything."

"I'm serious," Kristi said. "We can't stay here this weekend. There's nothing going on. Let's do something."

"What do you want to do?" Isabella asked. Abby stayed quiet. They were in her room, which always put her on edge. After freshman year, wherever the group of them lived, Abby always got a single. It calmed her to at least have a place where she could go and shut the door and not have to worry about anyone watching her. She hated when they gathered in here.

"Let's take a road trip," Kristi said. She rolled over and sat up. "I know! Let's go to Vermont." She pointed at Abby. "Come on, we've never been there. I want to see the farm." She started bouncing up and down on Abby's bed. "Come on! Please! Let's go to the farm!"

"You guys, it's so boring there," Abby said. She tried to stay calm. "You think it's boring here? You'll really die there."

But the girls kept insisting and Abby didn't want to protest too much, in case that would seem weird, and so it wasn't long before the three of them were in Kristi's car on the way to Vermont.

Abby knew as soon as they arrived that it would be a disaster. Her mom answered the door with unbrushed hair, wearing thermal pants and a T-shirt. "Welcome, girls," she said when they walked in. She hugged each of them, and Abby noticed that she wasn't wearing a bra. "We're so glad you could make it," she said. "Leonard is off somewhere, but he'll be back for dinner." The girls nodded and followed Abby upstairs with their bags. They stared out the windows at the farmland, and Abby wished she'd grown up in a suburb.

Her dad never returned, and so they started dinner without him. "I just don't know where he could be," her mom kept saying. They were almost done eating when he got back. "Mary Beth, I need your help," he said. Then he turned to look at the full table and said, "Oh, hi, girls. Welcome to Vermont." Isabella and Kristi smiled at him and said, "Thanks for having us," but he wasn't listening.

"Dad, what's going on?" Abby asked.

"The neighbors are neglecting their exotic birds," her dad said. He stood in the doorway and stamped his feet on the welcome mat. "The neighbors are neglecting their exotic birds," he repeated, and her mother just nodded, as though this was a normal thing to say. "I know," she said. "It's so sad."

"The neighbors have just let the birds out of the pen. They're wandering all over the property and we need to get them. Mary Beth, can you help me find a flashlight and a bag large enough to fit a peacock?"

Abby wanted to die. This was worse than she ever could have imagined. Isabella and Kristi sat in silence and her mom got up to gather supplies.

"The neighbors have these birds," Abby started to explain.

"Exotic birds," her dad said.

"Right," she said. "Exotic birds. And they aren't taking care of them." She turned to her dad. "Are you going to steal them?" she asked.

"No," her dad said. "We're just going to convince them to come here. Bob up the street is helping me."

"Bob's a vet," Abby explained to Isabella and Kristi. She felt like she was interpreting.

"We have to wait until it's dark," her dad said. "Peacocks are blind at night, so we can just put it in the bag and get it to the truck. The peahens are easy. They follow wherever the peacock goes. Did you know that?"

"Fun farm facts," Abby said under her breath.

"Be careful," her mom said. "I don't want you to get arrested because of the peafowl." Her dad nodded, took the bag, and he was gone. Abby looked at her friends and tried to think of something to say.

&

"Your parents are so cool," Isabella whispered to Abby later that night. They were lying in bed after smoking her dad's pot on the back porch. Kristi was passed out in the other bed. Abby had offered them the pot as soon as they were done with dinner. It seemed the least she could do after the exotic bird hoopla.

"They really aren't," Abby said. "They're horrifying."

Isabella laughed. "That's not true," she said. "You just can't see it because they're your parents."

"You wouldn't feel that way if they were your parents," Abby said. "Trust me."

"Maybe," she said. "But I think they're great."

When Abby stayed at Isabella's house, her mom made them spaghetti and meatballs and they ate at the kitchen table with the whole family. They watched movies in the basement, and Abby slept in a guest room with a flowered comforter that matched the wallpaper border in the room. Her mom wore a bra the whole time. It was the perfect weekend.

Later that night, Abby heard her dad's truck drive up the road. She got up and went to the window. Isabella got up and stood next to her. Kristi snored behind them. "What's going on?" Isabella asked.

"I think my dad has the birds," Abby said.

They watched as he unlatched the back door to the truck and then stepped back and began making a series of loud noises.

"Oh my God," Abby said. "He's making bird noises."

"How does he know how to do that?"

"He doesn't." But they watched as a peacock bobbed its way out of the truck and followed her dad to the pen.

"Oh!" Isabella said. "Oh!" The two peahens hopped out after him. "Look at that," she said. "Look at that, they're following him!"

They were both still a little stoned, and they stared as the birds made their way to the new pen. Once they were there, the peacock opened up his feathers into a tall spray of blues and yellows. The peahens stood on either side of him. They were pure white, which made his feathers seem brighter.

"Wow." Isabella sounded like she had just witnessed a miracle. Kristi snorted in her sleep.

"Don't tell anyone about this, okay?" Abby asked her.

Isabella nodded but didn't take her eyes off the birds. "Okay, sure."

Abby had asked her mom once why they'd sent her to the schools they had. Why couldn't they have put her in public schools? "We just wanted you to get a good education," her mom said. Abby found this a stupid reason. Didn't they know she'd be all alone? Didn't they know that as soon as they sent her away, she'd be separated from them and she could never really go back? Didn't they know that they couldn't send her to those schools and walk into the kitchen and say, "The neighbors are neglecting their exotic birds," and expect her to be okay with it?

When Abby met Matt, she knew that he was going to save her. He was the answer, of course, the thing that would make her really normal. He worked at Morgan Stanley, was from a suburb of Boston, and liked the Red Sox. He was so normal that it made her heart pound.

"He's a great catch," Kristi said to her. Abby knew this before Kristi told her, and for once she didn't care whether Kristi approved.

New York made Abby happy. This was, she thought, because she was not even close to the weirdest person there. Every day she was there, she started to relax a little more, and soon she wasn't looking around at people wondering what they were thinking of her. She left the apartment without looking in the mirror a hundred times, and when she walked down the street and tripped a little, she wasn't even embarrassed.

Abby and Matt moved in together after a few months of dating. "That's really quick," Kristi said to her. But Abby didn't care. And when they got engaged, she knew that all of her friends were surprised, but again she didn't care. She was on her way to a normal life, and she wanted to get there as fast as she could.

Matt came to the house in Vermont only once. He'd met Abby's parents twice before, when they came to the city for a visit. Out of their element, they could almost pass as normal. But after the engagement, Abby decided it was time to bring him home. She warned him that her parents were different in the house. "Abby," he said, rolling his eyes, "I get it, okay? I don't care if your parents are nudists. I can handle it."

"How did you know about the nudist part?" Abby asked him. He looked at her for a moment and then smiled. "You think you're so funny, don't you?" he asked. "Just relax. It will be fine."

Abby's sister, Thea, came home for the weekend too. "I should meet your intended," Thea told her on the phone.

"Sure," Abby said. "I guess you should."

Thea came home and brought her new baby girl, Rain. Thea and Rain lived on an organic farm in Vermont. "We work the farm and earn our keep," Thea explained to Matt that night. She was breast-feeding Rain and let her breasts wag back and forth as she switched Rain to the other side. Abby could tell that Matt was trying hard not to look at them.

"Is this making you uncomfortable?" Thea asked him.

Matt shook his head. "No. No, this is fine."

Thea smiled. "Breast-feeding is the most natural thing in the world, Matt. I forgot what it's like with most people on the outside. At the farm, if Rain is hungry and I'm not around, one of the other lactating mothers will feed her."

"What kind of farm does she live on?" Matt whispered to Abby in bed that night. They had shared a joint walking around the farm and now he was giggly. "That's like Jim Jones shit," he said. "Lactating mothers . . . what the hell is that?"

"So you don't want to move there with me?" Abby asked, and he laughed.

"I'd move anywhere with you," he said, sliding his arms underneath her shirt and around her stomach. He rested his head in her neck and she thought he was sleeping until she felt his shoulders shaking. "But I won't drink the Kool-Aid," he managed to get out above his laughter. He lifted his face to look at her. "Even for you, Abby. Even for you, I won't drink the Kool-Aid from the lactating mothers."

ॐ

After Matt's visit, Abby felt herself slipping back in time. It took her hours to pick out which shoes to wear, and when she finally did, she immediately regretted her choice. Her clothes seemed to fit differently, tight in places they never were before, too loose in others, and she pulled at them, trying to figure out why they didn't look right. "Do I look okay?" she asked more often. She stared at herself in the mirror until Matt grew impatient, telling her she looked fine when he wasn't looking at her at all.

Abby couldn't help what was happening. She needed Matt around all the time, felt confused when he was gone, followed him around the apartment, her toes hitting his heels when he stopped short. "Your wanting," he said one night, "is overwhelming." It sounded poetic, but Matt was not a poetic person. One night, she woke up holding a fistful of his shirt. Matt stared at her across the darkness, then shook his shoulders like a dog does when it's wet, and rolled over to face away from her. She knew he would be gone soon.

ॐ

Three months after Abby woke up holding Matt's shirt, she arrived alone at her parents' house. As she pulled into the driveway, she thought, "The neighbors are neglecting their exotic birds." That was not unusual. Ever since the peacock incident, that sentence came into Abby's head at the oddest of times. "The neighbors are neglecting their exotic birds," she wanted to say when there was a lull at a dinner party or a friend told her that she was pregnant. And so she wasn't surprised that on the night she came home to tell her parents that she wasn't getting married, it was that thought that ran through her head: *The neighbors are neglecting their exotic birds.*

It was no stranger than what she had come to tell them: that the wedding was off, that Matt had moved out, and that they would probably not be able to get a refund on anything. She turned off the car and thought about her options. "The neighbors are neglecting their exotic birds," she said out loud to no one. Her breath made little puffs of white in the winter air, and she sat in the car until it was too cold to bear, and then she walked inside the house.

"Mom, I'm not getting married," Abby said as soon as she walked through the door. Her mother was reading a book on the couch, and she marked her place with her finger before she looked up.

"What?" she asked.

"I'm not getting married." Abby made no move to take off her jacket or move farther into the room.

"All right, then," she said. "Why don't you come on in, and we'll talk about it?" She put the book down on the couch and stood up. "Would you like some tea?" she asked. Abby nodded.

Abby's mom didn't even look surprised to see her. She'd driven all the way from New York, walked into the house unannounced, and her mom acted like she'd been expecting her. Abby had never been able to shock her mom. Once, in college, Isabella had said, "Can you imagine if you had to tell your mom that you were pregnant?" She shuddered after she asked this and Abby made a sympathetic noise, but she couldn't really relate. Abby could have told her mom that she'd been arrested for heroin possession while carrying on a lesbian affair, and she would have taken it in and then suggested that they talk about it.

"So, will we still have the party then?" her mom asked. They were sitting at the kitchen table with their tea, and it took Abby a minute to realize that she meant the wedding. She and Abby's father were never officially married, of course, so maybe she thought they just decided to skip the legal part and live together forever.

"No, Mom," Abby said. "No party, no wedding."

"So you and Matt are . . ."

"Done. We broke up." She nodded and blew on her tea.

"I'm sorry, honey," she said. "That's a shame."

Abby wanted her to scream or cry or jump on the table. Tears of frustration came to her eyes, and she shut them tightly.

"Oh, sweet pea. Oh, Abby," she said. "Come here." Abby let her mother pull her onto her lap like she was a little girl. She cried for about two minutes and then felt like an idiot sitting on her mom's lap, and so she got up and went back to her seat.

"I'm fine," Abby said. "It was for the best."

"Then this is the right thing to do," she said.

"Mom, I don't think we'll be able to get much money back," Abby said. "It's only three weeks away. I don't know what they'll do."

Her mom was already waving her hands at her. "That is not

for you to worry about. Money is just money." Abby wondered, not for the first time in her life, if her mom would still think that money was just money if she didn't have so much of it.

"I have to stay here for a couple of days while Matt moves his stuff out of the apartment," Abby said.

"Of course," she said. "Do you need help with anything else?"

"Not now," Abby said. "But I have to start calling people soon, I guess, to tell them that the wedding is off. I guess that's what I should do."

"I can do that," her mom said. "These things happen all the time. No big whoop. We'll get it all straightened out."

"Thanks," Abby said. "Can I have a real drink?"

"Sure, honey. Wine or vodka?"

"Vodka," Abby said. "I think this calls for vodka."

The next morning, Abby walked downstairs to find her dad making eggs in the kitchen. He saw her and gave her a hug. "Your mom told me what happened, kiddo. I'm really sorry about that," he said.

"Thanks, Dad."

"Do you want some eggs? Sunny side up or scrambled?"

"Sure," she said. "Scrambled, I guess."

Her dad nodded and turned back to the stove. He whistled while he cracked the eggs and beat them with a fork. "If you like, you can help me feed the birds when you're done," he said as he put the plate in front of her.

"Sure, Dad," she said. She waited until he walked out of the kitchen, and then got up and scraped the eggs into the garbage.

Abby put on rubber boots that were by the back door, and borrowed her mom's winter jacket. Still in her pajamas, she slogged through the snow to the chicken coop. She thought about brushing her hair, but there was really no need to. She pushed open the door to the coop and smelled the coop smell of poo and bird dirt.

"Dad?" she called.

"Back here, kiddo."

She walked past the cages, wrinkling her nose at the dirty birds. Abby's parents had started raising birds when she was twelve. "We eat so much poultry," her mom explained. "And people are starting to talk about the way these birds are raised. This is much more humane, Abby. We know that the birds are fed right, and treated right."

Her parents didn't kill the birds themselves. They had someone come in and do it for them and prep the meat. Abby had never seen it happen, but less than a year after they built the coop, she stopped eating meat.

"Abby, don't be ridiculous!" her mother would say. "This is good for you. This is delicious meat!"

"It makes me sick!" she'd say. And it did. The thought of chewing chicken in her mouth made her want to gag. When she tried to eat it, it refused to go down her throat. Once, she got a bite halfway down and then promptly threw up on her plate. "Fine," her mom said after that. "You don't have to eat chicken anymore."

Abby's dad was pouring seed from a bag into a trough. "Want to start feeding them?" he asked. She took a plastic pitcher they kept there and filled it with the feed. She poured the right amount into each of the birds' feed bins. Every time a bird came clucking up to her, she stuck her tongue out at it.

Thea called that afternoon. "I heard what happened," she said. "Mom called and left a message. That's rough."

"Yeah," Abby said. "I guess you get out of your maid of honor duties, though."

"I guess." Abby could hear her light a cigarette and take a drag.

"Mom and Dad are being really calm," Abby told her. "It's like nothing happened."

"You know how they are," she said, exhaling the smoke and choking just a little bit. "Plus, they never really liked Matt."

"Yes, they did." Abby felt wounded to hear this.

"Oh, Abby. I don't mean that they hated him. But you know. He wasn't their type."

"Why? Because he showered and wore clean clothes?"

"No, because he always thought he knew everything. You could sense it about him. Not that I minded him. He had a really interesting energy."

"Right."

"Do you want to say hi to your niece? She's right here."

"Sure, put her on the phone."

Abby heard rustling and then she heard Thea say, "Say hi to your aunt Abby. Tell her hello!"

"Your mother is a moron," Abby said into the phone, and then she hung up.

"We should go snowshoeing," her mother said on the third day she was home. "It will do you good to get out in the fresh air."

"Okay," Abby said.

"You're so young," her mom said as they trekked across the snow. "You'll see that this is for the best."

"I'm twenty-five," Abby said. "When you were my age, you already had Thea."

"Well, I wasn't married."

"So you think I should get pregnant?"

"Oh, Abby," she said. "I hate to see you so sad."

"Thea called," Abby said. "She told me that you and Dad never liked Matt."

"That's not true. We like anyone that you bring home. Anyone you like, we like."

"But that's not the same thing. Did you really like him? Are you happy we're not getting married?"

Her mom sighed. "Abby," she said. "You have always known what you wanted. I never doubted you. But things happen for a reason, and if there was trouble, then yes, I am glad that you aren't getting married."

"I didn't say there was trouble."

"People don't call off weddings if everything is hunky-dory." Her mom's nose was dripping, and she wiped it with her glove. Abby looked down at the snow and pressed her weight forward on her snowshoes. "Come on," her mom said. "We should get back. Your father will be worried."

Abby watched her mom pat her arm, but she couldn't feel it through all the layers of clothes. She watched her go *pat, pat, pat* on her sleeve. Then her mom turned and started off ahead of her, stomping in the fresh snow. Abby waited until she was about ten steps in front of her, and then she followed.

Before Abby left New York to come home, she sent an e-mail to all of her friends that said: "The wedding is off. No one reason, just lots of little ones. I'll explain more later. Abby."

She was sure her friends had been calling and e-mailing, but she didn't get any cell service at her parents' house. For once, she was relieved. Usually it drove her crazy, and she would stand on chairs and hold the phone up in the air to try to get some sort of signal. "Come on!" she would say to the phone. "Give me something."

This time, Abby hadn't even taken her phone out of her bag. She knew she'd eventually have to go back to New York and face it. She would have to see her friends and drink vodka and listen to them tell her that it was for the best, that she'd be happier in the long run. She would exhaust herself, going out almost every night, deconstructing every part of her relationship with Matt until it wasn't hers anymore. She would do it, but just not yet.

"We can still live together," Matt said, after he told her about the wedding.

"No," Abby said. "No, we can't."

Abby's parents didn't have cable, so she watched old movies until she thought she could fall asleep. She read the books that were left in her room: *Anne of Green Gables, Little Women, A Day No Pigs Would Die,* and *Bridge to Terabithia.* She didn't remember them being so sad. They were all so sad.

Abby didn't want her mind to be free for even a second. Because when it was, she heard Matt saying, "Abby, I don't know about the wedding."

"What don't you know?" she asked him.

"I don't know if I can do it," he said. He didn't even sound mean when he said it. Actually, he sounded nice and a little apologetic. Like he was sorry for what he was doing. Like he was sorry for ruining her life.

When she didn't feel like reading anymore, she wrote. She made lists of things to do when she got back to the city. A list of things to buy for the apartment now that Matt was gone. A list of shows that she could watch now that he wasn't there. She wrote down names of people who had been through worse things than this: her aunt Eda, the war widow; her friend Crystal, whose parents were killed in a car crash; Helen Keller; Baby Jessica.

When she tried to go to sleep, her head was filled with the weird things people had said to her. She lay and listened to them, and then finally she got up to write them down. She thought maybe if she got them on paper, they would stop bothering her. She got out a pad of paper. *The neighbors are neglecting their exotic birds,* she wrote. Then, *I won't drink the Kool-Aid.* Then, *It's a more humane way to kill birds.* Then, *We can still live together.* Then, *I'm not getting married.* She read these over again and again, until the sentences didn't mean anything. Then she closed her eyes and fell asleep.

℘

Abby woke up to the sound of a child screaming and sat up in bed with her heart pounding. She'd been having a nightmare, but she couldn't remember what it was about. She walked downstairs, and found her mom peering out the kitchen window.

"It's the peacock," she said, without turning around. "He's been getting noisier. One of the peahens is sick, and we think he's upset."

The peacock bleated and bobbed around the pen, and the peahens followed. One of the peahens was slower than the other one, and she limped as she tried to keep up.

"Why is she following him like that?" Abby asked. "Why doesn't she just take care of herself?" It made her angry, that stupid fucking bird, using all of her strength to waddle after him.

Her mom shrugged. "If we knew that," she said, "we could solve all the mysteries in the world."

Abby watched the peacock raise his feathers, and they were beautiful. The peahens raised their feathers too, but they were shorter and not nearly as magnificent, which seemed unfair. The peahens waddled around, following the peacock wherever he went. He couldn't see in the night, so he wandered aimlessly in the pen. *Go the other way,* she wanted to scream at the gimpy peahen. *Stop worrying about where he's going and just rest.*

It seemed to Abby that the peacock was strutting, showing off his feathers to an invisible audience in the night. It didn't look like he was worried about the peahen. He looked selfish and self-absorbed, like he knew he was beautiful. Abby watched his feathers blow in the wind, and she watched as the peahens followed with all of their strength. They followed because it was all they had ever done; they followed because it was all they knew how to do.

Blind

When Isabella waitressed in college, she saw customers come in for blind dates all the time. "Has a man named Stuart come in yet?" they would ask. Or "Is there someone here who's waiting for a Jessica?" When Isabella would shake her head, they would look around nervously. "I'm meeting someone," they would explain, and she would nod. "Someone," Isabella would think. "Someone that you don't know."

Isabella always felt bad for these people, wandering into a restaurant, looking for something but not knowing what it was. "How sad," she always thought to herself. "How sad and a little pathetic." She remembered this as she agreed to go on her first blind date. "I can't believe I'm doing this," she said to Lauren.

"You promised," Lauren said. "You have to."

It was the summer of yes—that's what Isabella and Lauren decided. "We're going to say yes to every invitation that comes our way," they told each other. "We're going to be positive, and put positive energy out there, and then we will meet someone."

Mary decided that she would be a spectator for the summer of yes. She was studying for the bar exam and made it clear that she couldn't say yes to anything. "I'm going to have to pass," she said. "But I totally support you guys."

"You think we're crazy, don't you?" Lauren asked.

"Maybe a little," Mary said. "But it can't hurt to say yes, can it? Plus, if you get Isabella to go on a date, then it will all be worth it."

"That's what I was thinking!" Lauren said.

"You guys, I'm right here," Isabella said.

"Yeah," they said, "we know."

Isabella hadn't dated anyone since Ben moved out. "Get back out there!" her friends kept saying. Isabella didn't want to.

"Get back on the horse," her sister, Molly, told her.

"You get back on the horse," Isabella said to her.

"Nice," her sister said. "Very mature."

Her cousin suggested online dating. "That's how I met Roy," she said. Roy was a dentist with a beak for a nose, and he slurped his spit whenever he talked. "Wow," Isabella said. "I'll think about that."

"I think I miss Ben," she told Lauren one night.

"No, you don't," Lauren said.

"But sometimes, I really think I do."

Lauren sighed. "Isabella, you miss the essence of a boy. That's all."

"Are you sure?"

"Yes. It's better that he's gone. He was a pothead, remember?"

"What are you?"

"I'm a pot enthusiast," Lauren explained.

"Right," Isabella said.

Isabella had never lived alone before, not really, anyway. She'd gotten her own place years ago, but Ben was there almost every night, and then he moved in. Now that he was gone, it was just her and the dust balls.

Sometimes she talked out loud just to hear her voice. She missed having someone there to discuss what to eat for dinner. "I think I'll make a tuna sandwich," she would say to no one. "Or maybe a veggie burger," she would tell the couch.

She started sleeping with the television on at night. It blared reruns and gave her strange dreams. One night she woke up to a *pop!* and the TV screen was black. She sat up in bed and looked around. The air smelled like electrical burning, so she unplugged the TV and tried to go back to sleep.

"I could've died," Isabella said to Mary the next day. "It could have exploded and started a fire all over the place."

"I think you would have woken up," Mary said.

"Maybe."

"I wonder what happened."

"I killed the TV," Isabella explained. "I was too needy."

"You have to meet my friend Jackson," her coworker told her. "He's an accountant, he loves to go wine tasting, and he's a ton of fun."

"Okay," Isabella said. "Yes, okay."

Her coworker arranged it so that Isabella and Jackson would meet at a bar and then go to a Mets game. "You are going to have so much fun!" her coworker told her. Isabella smiled and felt sick inside. "Oh, one more thing, just so you aren't surprised," her coworker said. "Jackson is a little bit bigger than most guys."

"Okay," Isabella said. "Thanks for the heads-up."

It turned out that Jackson was, in fact, obese. And by the third inning, he was so drunk that Isabella couldn't understand him. He yelled at the guy in front of him for standing up, he yelled at the beer man for being too slow, and he yelled at the hot dog guy for running out of relish.

"What about me says, *Set me up with an obese person?*" Isabella wailed to Mary and Lauren later that night. She had made it through the game and then gone to chug wine at Lauren's apartment.

"Nothing," Mary said firmly. "Nothing about you suggests that you should date an obese person." Lauren nodded in agreement.

"Your coworker is obviously an idiot. Or an asshole," Lauren said. "I'm not sure which, but she's one of them."

"You guys, I mean he was really fat. Seriously." She took a Kleenex and blew her nose. "Great," she said. "I'm the meanest person. I date fat people, and now I'm obviously going to hell."

ßつ

Isabella's friend from high school came to visit. Kerry Mahoney was a chipper blonde who wanted everyone to be married. "I am totally setting you up with my cousin," she said. "He's cute and fun, and you guys totally have the same sense of humor. I'm going to give him your number, and maybe you guys can get together next week."

"Yes," said Isabella. "Can I see a picture of him? Okay, yes."

Isabella walked into Mexican Radio and looked around for someone who matched the picture she had seen. A boy with brown hair was at the bar, sipping a giant frozen pink drink with mango floating on top. He looked at her and smiled and she smiled back. "Isabella?" he said in a singsong voice, tilting his head to the right.

"Hey-a," she said. She meant to say hi, but it came out wrong. It was just that she was shocked that she was on a date with a gay man.

"First obese and then gay," she said to Lauren later that night.

"At least it wasn't both at once," Lauren said.

ßつ

"Are you ever afraid that you aren't going to meet anyone?" Isabella asked Lauren one night. They were finishing their last drinks at the bar, and Isabella finally asked the question she'd been thinking for a while now. She didn't want to say it out loud. She was embarrassed that she even thought it, and waited for Lauren to lecture her about being a strong woman. Instead, Lauren finished her drink, crushed an ice cube in her teeth, and said, "All the time."

"I'm exhausted," Lauren said. She was on two kickball teams, a softball team, and was an alternate for a beach volleyball league. "I have scabs all over my legs," she said, pulling up her pants. "Look! Look at this!"

"I don't think the summer of yes should be taken so literally," Isabella said. "It's not like you have to do everything people ask."

"Yes, I do," Lauren said. "That's what I set out to do, and now I have to follow through. I just didn't know that everyone was going to ask me to be on so many intramural teams. Am I that athletic?"

"Not really."

"I didn't think so."

Isabella met a guy selling art at a street fair on the Upper East Side. "I'm just trying to make a living doing what I do," he said. "I'm trying to perfect my craft."

He was handsome, and so when he asked her to hang out, she said okay. "I will ignore his weirdness," she told herself. "I will not be judgmental. This is the summer of yes." She gave him her number and he called the next day.

"A friend of mine from art school is having a party in Greenpoint. You want to go? You can bring some of your girls if you want."

"Yes," Isabella said. She hung up and went to Lauren's apartment to beg her to come with.

"Please?" she asked. "Please? For the sake of the summer of yes?"

"Fine," Lauren said. "But if anyone there asks me to play on any teams, then I'm saying no."

"Fair enough. Oh, and it's also a costume party," Isabella said quickly.

Lauren stared at her. "What kind of costume party?"

"Um, so Kirk kind of explained it as that—well, um, okay. So, what everyone is going to do is dress up as their spirit animal."

"Isabella, are you serious?"

"Yeah. He kind of sprung it on me at the end."

"He sounds like a freak," Lauren said.

"Yeah, he might be."

"I hate the summer of yes," Lauren said.

"I don't think I have a spirit animal," Isabella said.

Lauren ended up making out with a guy at the party who was wearing a green sweatsuit and shamrock antlers. "What are you?" Lauren asked him when they walked in.

"I'm the spirit animal of St. Patrick's Day," he said.

"That's really stupid," she answered.

"That's what I'm going for," he said. Twenty minutes later, they were grinding on the dance floor and Lauren was wearing his shamrock antlers.

Kirk was dressed up as a deer. "I'm gentle inside," he told Isabella. She wanted to hit him with a car.

"What are you?" he asked her.

"A bunny," she said.

"That's your spirit animal?"

"No, it's just the costume I had."

"Isabella, do you mind if I make an observation?"

"Go for it."

"You strike me as a closed-off person."

"Really?"

"Yes."

"That's too bad," Isabella said. She watched Lauren and tried to gauge how much longer she would have to stay.

"Would you like to have dinner with me?" Kirk asked.

Isabella thought for a moment. "Absolutely not," she said.

Isabella decided to quit her job at the mailing-list company. "I don't even understand what I do," she would say when people asked her to explain her job. "I organize lists, okay?"

The thing about this job was that Isabella was good at it. She had been promoted three times since she'd started. "I am now an account manager," she told Mary. "I am an account manager of a mailing-list company."

"It's a good job," Mary said. "Your salary is decent, the hours aren't bad. It's a good job."

"I hate it."

"Then you should quit. If you really hate it, you should quit. But you should do it now. You've been saying that you hate it for a long time, but the longer you wait, the harder it will be to leave."

"I want to work at a publishing house," Isabella said.

"Then you better get on it," Mary said.

Isabella nodded. She hadn't updated her résumé in five years.

It took her a week to find the file, and when she did, she realized that she should just start over. "The last thing on my résumé is an internship at *Harper's Bazaar,*" she said, looking at the piece of paper.

"You have to do it sometime," Mary said. "Just get it over with."

Isabella sent out e-mails to every single person she knew who might have a contact in publishing. She typed cover letters and perfected her résumé. She hounded the HR departments of every publishing house she could think of. She did not get one single interview.

"Why did I waste all this time?" Isabella moaned to Lauren one night. "Why didn't I do this two years ago?"

Lauren didn't say anything, and it didn't matter. Isabella already knew the answer. She hadn't noticed how much she hated her job when she was with Ben. He distracted her from the misery of list selling. And now, it just glared in her face.

"I will probably end up running the fucking company," Isabella said. "I will probably be the best list compiler and maker in the whole world. And I'll have Ben to thank for it."

"That should be your acceptance speech," Lauren said.

Mary called her, out of breath. "My brother's friend Andrew works at Cave Publishing, and he said that they need a new assistant. I have the e-mail of the woman who's doing the interviews, so e-mail her right now. Okay? Are you ready? I'll read it to you now."

"An assistant?" Isabella asked. At the list company, she had her own assistant.

"Isabella," Mary said, with warning in her voice.

"What?"

"Just take the e-mail and send her your résumé. You have to start somewhere, okay?"

"Okay."

ॐ

Isabella sweated through the entire interview. Her upper lip had never been so wet, and she was sure she wouldn't get the job. She assured the woman that she wouldn't mind starting over as an assistant, that she wouldn't mind a pay cut, and that she was eager to learn.

The woman took notes as Isabella talked. "I really want to make a change," Isabella said. "I'm not challenged at my current job, and I've always wanted to get into publishing." Isabella hoped she sounded desperate enough, but not pathetic.

She got the job and was offered a salary that was about half of what she was making. "So, I'll eat macaroni and cheese a lot," she said, trying to convince herself. Her parents told her they would help her out at the beginning. Isabella wished she could say, "No thanks, I'll make it work!" but her new salary barely covered her rent, so she just said, "Thanks. Hopefully it won't be too long."

ॐ

At her old job, people had treated Isabella like she was a savant. "So organized!" they would crow when they walked by her office. "So efficient!" they would cry when she doled out tasks. Now she sat in a cubicle that was covered in paper. "I don't even know what to do with most of it," Isabella admitted to Mary. "They keep handing me stuff, and I literally don't know what to do with it."

"You'll get the hang of it," Mary said. "Give yourself a break. It's only been a few weeks."

ᗷꝺ

At night in her apartment, Isabella talked out loud more often. "I'm tired," she said to the TV. "It's exhausting having no idea what you're doing all day," she told the rug. "I think I'm just going to order Chinese," she confessed to the coffee table, while lying on the couch.

"Maybe you should get a dog," Lauren suggested. "Or a cat."

"Lauren, if you ever tell me to get a cat again, we are not friends anymore. Okay?"

"Touchy, touchy," Lauren said. Then she considered it and said, "That's fair."

ᗷꝺ

"I met a guy," Lauren told her. "He's great." Isabella immediately hoped that it wouldn't work out, and then felt awful about that. Lauren was her friend, but she didn't want to be the last single one standing.

"Come out with us tonight," Lauren said. "He's going to bring some friends. What do you say?"

"Yes," Isabella said.

Isabella walked into the bar, and Lauren rushed up to her. "So, none of his friends could make it. Sorry! But I want you to meet him." She grabbed Isabella's hand and pulled her over to the table. "This is Brian," she said, and Isabella was relieved. He looked like Bert from Sesame Street—no, he looked like Bert with pockmarked skin. Isabella smiled. "It's so nice to meet you."

Isabella sat and drank her vodka soda, while Lauren and Bert held each other in long hugs. "How's the new job?" Lauren asked, with her face in Bert's shoulder.

"Great," Isabella said. "Everything I hoped."

ϑ

Isabella's new boss was called Snowy. She had a skunk stripe in her hair and was frighteningly skinny. Sometimes when she walked down the hall, Isabella was sure her legs were going to pop right off, like a Barbie doll's. Snowy was only ten years older than Isabella, and a star in the publishing world. When Isabella started, Snowy told her that she wanted to be a mentor, not a boss. "I want to help you learn, to help you become a star here."

Snowy had two assistants, and Isabella was hired to be the second one. The first assistant was a twenty-two-year-old named Cate, with shiny brown hair and an amazing wardrobe. The day Isabella started, Cate took her to lunch at a fancy French place and used Snowy's credit card. "I used to be the second assistant, but the first girl left because she said Snowy was impossible to work for," Cate told her.

"Is she?" Isabella asked.

Cate shrugged. "I mean, yeah, she's a nightmare. But don't worry. Just do your job and try not to get upset when she yells."

"Okay," Isabella said. They went back upstairs and Cate showed Isabella how to do Snowy's expenses.

That night, when Mary asked Isabella how work was, she said, "Today, I got career advice from a twenty-two-year-old."

"It'll get better," Mary said.

"God, I hope so."

About three times a day, Snowy dropped a pile of little scrap papers and Post-its on Isabella's desk. They had handwritten notes on them, most of which made no sense. "Here," Snowy would say as she gave them to her, "file these." Isabella, unsure of what to do with the notes, typed them up and kept the originals in a file folder, in case Snowy ever asked for them. One time, Isabella found a Kleenex in the pile of papers. "What am I supposed to do with this?" she asked Cate.

Cate just wrinkled her nose and said, "Gross."

One morning, Snowy dropped a manuscript on Isabella's desk. "Why don't you read this and get back to me?" Isabella held it with both hands on the subway home, afraid that she was going to lose it. She stayed up most of the night, reading it and writing out notes. Everything she wrote sounded stupid. *The main character is too one-dimensional,* she wrote. Then she crossed it out. *The main character does not have enough depth,* she wrote instead. "At one point in my life, I was smart," she thought.

In the morning, Isabella's head and eyes hurt. When she went into Snowy's office to drop off the manuscript, she thought she was going to wet herself. She felt homesick for the list company, just for a second, and then handed her notes to Snowy. When Snowy handed them back to her later, Isabella could see that she'd crossed out almost every note Isabella had written. *No,* she'd written in mean red pen. *Not clear enough.*

"You'll get the hang of it," she told Isabella. Isabella went to the handicapped bathroom and cried for ten minutes. Then she got up, splashed her face with water, and went back to her desk. Cate smiled at her sadly.

ॐ

Cave Publishing was closed the last week of August, and Isabella decided to go home. Her mom had suggested it, and Isabella almost wept with relief when she did. She was tired of getting Snowy coffee. She was tired of having Snowy tell her that she was doing her job wrong. She was tired of the name Snowy.

"That would be great, Mom," Isabella said. She was looking forward to having someone cook for her. She could stay in sweatpants all day if she wanted.

"Oh, that will be fun!" her mom said. "Plus, you can help out with Connor. I'm sure he'll love to see you."

Isabella's nephew Connor was spending most of the summer at her parents' house. He had been asked to leave camp after he screamed at a counselor for changing the schedule. Apparently, the Guppies were supposed to have free swim after crafts, and the unassuming teenager had tried to mix it up and take them to archery instead. Connor flipped out and charged the counselor, head-butting him and screaming, "You idiot asshole!" The head of the camp thought that Connor showed signs of "unusual aggression," and that it would be better if he didn't come back to camp. With no backup child-care plan for Connor, Joseph had asked his parents for help.

"I didn't know you could get kicked out of camp," Isabella said to her mother.

"I didn't know either," her mom said. "But it would be great if you were here to spend some time with him. He's a little difficult these days."

༄

Every morning at eight-thirty, Isabella's brother dropped Connor off. Joseph was balding at a rapid rate. He looked old and tired to Isabella. He was probably upset, but he appeared formal and detached; that's how he always was. "Good morning, Isabella," he would say. Then he would bend down to talk to Connor, who scowled and remained silent.

Connor had been tested for every behavioral abnormality under the sun and had been diagnosed with some frightening acronyms. Now they were working with a therapist to "overcome his challenges." He was odd. Isabella couldn't deny that. But she'd always had a fondness for Connor. He was her oldest nephew and always told her she was his favorite aunt. He always chose to sit next to her. He was sensitive. (Plus, his mother had run off with a man she'd met on the Internet, leaving Connor and his sister with their dad. You had to cut the kid some slack.)

Last Thanksgiving, Connor made up a game. He would draw a box, then draw three objects. "Okay," he'd say. "You're locked in a room with a gun, a bomb, and a phone. What do you do?" No one else but Isabella would play the game.

"What would you do, Auntie Iz?" Connor asked.

"I would use the phone to call outside," Isabella said. "I would warn them to get away, then I would blow a hole in the wall with the bomb and have the gun just in case anyone dangerous was out there."

Connor looked pleased with her answer, and said quickly, "Okay, good one." He nodded his head four times. Then he started drawing another room with three new objects.

All week, Isabella tried to keep Connor occupied. She took him swimming, she took him to play tennis. They went to see a movie, and went to check out books at the library. But on the last day Isabella was there, they ran out of things to do. They sat in the playroom, staring at each other.

"Do you want to play a game, Auntie Iz?" Connor asked. Isabella didn't, but she said yes.

"Okay, so here's the game. It's called Deaf or Blind. So first, you tell me if you would rather be deaf or blind."

"Blind," Isabella said. Connor looked annoyed. He was holding earplugs he'd found in her dad's room.

"You should choose deaf," he said. "It's better."

"But I want to make sure I can still hear music. I'm going to choose blind."

Connor shook his head like he couldn't believe she was making this choice. "Okay," he said, "hold on." He went over to the dress-up chest and rummaged around for a while, until he found a bandanna that had once been part of a cowboy costume.

"You know," he said, "it's a lot scarier to be blind." Isabella nodded. "Okay," he said. "Okay. I've never picked blind before. It seems scary."

"I think I'll be okay," Isabella said.

"Are you scared?" he asked.

"Just a little bit, but not too much." Connor looked at her with admiration.

He stood behind her and wrapped the bandanna around her eyes and then tightened it. Isabella saw the blackness, and then, as he pulled it tighter, bursts of light started to explode. "You can't see, right? Auntie Iz, you can't see anything, right?" Isabella shook her head no.

"Okay," he said. "Here's what we're going to do. I'm going to go in another room and you have to count to a hundred and then come find me. You can call my name three times. Wait, no, only two times. If you call my name three times, then you lose points, okay? And I'll answer you so that you can try to hear where I am."

"Got it," Isabella said.

"Okay. This is hard, though, Auntie Iz. You have to listen with your insides. You can listen in a way that you didn't before. Okay?"

"Okay."

Connor walked out of the room and then Isabella heard him stop. "But Auntie Iz? If you get scared or fall down, you can take it off, okay? That's okay." Isabella nodded. She felt Connor touch her eyes softly. "You really can't see, right? Okay, here we go."

Isabella heard him run out of the room and shout, "Okay, go!" She was counting to one hundred in her head, and then she heard him say, "Auntie Iz, you have to count out loud!" So she started over. "One, two, three, four," she said, and then she heard him scream, "Slower!" so she slowed down.

She heard a door slam downstairs and then voices. Her mother was talking to Connor. Isabella could tell that he was frustrated that she was interrupting the game. Then she heard her brother's voice. They were talking to Connor like he was younger than he really was, and Isabella felt bad for him. She hadn't noticed how their voices changed when they talked to him. She heard them ask him about where she was.

"No," she heard him say. "No, you can't get Auntie Iz now. She can't come in here yet. She's blind," and Isabella was struck by how he said that last word. He said it like he was proud of her for choosing the blindness, like he was amazed that she would choose not to see.

She could hear Connor's voice start to rise. His pitch got higher and his volume louder as he said, "No, you said three-thirty and it's only three o'clock. I'm not ready. I'm not finished." Isabella knew that he was shaking his head as he said this, tightening his arms and shaking them back and forth with quick, little movements. She had seen him work his way into a fit a number of times in the past week, but now she just listened.

"I'm not done, I'm not ready!" he said. "Izzy is still blind, and I didn't know you were coming yet. I'm not done! I'm not done!"

Isabella listened to him as he shrieked so high and loud that she knew the neighbors could hear. "This isn't how it was supposed to go!" he yelled. She listened to her mother and brother try to quiet him down, try to plead with him to settle himself. But he didn't. Connor screamed with all of his might. He fought against it with everything he had. All he wanted was to know what to expect. His world didn't look like he'd thought it would, and she understood. How could he keep calm if he couldn't see? Isabella lay on the floor of the playroom upstairs and listened. She heard the screams and she knew exactly how he felt. He was right—she could hear it on her insides.

An Animal Called Ham

The bartender at McHale's was sleazy in an attractive way. This annoyed Lauren. She couldn't make sense of it. She was disgusted with Preston, yet still happy whenever he threw a lime at her from behind the bar. "He's gross," she tried to explain to her friends. "He has dirty blond hair that he slicks back behind his ears with little curls at the end. It always looks greasy. His eyes are a filmy blue, like he's thinking pervy things. And he has this big scar on his chin that I just always want to touch."

"So he's dirty sexy," her friend Shannon said.

"Yes!" Lauren said. "But why?"

"Dirty sexy can't really be explained," Shannon said. "It's kind of like ugly sexy. Only you feel worse about it because you think you should be above the sleaze."

Lauren felt better for the explanation, but it still unsettled her to be around him. "I will not sleep with him," she told herself. Two weeks after she started working there, she stayed with Preston to have a drink after work and found herself having sex with him in the walk-in fridge. One second she was drinking a vodka soda, and the next thing she knew there was a bin of lettuce shaking above her head. She couldn't serve a salad for weeks without feeling trashy.

"So much for that," she said to Shannon. Shannon just shrugged.

Lauren was sure that Preston was not the right guy for her. But still, she found herself in his bed. She lay behind him and sucked his blond curls when he was sleeping. She knew it couldn't end well.

Lauren was almost out of money when she decided to be a waitress. She had been looking for PR jobs in New York for a month and hadn't even gotten an interview. So she started applying at bars in SoHo and gastropubs in the West Village. (She figured if she was going to be a waitress, she would like to do it in a place where she might see famous people.) But none of those places wanted her. It turned out that being a waitress in New York was more competitive than being in PR. Aspiring models and actresses flooded every restaurant, elbowing one another with bony arms to win the right to serve food. Lauren didn't have a chance.

A friend suggested that she apply at McHale's, an old-fashioned restaurant in Midtown with a wood-paneled dining room and a meatloaf special on Wednesdays. McHale's was the kind of place that made people nostalgic for a time when businessmen drank at lunch and people ate pot roast on Sundays. It had a bar with red leather stools and a mean vodka gimlet. They offered Lauren a job the day she walked in and she took it.

And just like that, Lauren was a waitress. It was only temporary, of course. It was just an in-between job, something to make money while she was looking for her next move. She could tell that it made the customers happy when she told them this. They were more comfortable once they knew that Lauren had plans. She was just too pretty, too charming to simply be a waitress.

Lauren figured she would work at the restaurant for three months, maybe six months max. But a year went by and she was still there. She stopped sending résumés out to PR firms. She couldn't even remember what she thought she had wanted to be.

At the very least, Preston was a distraction from the detour her career had taken. He wasn't a big talker, and Lauren found herself filling up the silence when they were together. That was how she came to tell him the story of the ham.

In her high school biology class, Lauren dissected a pig. Each pair of students got their very own formaldehyde-soaked piglet to cut up. As they sliced and dismembered the little porkers, the teacher told them different facts about the pig's stomachs and reproductive organs. He walked over to Lauren's pig and pointed to the rump. "This is where ham comes from," he told her. Lauren looked up. "Ham comes from pigs?" she asked. "Doesn't ham come from a ham?" Everyone laughed. As soon as the question was out of her mouth, she knew it wasn't right. A ham wasn't an animal, of course. She was only confused for a second or two. But the thing was, she knew what the ham would look like if there was such a thing. She could picture it perfectly, as though she had actually seen it before.

She told Preston this story when they were lying in bed together. She didn't know why she told him. Lauren hated the story, hated explaining how she'd thought a ham was an oval-shaped hunk of an animal that slurped across the ground. "You know," she said, "I thought it would be a ham." As she said this, she moved her hands in an oval motion. "A *ham*," she emphasized, as though this would explain it.

Preston laughed so hard that he cried. "Did you think it had just that one bone?" he asked. "I don't know," she said. "I guess I didn't think about it." He held his stomach and rocked back and forth. "Ow," he said, wrapping his arms around himself. "Ow, it hurts! I can't stop!"

A week after that, he woke up and said, "I don't think this is going to work." She was still in his bed in a T-shirt and underwear and didn't know what to say. Immediately she felt sorry for the ham—it had been a mistake to tell him about it. That much she knew.

After Preston broke up with her, Lauren started going to the park during the day. All of her friends worked in offices and she couldn't stand to be in her apartment alone. She would go to the park and lie on the grass, waiting for the day to be over so that she could start her shift at the restaurant. She liked watching the clouds. She liked the way they always kept moving, even if it was so slowly that you couldn't tell which way they were going.

Lauren bought a book about weather and learned the names of the clouds. She would chant them under her breath as she looked up: "Cumulus, stratus, cirrus, pileus." She learned everything she could about clouds to fill up her time. She learned that *cirrus* was a Latin root meaning curl of hair. "Cirrus," she'd whisper, standing behind Preston, staring at his hair. "What?" he'd say. "Nothing," she'd answer. Her favorite cloud was cumulonimbus. It sounded like a magic word. It sounded like something dirty.

Her friends were concerned that she was going crazy. "You should quit your job," Shannon told her.

"Yeah," Isabella agreed. "Don't make yourself sick over this guy. He's just a dirty bartender."

"A dirty sexy bartender," Lauren said.

Shannon nodded sadly. "Yeah, he is. You should definitely quit."

Preston walked in late for the lunch shift and slid behind the bar to start cutting fruit. Lauren raised her eyebrows at him from across the room, where she was rolling silverware. "You're late," she said to him.

"Really, my dear?" Preston asked. "I thought I was right on time." Preston was a person who got away with saying things like "my dear" to girls he'd just dumped. Lauren hated him for this.

"Late night?" Lauren asked. "You look like shit." Preston laughed because he knew he didn't and tucked in his shirt.

Carly, the other waitress, burst in and threw her bag down before running to the bathroom. On Lauren's first day of work,

Carly had told her that she had a tattoo of a lawn mower on her pubic bone. "See, the lawn mower is right here," she said, touching the space right above her crotch. "And then I shave the hair in front of it to make it look like it mowed a path. Upkeep's a bitch, but guys love it. Want to see it?"

"No thanks," Lauren said. "Maybe another time."

Lauren was sure that she would die young. Maybe she would get a tumor or die in a freak subway accident. More likely, she would be murdered by a serial killer. *Dateline* would do a special and interview everyone at the restaurant. "She was a pretty nice girl," Carly would say. Maybe she would offer to show the cameraman her tattoo. Preston would pretend to be upset, but would really be excited at the thought of being on TV. "We dated," he would tell them. "She was a special girl," he would say, and then look down for dramatic effect.

People who knew Lauren from college would watch this and wonder what the hell happened to her. They would ask each other why Lauren was hanging out with Ms. Lawn Mower Tattoo and Mr. STD Bartender. They would be sad for the way things turned out for her, and then they would turn off the television and forget about it.

Lauren tried to go out with her friends and have a normal social life. She would meet them after her shift ended and pretend that she wasn't exhausted and didn't smell like hamburger meat. She told herself that she needed to keep doing this.

"I have to find a real job," she would tell her friends.

"So find one," they would say. They didn't understand. They talked about e-mail programs and corporate retreats. They compared health plans and 401(k)s and Lauren felt lonely.

⌘

Carly came out of the bathroom and asked Preston for a glass of cranberry juice. "I have a UTI," she confided to Lauren. Lauren just nodded and continued to roll the silverware.

"It's that new guy I'm seeing. I can't get enough!" Carly bumped her hip against Lauren's as though they were old friends, two gossiping gals trading sex stories.

Lauren excused herself from the UTI talk to go back to the manager's office. She had requested next weekend off and wanted to make sure that Ray hadn't put her on the schedule. Lauren had to go to her friend Annie's wedding on the Cape. Annie and her fiancé had bought a house in Boston and e-mailed pictures of the renovation of the rooms as it went along, with commentary like "Mitchell put in the tile in the upstairs bathroom all by himself. I knew there was a reason I'm marrying this one!"

Annie was the kind of friend who needed to do everything first. Lauren knew what she must have been like in third grade, filling out tests and raising her hand for the teacher, shouting, "Done! I'm done!"

When she'd gotten the save-the-date card last year, Lauren had been sure that she would have a job by the wedding. When she'd gotten the invitation two months ago, she'd still thought there was hope. Now she knew that she would have to see all of these people and tell them that she was a waitress. A waitress who had sex in walk-in refrigerators.

⌘

Lauren's first customers of the day were two women, a brunette and a blonde. They had a young boy with them who belonged to the blonde. Lauren could tell by the way he kept trying to impress the brunette that she wasn't his mother. He wiggled in his seat and said things like "A horse says, *Neigh!*" Then he laughed and slid down the booth to the floor, pretending to be embarrassed when she noticed him.

Lauren didn't dislike children, but she also couldn't say that she liked them. She was sure this was going to be a problem. Shannon assured her that it was normal, but her friend Kristi told her it was not. "That makes me sad," she'd said to Lauren, and Lauren felt ashamed.

The two women each ordered a chicken salad with fat-free raspberry vinaigrette, and the little boy ordered bacon and French fries. His mother laughed like he had done something clever. She looked at her brunette friend and shook her head and smiled as if to say, *Isn't he a riot? Isn't he the most adorable thing you've ever seen?* Lauren waited with her pen above her pad for the mother to make him order something else. The mother didn't say anything.

"So, you want me to bring an order of fries and a separate order of bacon?" she finally asked. The mother looked at her like she was stupid and nodded.

Lauren walked to the computer to put the order in. She didn't even know how to place an order of bacon. At McHale's, bacon was something that went on a burger or a BLT. It was not something that people ordered a plate of.

"Preston?" she called to him down the bar. "Do you know how to place an order of bacon?"

"Bacon? Where does bacon come from? A ham?" Preston asked, and then laughed.

"Don't be such a shit," Lauren said.

"What's with the attitude, peaches?" Preston asked. "Just a little joke. You like jokes, don't you?"

Lauren sighed and turned back to the computer. Finally she ordered a BLT with extra bacon, hold the bread, tomato, and lettuce. Then she walked back to the kitchen to explain to Alberto what the order meant before he came out yelling.

When Lauren got back, there was another customer in her section. "He just sat there," Carly said. She sat on a bar stool and sipped cranberry juice, looking miserable. Lauren didn't feel like fighting with Carly today, or hearing the details of her UTI, so she picked up her pad and went over to the table.

"Hi," Lauren said.

"Hi," the man said back. He was about thirty, but he was dressed like he was older; his hair was swirled in an old-fashioned part and his suit was impeccable. He wore heavy-looking cuff links of a bear on his right wrist and a bull on his left. Lauren hated him on the spot.

"Can I get you something to start?" she asked.

"Well, to start with, you could smile. Would that be too much to ask?"

Lauren looked up and locked eyes with him for a second. People were always telling her to smile. Construction workers on the street and random guys in bars would just call out to her, "Hey, beautiful, smile!" They said it like they were doing her a favor, like they could make her happy with this little tip.

"My mouth turns down," Lauren said. "I'm not unhappy."

"Whoa, okay. That's more information than I asked for."

Lauren sighed. "You told me to smile, implying that I was

unhappy. But I'm not. My mouth turns down and sometimes it looks that way."

"So what are you?" the guy asked.

"What do you mean?"

"Well, you said you're not unhappy and you clearly aren't happy. So what are you today?"

"I guess I'm neutral."

"Well, neutral, it's lovely to meet you. Can you get me a Glenlivet on the rocks?"

Lauren nodded and turned away. She was used to creepy customers. And she knew from experience that this guy was a self-important creeper, which was the worst kind. He thought that Lauren should be thrilled to be his waitress. He thought he was different from every other customer.

Lauren placed the drink order at the bar and then went to deliver the food to her other table. The boy clapped his hands when she put down his plates of fries and bacon.

"And pickles!" he cried. "I want some pickles."

Lauren wanted to tell him about the rise of childhood obesity, but she went back to the kitchen and pulled four pickles out of the pickle tub and put them on a plate. When she placed them in front of the boy he said, "You're a pickle," and pointed to the brunette. Then he clamped both hands over his mouth and laughed and bounced on his seat.

She picked up the Glenlivet from the bar and deposited it on the table. "Are you ready to order?" she asked. She looked down at her pad. She didn't want to meet his eyes.

"I know you from somewhere," he said.

"I don't think so," she answered. "People say that a lot. I'm a familiar-looking person."

"No, I definitely know you from somewhere. What's your name?"

Lauren looked up at him. She debated giving him a fake name. Maybe this would be the serial killer who would murder her. Carly could tell the cameras that she felt guilty for not waiting on him. "It could have been me," she would cry through purple mascara.

"Did you forget?" he asked.

"What?"

"Did you forget your name? It's taking you a long time to answer."

"Lauren," she said. She figured if he was going to murder her, he was going to do it whether or not he knew her real name.

"Lauren," he said. "I don't know any Laurens." He looked at her carefully.

"I told you, I'm a familiar-looking person," she said. His stare was upsetting. She wanted him to stop looking at her. He ordered a steak sandwich and another drink. Lauren looked down, surprised. She hadn't realized he had finished the first drink while they were talking. She took the empty glass and walked away.

"Lauren, who's the hottie over there?" Carly was looking much perkier after her third glass of cranberry juice.

"Just some guy. He's kind of a creep," Lauren said, and waited for Preston to look her way so that she could order the drink.

"So you're taking next weekend off?" Carly asked. "Ray asked if I could cover your shift."

"Yeah, I have to go to a wedding," Lauren said.

"Oh, fun! I love weddings," Carly said, and then she sighed. "I want to get married."

"Is that a proposal?" Preston asked.

"Yeah, right, Preston. Like you could handle all this!" Carly did a shimmy to make her boobs swing back and forth and Preston laughed.

"Preston, can you get me this drink?" Lauren pushed the slip across the bar.

"What's with you, sourpuss?" Preston asked.

"Why is everyone saying that to me? I'm fine," Lauren said.

"Clearly," Preston said.

"It's just these customers are bugging me today," Lauren said. "See that table over there? The mom let her son order bacon for lunch."

"Grody!" Carly said.

"Yeah, grody!" Preston mocked her. "Plus, do you know how many little bacons had to die for that lunch? It's really a shame."

"Shut it, Preston."

"Here's your drink, sunshine!"

The man smiled at Lauren as she carried his drink over. "Is that man your lover?" he asked.

"Lover?" Lauren asked. "No, that man is not my *lover*. Where are you from? Who talks like that?"

"I do," he said, and sniffed.

"I didn't mean to offend you," Lauren said.

"You did mean to, and you didn't, so don't worry."

"Oh, okay."

"I'm a very successful man," he said.

"That's great."

"It is. A lot of people are jealous of me. I make a lot of money."

"Great."

"A lot. More than you could probably guess."

"Is that right?"

"Yes," he said. "I thought of where I knew you from, by the way."

Lauren's heart started pounding. "Really?" she asked.

"Yes," he answered. "I used to see you in the park."

"The park?"

"Yes, Madison Square Park. You used to lie there and talk to yourself."

"What?" Lauren felt dizzy.

"I used to work right there, and we'd see you on our lunch break. One of my buddies thought you were retarded."

"I didn't—that wasn't me. I don't know what you're talking about."

"Oh, come on, Lauren, give it up! I saw you. I saw you every day. Don't be upset about my buddy calling you a retard, he was just playing around. Anyway, when he said that, I told him, 'I'd still sleep with her. She's still hot, even if she is a retard.' "

"I didn't" was all Lauren could say.

"So, what were you doing there anyway? You were there every day and then one day you weren't there. I always wondered what happened to you. I always wondered what you were doing, lying there and talking to yourself."

"I wasn't doing anything," Lauren said.

"Well, Lauren, you must have been doing something."

Lauren wished she hadn't told him her real name. She didn't like the way it sounded coming out of his mouth.

&

Lauren never told her friends how much she went to the park after Preston dumped her. They wouldn't have understood that it was the only place she wanted to be. She figured she'd just keep going there forever, lie on the grass and look at the clouds, happy in her own world. But then one day she went to the park and it rained. It rained big, thick drops that made noise when they hit the ground. Lauren watched as the white light clouds soiled themselves, turning an army brown and finally a slimy black. She lay there, feeling the people around her gathering their things and leaving. But she stayed, watching the clouds quiver and finally release. She kept her eyes open the whole time. She didn't even blink.

One drop hit her chest and stayed intact, a tiny puddle of rain wobbling on top of her skin. Others fell on her face, sliding off the grooves of her nose and mouth. Some hit her eyeballs, and she thought they ran right inside her head, through her eyes and all the way to her brain. She let them all fall on top of her, let them soak her one at a time.

She watched a cloud turn into a shape that she recognized. It was a ham—but not the ham she had seen in her head. No, this was an ugly ham, a deformed ham. She watched it float along the sky and she was repulsed. It had bumpy skin and big nostrils. It was so fat that it looked like it was going to burst. She stayed there and watched as it floated away and got eaten by the other clouds. And then she left.

Lauren didn't go back to the park after that. She hadn't wanted to. She wasn't totally over Preston, but something in her shifted. Wanting him back was like wanting to cut off your arm or have your toes poked with needles. It didn't make sense. Her friends never knew exactly what had happened, but they were just happy she was getting back to normal.

"Breakups are tough," Isabella said. "But you got through it!"

"I'm glad you're over him," Shannon said. "Now you need to go find another asshole to fuck with your head."

But none of them knew that it was the ham that had done it. How could something that Lauren made up in her own head turn so ugly? How could her creation get so out of hand? It was that ugly ham that made her move on.

Lauren was still standing at the man's table. She couldn't seem to make herself walk away.

"Would you like to have dinner with me sometime?" He smiled and sat back, like he was sure she would be flattered at this invitation.

"No," she said. "I really wouldn't."

"I'm very successful," he said. He slurred a little.

"Why are you here alone?" Lauren asked.

"I'm celebrating. I'm celebrating a big deal."

"Alone?"

"I'm very successful," he said, sounding impatient. "I told you that already."

"Well, you're not the type of guy I want to go to dinner with."

"Oh no? Who is, then? That bartender over there?" He said the word "bartender" like he was saying "pimp" or "homeless person."

"No," Lauren said. "He's not my type either."

"Oh, well, look at you, Miss High and Mighty! Are you going to meet someone in the park?"

"You're a jackass," Lauren said.

"And you are a rude waitress," the man said. "A rude waitress who just lost herself a tip."

"Good," Lauren said. "I wouldn't have it any other way."

"Why don't you just sit down for a minute?" the man asked. "I feel like we got off to a bad start."

Lauren rested her hands on the back of the chair across from him. Her knees felt wiggly. "I'm okay," she said.

"I didn't ask if you were okay," the man said. "I asked if you would like to sit down. I would buy you a drink if you did. I just closed a huge deal."

"I know," Lauren said. "You told me. Why do you keep telling me that?"

"It's the kind of thing people like to know," he said. "It's the kind of thing you want to tell someone about yourself."

Lauren straightened herself up and looked him in the eye. She smiled widely, showing him all of her teeth. "Thank you, then," she said. "Thanks for sharing." She walked away from the table. The man sat there holding his drink.

ß

"Carly, I need you to finish up that table for me," Lauren said. "I can't wait on that guy anymore."

Carly nodded. "Sure. Is he rich?"

"He might be," Lauren said. "You should ask him."

"Hey, Lauren," Preston said. "This guy at the bar just ordered a grilled ham and cheese. You want to go tell him that he shouldn't eat the precious ham animal?"

"You are a moron," Lauren said. "You know that?"

"I'm just saying, there are a lot of hams getting slaughtered around here today," Preston said and smiled.

Carly looked back and forth between them, like she was waiting for a fight to break out. "What's going on?" she asked.

"Nothing," Lauren said.

At the other table, the little boy was standing on the seat of the booth wiggling his hips and singing, "Ooh, baby, baby. Ooh, baby!" His mother clapped and laughed until his knee knocked over the water, and then she told him to sit and motioned to Lauren that they needed help cleaning up.

This was not what Lauren went to college for. This was not where she was supposed to be. These were not the kind of people she was supposed to be around. She took a deep breath and whispered, "Cumulonimbus." She closed her eyes and saw the Ham—the real Ham—basking in all of its glory. It looked nothing like the monster she'd seen at the park. This was a handsome Ham. It had whiskers that blew in the wind, and Lauren thought it was smiling at her. She opened her eyes, feeling better. "Did you say something?" Preston asked her, and she shook her head. She picked up a towel from the bar and went to go clean up her table. She had the Ham back. Tomorrow, she told herself. Tomorrow she would quit.

Cigarettes at Night

When Mary was nine, she stole a prayer. It happened by accident, but it happened just the same. She was kneeling in front of the prayer candles at church, blowing softly out of her mouth, and watching the flames flicker. She made a little circle with her lips and held her hands folded in front of her mouth, as though she were praying. Mrs. Sugar watched her closely, giving her warning looks with her thick eyebrows, while she tried to pay attention to the rest of the class, which was still lined up to give confession. Mrs. Sugar had a nice-sounding name, but really she was a witch. Every time she looked over, Mary pressed her lips together.

Mary had gone to confession first, and had already said her two Hail Marys and her three Our Fathers. Now there was nothing left for her to do except kneel quietly and blow at the candles. She sent the flame to the left, to the right, and then straight back. It leaned and bounced but always came back to the center, standing straight and tall. And then, it happened. She breathed a little too hard, and the candle sputtered out.

Mrs. Sugar was by her side before she even realized what had happened. She leaned down and grabbed the top part of Mary's arm, whispering because they were still in church, but whispering meanly. "Do you know what you did?" she said. "You stole someone's prayer. Someone lit that very candle with a personal prayer, an intention. And now it's gone. Vanished. And it's all because of you."

Mary cried and was sent to sit on the bench in the vestibule to wait. She sniffled as she sat, wondering what Mrs. Sugar was going to do to her. But while she was back there, James Lemon farted loudly, making the rest of the class laugh and scream, and Mrs. Sugar got distracted as she ran around trying to calm everyone down. For the rest of the day, Mary waited for her punishment, but it seemed Mrs. Sugar had forgotten all about the candle and the stolen prayer.

Mary, on the other hand, never forgot. Anytime she lit a candle, she felt guilty. She kept thinking that this feeling would go away, that eventually something bigger and more important would come and take the place of this memory. But it didn't. For years, anytime that she went to church, she put a dollar in the box to light a candle. "For the one that I stole," she would whisper, and then she would light it. She lit a candle in Rome her junior year, and another in Ireland. When she moved to New York, she lit one in St. Patrick's, and that was her last one. She stopped partly because she was rarely in church anymore, but also because she figured that however big the prayer was that had been attached to that candle, she'd more than made up for it by now.

℘

Mary was quitting. That's all there was to it. She'd always said that as soon as she passed the bar, she was done. No more cigarettes. She'd never been a real smoker anyway. It was just something she did when she studied late at night. And when she drank. But that was all over now, she told herself. She was a lawyer now. A lawyer who didn't smoke.

Mary was hired at Slater, a big law firm right in the middle of Times Square. Its real name was Slater, McKinsey, Brown, and Baggot, but no one ever got past the Slater. She was hired along with nine other brand-new eager lawyers, and all of them were taken out on a boat cruise, where they were served piña coladas and reminded that they were incredibly lucky, that this was the job of a lifetime, that they better live up to their promise, and that they must pass the bar.

She spent the summer studying for the bar, holed up in her apartment drinking Red Bull and eating bananas, because she'd heard that they were good for concentration. Her friends sometimes dropped in to check on her, and while she knew they were being nice, she wished they would just ignore her until it was over. "It's not normal how long you can stay in one place," Isabella told her one night. She'd stopped by and found Mary sitting at her desk, where she admitted she'd been since that morning. "I think you should at least get out of the apartment once a day. Maybe we should go for a walk?"

But Mary refused. She didn't have time to leave her apartment. She went to the store once a week for supplies, jumped rope for exercise, and treated herself by leaning out her window and smoking out into the darkness. "Just until I finish the bar," she would sometimes say out loud, and then stub out her cigarette with purpose and force, so that it bent in half, as if to say, *See, cigarette, I won't need you for long.*

After she took the test, Mary thought she would feel relief. But all the weeks of studying had taken their toll and all Mary felt was strange. She could feel all the caffeine she'd drunk still throbbing through her system, and her hand seemed unfamiliar now that it was no longer holding a pencil all the time. Sometimes Mary was sure she could still feel the pencil in her hand, the way she imagined people with missing limbs would feel.

It was because of all of this that Mary decided that she would not throw away her half-finished pack of cigarettes right after the bar, as she had originally planned. She would finish this pack she had, and then she would quit when she started at the firm. No sense in making too many changes at once.

But when Mary started at Slater, she found she needed her cigarettes more than ever. All of the other new lawyers, who she'd imagined would be her friends, were competitive and nasty. Some of them were secretive about their desire to be the best. Others, like Barbara Linder, followed Mary around, asking her what she was working on, how many hours she had logged that week, and what the partners had said to her.

Slater had a tradition of announcing congratulations to the new lawyers who passed the bar over the loudspeaker, and then having a cocktail reception. For weeks, Mary wondered what it would be like if she didn't hear her name, if she was the one person of the group to fail. Until she heard the results of her test, there was no way she could stop smoking. And then when she did find out that she'd passed, the relief was so immediate and overwhelming that she made a weird noise and got tears in her eyes. Also, she wet herself just a little bit and so she let herself have a cigarette. If you pee in your pants, she thought, you deserve at least that.

℘

Mary was at the office until at least nine every night, and that was if she was lucky. She was exhausted and sad to go to sleep at night because she knew it would mean the whole thing would start all over again soon. Each morning, as she walked from the subway to her building, she thought, "If I get hit by a car today, I won't have to go to work." She didn't want to get seriously hurt, of course. She just wanted a minor bump that would send her to the hospital for a week or two, where she could watch TV and eat Jell-O.

No one had told her it would feel like this. She'd gotten so much advice about her first year at a law firm, but no one had ever said, "You will be constantly afraid." And that's what she was. She was afraid that someone would come to her with work to do, and she was afraid that no one would come to her with work to do. She was scared that she was missing something in her research. She went over each assignment she was given, and then she was terrified that they would all think she was slow. Whenever someone said "case law" or "document review," her first instinct was to hide underneath her desk.

Sometimes, just as she was finishing up one project, feeling like she'd accomplished one thing, someone would come to her office to give her a new task. She was sure she was failing.

At night, Mary would take breaks and leave her office to go to the roof for a cigarette. It was wrong, she knew, but she couldn't help it. She only smoked at night. During the day, there were too many people around and she didn't want them to think that she was actually a smoker. She looked forward all day to standing outside and lighting her cigarette. She loved those five minutes of quiet, standing and blowing smoke. She breathed in and out, and told herself that smoking, for her, was a little bit like meditation. It was keeping her sane.

☙

There was a lot to worry about those first few months, but one of the biggest things was this: Mary was afraid that she was getting fat. Each night that she ate dinner at the office, she felt her ass getting bigger. When it came time to order, she would look through the menus in disbelief that she was staying for dinner again. Sometimes, in a fit, she would order lobster or two different entrées. "They want me to stay, they can pay for it," she would think as she clicked in her order on her computer. Other times she'd order from the diner, cheeseburgers and fries, and a milkshake for good measure. After these giant meals, she would go up to the roof and smoke. Breathe in and out, she would repeat. Breathe in and out.

In the bathroom, she examined her butt, turning to the side and running her hands over it, trying to measure how much bigger it was than the day before. She'd seen her cousin Colleen gain fifty pounds during her first year at a law firm. Colleen went from normal to almost obese in a matter of months, and she grabbed the weight and held on to it. "It's worse than having a baby," she'd said last Thanksgiving. "It's just part of the job," she'd told Mary. And then she'd eaten two pieces of pecan pie.

Mary had sworn that it wouldn't happen to her, but she hadn't known it would be so hard. She always wanted to leave the office and she always wanted to stay. She wanted all of the partners to like her, to praise her. She lived for one of them to say, "Nice job" or "Thanks for the help." It didn't come often, but when it did, it felt like getting an A. Or at least a B. And there was nothing that Mary loved more than getting good grades. Maybe that made her pitiful, but she couldn't help it. And so she stayed, and she sat in her chair for fifteen hours at a time, eating Chinese food, popping dumplings into her mouth, slurping up sesame noodles, and hoping for someone to notice her work. And then she would go home and look at herself in the full-length mirror, studying the bulge that was threatening to explode, wondering how long it would be before she erupted into a truly giant person.

Each time she bought a pack of cigarettes, she said, "Last pack," as she unwrapped the plastic at the top. She was basically done smoking, she told herself. It was really just a formality until she was an official nonsmoker. And so when Isabella came over to her apartment, sniffed the air, and said, "Were you smoking in here?" Mary said, "No, I quit."

She knew she'd gone too far. Once she started lying about it, there was no going back. "I don't care if you smoke," Isabella said. She gave Mary a strange look. "I was just asking." But still, Mary denied it. She hid her cigarettes in her bedside table, tucked in the back of the drawer, wrapped in an old bandanna. Each time after she smoked, she wrapped up the pack of cigarettes with the lighter, folding them in the cloth, and carefully placing them back where nobody could find them.

Brian Sullivan was made a junior partner at thirty-three. He was the one all of the first years wanted to be, the one they all talked about. He was handsome in a prep school way and looked like every cute boy that Mary had a crush on in high school. He was the first person to ask Mary to write a memo, and she was flattered. "Really," she asked. "A memo?" She sounded like a parrot.

He laughed and leaned on her desk. "Look," he said. "I know it feels impossible now, but it'll get better. I promise." He put his hand on her shoulder, and Mary almost turned her head and leaned down to kiss it. It was the first time in a week anyone had touched her, not counting the toothless woman who'd pulled on her leg as she was going down to the subway. Her face got hot, as though she had actually leaned over and placed her lips there. Brian removed his hand before she could think much more, and she was left in her office with her embarrassing thoughts.

Mary had always been scared of her imagination. When she was younger, she used to think, "What if I stood up in the middle of class and told Mrs. Sugar to go to hell?" Then her cheeks would flush at the thought and her heart would start pounding, as if she was really going to stand up and scream. "I'm not going to do it," she would tell herself. She would try to calm down, but then she would think of it again, how she could have just screamed, how no one would have stopped her, and she would get nervous again. It was the potential of what could happen, the possibility that she could do something so reckless. That's what scared her.

Brian Sullivan brought all of that back. Every time he came into her office and stood next to her desk, Mary imagined what would happen if she put her hands on his belt buckle and started to take off his pants. Her blood pounded in her ears, and she tried to reassure herself that she wasn't going to do any such thing. But then she'd pass him in the hall, and she'd think, "What would happen if I just went up to him and said, 'Let's have sex right now'?" She tried to tell herself that she was in charge of her actions, that her brain couldn't take over. And then she thought, "This is what happens to people right before they go insane."

Brian found Mary on the roof one night, sitting on one of the stone benches, her head leaning back as she smoked her Marlboro Light very slowly, letting the smoke trickle out of her mouth and escape into the air. "Hey," he said. "So, you're a smoker."

Mary snapped her head up quickly, causing her to cough and choke for a few seconds before she could speak. "No," she finally said. "I'm not a smoker. I'm quitting."

"Oh," he said. "Okay." He pulled out an unopened pack of cigarettes and hit them against the heel of his hand, then unwrapped the plastic and crumpled it into a ball, never looking away from her. "I've been quitting for years." He raised his eyebrows and took a cigarette out of his pack, held it in his teeth, and smiled.

Mary gave a weak laugh and held her cigarette low. "I really thought I would've quit by now," she said. "But it's been a harder adjustment than I planned on."

"Because I make you nervous?" Brian asked.

"What? No!" Mary said. She sounded too forceful. She'd meant to sound calm, but it came out in a little yell.

Brian laughed. "It's okay," he said. "I mean, when I first started, even the secretaries made me nervous. Everyone knew more than I did."

"Oh," Mary said. She realized that he had meant something very different, and she made herself laugh again. "Yeah, well. I guess it goes away eventually, right?"

"That it does," Brian said. He blew circles in the air.

Brian and Mary started smoking together at night. She always hoped she'd see him and she always felt sick when she did. She should not be doing this, she told herself. He was a partner. He was her boss. But she looked forward to their conversations all day. When two days in a row passed without them running into each other on the roof, she felt desperate. When he returned on the third day, she almost jumped off the bench.

Every piece of information she got about him felt like a gift. She gathered all that she knew and went over it in her head. He had two brothers, he was the youngest, he liked gherkins and sour Altoids but hated any kind of soda. He was a Yankees fan, called his grandfather "Oompa," and looked best in light pink shirts.

They talked about college, and she found out that he'd played lacrosse. "Well," she said, "that's no surprise."

"What's that supposed to mean?" he asked her.

"Just that, you know, you kind of look like a lacrosse player," Mary said.

"Really?" Brian asked. "How do you mean?"

"I mean, you just look like you went to prep school and played lacrosse. I don't know." Mary took a drag of her cigarette and tried to sound not stupid. "All the boarding school boys at my college, they all played lacrosse and just had a look."

"Well, I did go to prep school," Brian said. "But I didn't go to boarding school. My roommate did, though, and he was weird." Brian stopped talking and Mary wasn't sure if he was done. Then he flicked his cigarette and continued. "I'd never send my kids to boarding school," he finally said. "It fucks them up."

Everything she learned in these five-minute conversations just made Mary like Brian more. And once when she was assigned to his case in a big meeting, he winked at her, and she thought that maybe she didn't have control of her brain anymore. With each day, there was a greater chance that she was actually going to act on one of her totally absurd thoughts. There was no going back.

இ

Mary told her friends that there was a cute lawyer at the firm, but that's as far as she let herself go. They were out for drinks one night and she just wanted to say his name, so she said, "There's this guy at my firm, Brian, who's pretty cute. He's a partner, though." Then, because she regretted saying his name, she said, "I'm not interested in him or anything. Maybe he's not even that cute. I can't tell anymore."

Lauren nodded and said, "It's probably the cutest-boy-in-the-class syndrome."

"The what?" Mary asked.

"Cutest-boy-in-the-class syndrome," Lauren repeated. "You know, when you spend all your time in a class and it's boring and you get a crush on a guy, who looks super cute in the class but then when you go out in the real world, he's not. It's just that you were only comparing him to that small group, so there was a curve."

"Huh," Isabella said. "I never thought about it like that."

"I mean, that's just the name, but it applies to all sorts of things. Like why camp boyfriends always turned out to be nerds. Or how a work crush can happen on a guy that's really not all that great." She shrugged and tried to look modest, as though she were the one to discover this phenomenon. "It's good to remind yourself of it, though," she said. "So you don't end up sleeping with a bartender who's a total life loser, or something like that."

"Or something like that," Isabella said. Mary nodded, as though they had figured it out, but she knew Brian didn't fall into that category. She didn't know where he fell, but it wasn't there.

ॐ

They kissed one night in her office, late, after everyone else had gone home. The two of them had ordered Thai food, and Mary had eaten very little, afraid that her skirts were going to stop fitting soon, and sure that when Brian looked at her, all he saw was a big ass.

He came into her office and stood behind her so that she couldn't breathe. When she got up to go get a piece of paper from the other side of the room, she turned and was facing him, their mouths close. And then they were kissing, and she tasted the curry he'd eaten that day. It made her dizzy, but it all seemed a little unreal, like walking outside in pajamas.

When she got home, it was hard to remember if it had happened or not. She barely slept, and when her alarm went off she was happy to get up. She laughed in the shower as she got ready; giddy and tired, she lathered her hair and laughed.

She didn't see Brian all day. He wasn't on the roof that night, and she knew something was wrong. Two more days passed and the only time she saw him was from down the hall as he went into a meeting. She was such an idiot. He was her boss. This was not something she would ever do, and she decided that she would clear it up as soon as she got the chance.

A few nights later, she was in her office and he walked by. Before she knew it, she was calling out his name. He looked surprised, but just raised his eyebrows and stepped inside. "Yes?" he said.

"Hi," Mary said. "So, I just wanted to apologize for the other night. It wasn't professional, and I regret it."

"Okay," Brian said.

"Okay," Mary said. He looked like he was going to leave, but Mary wanted to say more. "I mean, if there were different circumstances, maybe. But you're my boss, and we work together."

"That's the least of it," Brian said.

"What?" Mary asked. "What do you mean?"

"Mary," Brian said, "I'm engaged. You knew that."

"I didn't know that," Mary said. "How could I have known that?"

Brian laughed. He sounded a little evil. "You knew," he said.

"I didn't know," Mary said. Her voice sounded like she wasn't sure if she believed herself or not.

"Of course you knew," Brian said. He sounded impatient. "Remember the week after you started when everyone had cake in the big conference room? It was for my engagement. Carla arranged it." Mary vaguely remembered standing with plastic plates, eating white frosted cake that wasn't good but was better than sitting at her desk.

"No," she said. She shook her head. "No, I don't remember."

Brian laughed meanly again, and Mary realized that he was maybe the kind of guy who contained the potential to be very cruel, the kind of guy who believed the lies he told. "Look," he said. "Whatever you need to tell yourself. Just don't repeat it around here."

"I wouldn't tell anyone. Don't you tell anyone." This came out sounding stupid, like a child deflecting an insult by repeating it.

Brian just nodded. "Okay," he said. He turned and walked out of her office.

Mary sat at her desk for a while, not knowing what to do. She'd never done anything this bad in her life. She'd never cheated on anyone, never stolen a friend's boyfriend, never kissed a guy who was taken. Engaged. The word was weighted.

Had she known? She didn't think so, but maybe she was just trying to make herself feel better. She considered going to confession and then decided against it. She'd always hated confession, ever since the first time she went, when she told the priest that she was afraid of the albino janitor who cleaned the school.

"I'm afraid of Andy the janitor," she'd said. "Because he's an albino."

"That's not a sin, Mary," Father Kelly had said. He'd sounded annoyed, like she didn't understand what it was she was supposed to tell him. But Father Kelly was wrong. Mary knew that it was a sin to be afraid of Andy the albino. She didn't want to look down when she saw him, didn't want to go to the other side of the hall when they passed each other. He always smiled at her, like he understood, and that made the whole thing worse. She wanted to cry when he did that. She didn't want to be afraid of him, but she couldn't help it and it made her feel awful, like she was the worst person in the world. And no matter what Father Kelly said, it was a sin. She knew that much.

Mary turned back to her computer as if she was going to do more work, and then she decided against it. She had to get out of the office. She walked all the way home, even though it was so cold that she couldn't feel her toes after the first block. She didn't want to stop for anything, didn't want to wait for the train to come. She just wanted to keep moving, and so she did. She walked forty blocks to her apartment, and by the time she got there, her nose was running and her eyes were watering, spilling down her face. She wasn't crying, though she wished she were. It was just the cold.

She went up to her apartment and started running a bath, which she'd never done the whole time she'd lived there. She had trouble unbuttoning her blouse because her fingers were numb, but she managed, and got into the bath, which was so hot it burned her skin for the first few minutes. Mary stayed in the bath for over an hour. Whenever the water started to cool, Mary drained a little bit and added more hot water. When she was sure she could feel her fingers again, she got out and put on her most comfortable pajamas, thin flannel pants and a long-sleeve T-shirt that was worn and soft. She curled up on her couch underneath the blanket. She wanted a cigarette. But she wouldn't let herself have one. Not tonight and not ever again. She sat there for a moment, and then she got up and started lighting all of the candles in her apartment. This would have made her mother very nervous. "You'll fall asleep and burn the place down," she would have said. But Mary was wide awake and not afraid of starting a fire. She turned off the lights and sat on the couch, watching all of the flames light up the room. She breathed in and out until she didn't want a cigarette anymore. She sat there for a while, and then she leaned over to the candle closest to her and blew, softly at first, and then harder, so that the flame vanished. She got up and walked around to each candle, blowing them out, watching as the flames turned into long winding tails of smoke, and she watched them curl and twist, up in the air, until they were gone. And then she went to bed.

Black Diamond, Blue Square

His name was Harrison, but no one ever called him Harry. Isabella learned that right away.

Isabella was drunk. It was happy hour and her friends had ignored her requests to go somewhere that served food. She'd ended up sitting on a bar stool in her rumpled work clothes, plotting to stop for pizza on the way home, when Harrison approached her and introduced himself. And because she could think of nothing better to say, she asked, "Do people call you Harry?"

"No," he answered. He looked as though she'd asked if people called him Bob or Walter.

"Oh," she said. She shouldn't have had the third dirty martini. She could hear her voice from somewhere deep inside her head. And from in there she sounded retarded.

Isabella was tired. It was already almost eight o'clock and it would be a lot of work to talk to someone new. She had to be at the office early the next day. She contemplated excusing herself, getting up, and leaving. She could be home in her pajamas with pizza in thirty minutes.

But then her plan seemed too hard to carry out and so she let herself sit there. And after a few minutes, she leaned forward on the stool in a wobbly way and kissed Harrison in a crowded bar.

And that was how Harrison and Isabella met.

Her friends called him handsome, but what he was, was pretty. He had high cheekbones, delicate features, and flawless coloring—porcelain skin and cheeks that flushed naturally when he was excited. His shirts were never wrinkled. Even untucked at the end of a day, with his tie pulled loose, he looked staged, like somebody had gotten him a wardrobe for "end of the workday."

Around him, Isabella felt sweaty and bloated more often than not. She wanted to apologize when she got a pimple or had to blow her nose. She was fairly certain he never had boogers.

Harrison met new people gracefully, shook guys' hands and grasped their arm with his left hand. He kissed girls on the cheeks and remembered names. He was always interested in conversation, tilting his head at whoever was talking, nodding and interjecting every so often, but not enough to be obnoxious.

"He's the one!" Isabella's friends said. "We can't believe you found him!"

The ones with boyfriends and fiancés were relieved for Isabella. She was twenty-seven and they all agreed it was about time. The single ones were sort of happy and a little annoyed. They'd been at the bar that night too. Isabella was pretty, but not gorgeous. Where had they been when he'd come up to her? (But for the most part, they were happy, of course.)

࿇

Harrison knew how to date. He made plans to go to dinner at restaurants where they could drink margaritas and hear each other talk. He took her to movies and then to a diner for grilled cheese. He always paid. He called when he said he would, and held the door for her. The first night she stayed at his apartment, he woke up early and came back with two cups of coffee.

"I like him," Isabella told her friends. She sounded miserable. "He's really fun. It makes me feel sick."

Isabella knew enough by now to know that this wasn't a common occurrence. You didn't just bump into a nice guy that you liked every day. She was positive that she was going to mess it up.

࿇

Harrison and Isabella had been dating for three weeks when he mentioned the ski trip. He brought it up casually one day, as though the thought had just occurred to him that very moment, asking, "Do you want to go skiing for New Year's?"

Isabella was in a panic almost immediately. She had been up most nights wondering if they would exchange Christmas presents, imagining the horror of handing him a wrapped box and being greeted with an uncomfortable look. New Year's hadn't even entered her mind yet. She was trying to deal with one holiday at a time.

"Isabella?"

"What?"

"New Year's? A bunch of my friends are renting a house in Vermont. It should be fun."

"Fun" was a relative term, Isabella knew. Something that seemed fun when compared to doing nothing could really end up being a horrific mistake. And a weekend with strangers could be up there with a car crash.

"Do I know any of them?"

"Um . . . I'm not sure. You met Parker, right?"

Isabella shook her head.

"Oh, I thought you did. Well, look, they're a fun group. It's not that big of a deal. If you want to go, great. If not, don't worry about it."

"Do you even want me to go?"

"Yeah."

"It just kind of sounded like maybe you didn't really."

"If I didn't want you to go, I wouldn't ask you."

"Oh."

"Stop being so weird," he said, and poked her in the stomach. "It's really not a big deal. Just let me know."

"Okay."

გ

Isabella wondered what it would be like to be a boy. She knew that Harrison meant it when he said it wasn't a big deal. He really wouldn't care. He didn't have to obsess over her response or if she would go or not. If she were a boy, she would be much more successful. She was sure of it. As it was now, she wasted days at work analyzing things that Harrison had said to her.

When he told her it was interesting that she had a goldfish, she lost a week of productivity.

What did she know about dating, anyway? Nothing. She thought back to the sixth-grade sex-ed class they'd had at St. Anthony's. The girls were put in a room with the school nurse and forced to read scenarios out of an old pamphlet. "Kate and Michael have been going steady for a month," the book read. "Michael wants Kate to try heavy petting, but Kate doesn't feel ready. What do you think she should do?"

The nurse cleared her throat, blushed, and addressed the girls. "So, does anyone have a thought on what Kate should do?" The room was silent. Finally someone asked, "What's heavy petting?"

In the other room, the boys told them later, a priest had drawn a large dome on the blackboard. "Do you know what this is?" he asked them. He sounded angry and annoyed. He put a dot on top of it. "That's a penis," he said.

That was her education? How was she prepared for this? There was no scenario in that book about starting a new relationship with a Harrison. There were no tips on whether or not to go on a trip so early in a relationship. (Or if there were, they never got to them. Because once they found out what heavy petting was, they laughed for a week and a half.)

"You should go," her friends all said. The fact that she hadn't skied in years and didn't really miss it wasn't something they were concerned with. The drive up there would take almost five hours. What would they talk about? They had never been in a car alone that long. What if it was just silence? After sleepless nights and countless conversations, she agreed to go. Immediately after, she felt sick.

ℬ

The ski house was built to sleep as many people as possible. Most rooms had two sets of bunk beds and stairs that led to another room with a futon. When they got there, it was already dark and she could hear laughing as they stood outside the door. It was so cold that Isabella could feel the inside of her nose freeze when she breathed. The night seemed darker after coming from the city, and it made Isabella shiver. More than anything at that moment, she wanted not to be there. What had she been thinking coming up here? She didn't know these people.

Isabella let Harrison walk in front of her and she walked behind him, pretending to look for something in her purse. There were about a dozen people in the kitchen and living room, sitting around, drinking and laughing. There was a football game on the TV, which no one was watching.

Everyone smiled and there were shouts of "Hey" and "What's up?" Isabella waited for Harrison to introduce her and then stood there while he pointed to everyone and said their names. She didn't remember any of them.

Harrison grabbed her bag to take it upstairs and she followed him. They peeked in the rooms, looking for an empty one, but there were bags on all of the double beds. The only thing free was a set of bunk beds in the corner of one of the rooms.

"Looks like this is us," Harrison said. "Do you want the top or the bottom?"

Isabella wasn't sure. If she slept on the bottom, she would be eye level with the other couple staying in the room. If she took the top, she ran the risk of falling out of bed and paralyzing herself while waking the whole house up.

"Um, the bottom, I guess."

"Okay."

Harrison threw the bags on top of the beds and turned to her. "You ready for a drink?" he asked. She nodded and followed him downstairs silently.

That weekend, Isabella sat close to Harrison, holding his hand and resting her head against his shoulder, which she never did. When he left the room for more than two minutes she started to panic at the thought that she was stuck with these strangers. She acted like a different girl than she was. Harrison didn't seem to notice.

The first night there, Isabella was cornered by one of Harrison's friends from college. Her name was Jocelyn. She was drunk and a close talker.

"I don't really know my dad," she confided to Isabella. "He never really wanted a daughter and I'm not sure he ever loved me."

She was leaning in so close that her giant boob was resting on Isabella's arm and her breath was on Isabella's cheek. Was this girl hitting on her? Isabella felt like crying. She kept trying to catch Harrison's eye so that he could save her, but every time she did he gave her a look like, *I'm glad you're fitting in.*

At the end of the night, Jocelyn held Isabella in a too-long embrace and muttered something about how glad she was to meet her. And then she said, "I love you." Isabella was in a loony bin.

๛

"Isn't Jocelyn nice?" Harrison asked. They were standing side by side in the bathroom, brushing their teeth. The floor was freezing and it made Isabella's feet cold right through her socks. She was drunk and had to close one eye so that the reflections of her and Harrison in the mirror would stop moving.

"She would be nice if she was in therapy," Isabella said. She stumbled a little bit and leaned on the sink. Harrison caught her arm.

"So judgmental," he said. He tried to make it sound like a joke, but she knew he was annoyed.

She spit out her toothpaste and rinsed off her toothbrush. "Do you realize that at the end of the night, she said, 'I love you' to me? That doesn't strike you as a little strange?"

"She's an emotional girl. You just need to get used to her."

"Did you use to date her?"

Harrison laughed. "I wouldn't call it dating. It was a long time ago."

Harrison rubbed the back of her thermal shirt and she leaned her head against him. All she wanted was to be back in the city at one of their apartments, where they could sleep in the same bed.

"Good night," Harrison said and swung up to the top bunk.

"Night," Isabella whispered into her pillow.

๛

Isabella didn't really want to go skiing, but the alternative was staying in the house all day with the few people who weren't going either. Jocelyn was one of them, so Isabella put on her long underwear and ski pants, her thermal shirt and her puffy jacket. She looked like a marshmallow.

Isabella had skied when she was younger, but lately had realized that she didn't like it all that much. It was scary—absurd, actually—to climb onto a metal contraption that would take you up a mountain so that you could zip back down again.

It became very clear while talking about this trip that Harrison was an excellent skier. He mentioned winters in Vail and Beaver Creek, and spring skiing in Aspen. He knew the names of his favorite runs, and would say things like "The speed you can get on Pepe's Face is crazy." Isabella just nodded.

"You can go ski with your friends if you want," Isabella offered. She was relieved when he declined.

"The whole point is for us to hang out," he said, and pulled her hat down over her eyes like he was one of her older brothers.

"Okay," she said. "I'm just not sure that I'll be able to keep up with you. It's been a while since I skied."

"No problem," he said. "We'll start on some blues until you get the hang of it."

By the second run, Isabella was pretty sure that she'd never get the hang of it. Harrison skied ahead of her, swooshing in the snow like a professional. Isabella made a snowplow and took wide turns down the mountain. Every time she felt like she was going too fast and about to lose control, she let her knees buckle and fell to the ground.

"Just trust yourself a little more," Harrison advised her. "The fun part is when you start going really fast."

"Fun until you crash," she said.

How could she not have remembered how terrifying it was to ski? Even the chairlift scared her as it chugged high off the ground with nothing to keep them from falling out.

"Could you not swing your legs so much?" Isabella asked Harrison. She tried not to sound so panicked.

"Such a little worrywart," he laughed.

The day seemed impossibly long. The snow was icy and Isabella's gloves were wet from falling. She sat inside the lodge to warm up while Harrison went on a couple runs by himself. When Harrison came back in to get her, she tried not to look sad and followed him back out to the slopes.

Isabella kept waiting for it to come back to her, but her legs kept buckling and shaking. And when Harrison said, "One more run and then we should go in," she was so happy that she almost cried.

They were the last ones back to the house and there was no more hot water. Isabella shivered in the lukewarm spray and told herself the weekend was almost over. Everyone was tired from skiing, and wore sweatpants and pajamas. Isabella came downstairs in jeans and a sweater and felt like an idiot.

They played old college drinking games, and Jocelyn claimed Isabella for her flip-cup team. Isabella was relieved. Skiing was not her thing, but flip cup she was good at. She didn't even mind that Jocelyn hugged her every time they won. She figured that Jocelyn was trying to make it up to Isabella for sleeping with Harrison. It was sort of nice, in a weird, messed-up way.

Isabella got drunk and happy. These people weren't all that bad. She dragged Harrison to the middle of the room and danced with him. She was fun! Harrison's friends would know that now. She made everyone do tequila shots and tried to suggest body shots, but Harrison shut that idea down.

"Time for bed, little lady," he said, and picked her up over his shoulder. He smacked her behind, and the last thing she remembered was Harrison dropping her on the couch because they were laughing too hard.

The next morning, Isabella woke up with a headache and waited for Harrison to climb down the bunk bed ladder, but he kept sleeping. The other couple in the room got up and got dressed, and Isabella faced the wall and pretended to sleep until they were gone. She lay in her bunk and listened to the sounds of everyone else in the house as they started their day. She heard pots being clanked around, smelled coffee. She heard the television being switched on and cheers for some game.

"Harrison, are you awake?" she whispered to the top bunk.

Isabella could hear half snores coming from above. This wasn't like Harrison to sleep so late. She slid out of her bunk and peered up at him. He was sleeping on his side with his mouth wide open. He looked like a little boy.

"Harrison," she said, and poked him on the shoulder. He made a gurgling sound and opened and closed his mouth a couple of times, but didn't wake up.

What was she doing here? She had been wondering it all weekend, but now she just wanted to cry. She thought of all the places she could be, with people she knew. Instead she was in a house of strangers. Pieces of the night before came back to her and with each flash, Isabella was more and more mortified. She couldn't face these people. Harrison probably didn't even like her anymore.

She climbed up the ladder and sat in the bunk at the edge of Harrison's feet. She willed him to wake up for seven minutes. Then she lay next to him so that she was closer to the wall. She put her head on his pillow and stared at him. When he finally opened his eyes a few minutes later, he let out a startled scream.

"Isabella, what the hell?" He half sat up and looked around, trying to figure out where he was. When he had calmed himself, he lay back down and crossed his arm over his eyes.

"My head," he said, "hurts like a motherfucker."

Isabella laughed. She'd never heard him talk like that. He uncovered his face and smiled at her. "Oh, you like that? You think that's funny? You can't be feeling too great yourself, Little Miss Tequila."

"Don't say that word," Isabella warned. The only thing worse than being in a house full of strangers was throwing up in a house full of strangers.

Harrison smiled and closed his eyes again. "I don't think I can go skiing today," he said.

"Oh, thank God," Isabella said. She was so sore from yesterday that it hurt to talk. "Maybe we can go get lunch in town?"

"Isabella, I don't think I can move right now."

Harrison never called her Iz or Izzy. It was always Isabella. It was always formal. It made her think of Ben and the way that he would sing to her in the mornings, "Izzy, Isabella," kissing her stomach until she woke up. Thinking of Ben made her lonely, which wasn't what she'd expected. She hated Ben. But she knew him, at least. She wouldn't have to be polite with him if he were here right now. She could tell him to get up and go downstairs with her. Instead, she was stuck here with Harrison, who called her by her full name and was never mean. It was basically like being with Miss Manners.

Isabella lay next to him while he slept. Once she got up to go to the bathroom and ate a granola bar she had in her bag. She sat in the bottom bunk for a little while and read her book, but she couldn't concentrate so she climbed back up the ladder and lay down next to Harrison again. Maybe she didn't really know him, but compared to the people downstairs, he was her closest friend, her ally. She wasn't leaving his side.

Sometime after the sun went down and it was night again, Harrison woke up. Isabella was staring at the ceiling. "What are you doing?" he asked her.

"Thinking," she said.

"You look like a crazy person," he said and laughed a little bit. "Have you been here all day?"

She nodded. "I didn't want to go downstairs," she said. Her eyes started to fill with tears. "I didn't know anyone, so I just stayed here."

Harrison turned toward her and smoothed back her hair. All she wanted was not to cry. She couldn't cry; they hadn't been dating long enough. He would think she was crazy, a nut.

"Sorry," he whispered right next to her ear.

"That's okay," she said. "You know, they probably think we're making out up here. No one's come up all day."

Harrison smiled. "Then maybe we should prove them right," he said and slid himself on top of her carefully.

"I've never had sex in a bunk bed," she said.

"There's a first time for everything," he said. "Just don't fall off."

ᗡ

Harrison stayed by her side that night, and she was grateful. They went to a local bar, for which she was also grateful. She stayed even closer to Harrison than she had the night before. Part of her was touching him at all times.

"So, you want to go skiing tomorrow?" he asked. "It's our last chance. Plus, I think we can go on some diamonds."

Isabella said, "Absolutely."

ᗡ

The second day of skiing started off better. It had snowed the night before, so when Isabella fell, she fell on soft snow instead of the ice. It was also a little warmer, and Isabella even started to have some fun.

Harrison was conscious of her at all times. He was faster than she was, but he always waited at certain points to let her catch up. This was a big mountain, and there were different forks and turns you could take. Harrison always pointed out the path they were going to take on the map before they went.

For the last run of the day, Harrison wanted to try something different. Isabella felt bad that she had been holding him back on the easier mountains and so she agreed. They had to take two chair lifts up and would ski down a blue, then a black, then finish on a blue. "It's easy, see?" Harrison said, running his finger along the map. "Just keep staying to the right and you'll get to the next run. I'll wait for you at the top of each."

Isabella nodded. She was cold again and ready for this day to be over. Just one more run and the whole day would end on a good note.

The second chairlift was higher than any of the other ones they had been on. It stopped halfway up the mountain and Isabella started seeing black.

"Scared?" Harrison asked.

Isabella nodded and Harrison just laughed. He thought it was really funny. She felt like she was dying. The metal creaked and kicked and the lift started moving again. Isabella waited for the whole chair to plummet to the ground, and was surprised when they skied off at the top.

"Okay, so you remember the way?" Harrison asked. He put his sunglasses down and smiled at her. She nodded. Almost over. It was almost over.

They started down the mountain and it was going okay. Isabella had gotten used to the blues and her snowplow wasn't such an embarrassing giant wedge anymore. She even let herself go a little fast sometimes. She finished the run and skied up to Harrison.

"Awesome," he said. "Ready for the next one?"

He was already moving before he finished talking. There were moguls at the top of the run and Isabella hesitated. She saw Harrison flying down the mountain, and then the next second she was on the ground, rolling down the steep hill. One ski came off and all she could see was black when she hit the ground.

She knocked over another skier and the two of them tangled up together and slowed down to a stop.

"You okay?" the guy asked her. She nodded.

"Well, then watch it next time. You shouldn't be on this slope if you can't handle it," he said and stood up and skied off.

Isabella sat in the snow. She only had one ski and couldn't even see where the other one had gone. That guy had been such an asshole, she thought as she climbed back up the hill. What a jerk. They could have been killed. It wasn't her fault, totally, was it? No, he had gotten in her way.

The whole time she climbed back up the hill and struggled to put the runaway ski back on, Isabella thanked God that Harrison hadn't been there to see it. That would have been mortifying. She crawled up and snapped her boot back into the ski. She sat for a moment to get her bearings, and then she stood up. She had to ski down. There was no other way off the mountain. She was a little turned around, but stayed to the right. That was what Harrison had said to do.

She skied down the rest of the mountain and didn't see Harrison once. Maybe she'd taken too long after her fall. She skied right up to the lodge and took her skis off. She was done.

Isabella clomped into the lodge in her boots and took out her cell phone to call Harrison. "Where are you?" he asked when he answered. "I was getting worried."

"I'm at the lodge," she said. "I fell."

"I'm at the lodge too," he said. "Where are you?"

"I'm right by the food counter."

"I don't see you."

Isabella looked around for Harrison and then realized that

this lodge looked very different. "Um, Harrison, I think I'm somewhere else. The sign says the Blackbear Lodge. Do you know where that is?"

Harrison was quiet for a moment. "That's on the other side of the mountain. How did you get there?"

Isabella could tell he was laughing. Her eyes started to fill with tears again.

"I don't know! Where am I?"

"Stay there, okay? I'll come to you," Harrison said and hung up.

Isabella limped over to the counter and ordered hot chocolate. She had started crying a little, which made her nose run even more. The cashier was a high-school boy and he looked frightened of her. He was probably scared she was going to talk to him and tell him her problems.

She took as many napkins as she could and walked with her hot chocolate back to her table. On the way, she spilled hot liquid on her hand. Now the tears started again. She was pathetic. She was a pathetic person.

Isabella was blowing her nose when Harrison walked in.

"Hey there," he said. "There's my little Rand McNally."

Isabella laughed and then started crying again. She couldn't stop. Now this really would be the end of them. Harrison would see how crazy she was and he would have to break up with her. Then they would have to drive back to the city together. This was a nightmare.

"Hey, what's wrong?" Harrison pulled up a chair and took her hand.

"Nothing," she said, wiping her face with the back of her

hand. "Nothing, it's stupid. I'm just really tired and I got so cold. And I'm embarrassed that I got lost."

Harrison laughed in a kind way and leaned over to kiss her cheek. "That's all? You'll be fine, my little ski bunny. My little lost ski bunny."

Isabella laughed and then felt stupid for crying. "So how do we get out of here?"

"We have to go back up the lift and then back down the other side of the mountain. It's a good run, though," he said quickly.

"I don't know if I can go back up there," she said.

"Well, I could go by myself and then ski back down to the main lodge and get the car. But it would take a while."

Isabella leaned her head back.

"You know," Harrison started and cleared his throat. "I'm really glad you came this weekend."

Isabella righted her head and looked straight at him. "Really?"

"Yeah," he said. "I really like you, you know."

Isabella smiled at him. "Probably just because of my navigational skills," she said.

"Probably. So whadya say? You want to brave the mountain? I promise not to rock the ski lift," he said, holding up his right hand.

Isabella was tired and cold and she didn't really feel like skiing and was still terrified of the actual ride on the ski lift, but it seemed ridiculous to sit here and wait and do nothing while Harrison got the car. How bad could it be?

"Are you up for it?" he asked. He looked hopeful.

"Yeah," she said. "Okay, let's do it."

The Day They Captured the Pigeons

*B*ridget Carlson was the kind of friend you couldn't get rid of. You could try—you could ignore her e-mails, let her phone calls go to voice mail, move to a different city, let her birthday pass unnoticed, take her number out of your cell phone—but she would find you. She was persistent, if nothing else. She tracked down new addresses, new phone numbers, new e-mails, and she would claw her way back into contact with you, until you had no choice but to acknowledge her.

This was how Cate found herself, against all better judgment, agreeing to have lunch with her. For weeks, Bridget had been leaving messages on her voice mail. "Caitlin, it's me," the messages said. "I'm coming to New York and we are meeting up if it's the last thing we do. It's been too long." The messages almost sounded like threats. They could, at the very least, be perceived as mild harassment. Cate's cell phone had a message almost every day, and then somehow Bridget found Cate's work number and started calling her there too.

"Why aren't you answering your phone?" Isabella asked her. Cate was peering at the caller ID, letting it ring and ring.

"It's this girl from college," Cate said. "She won't leave me alone."

"Is she a friend?" Isabella asked.

"Not really," Cate said. "Sort of, I guess. But no, not really. I just need to wait until her trip is over and then I'll call her back."

And then one day, the caller ID said "Unavailable" and Cate picked up. "Gotcha," Bridget said on the other end. "Caitlin Johnson, you are one hard person to get a hold of. You have got to meet me for lunch!" Cate was so surprised that she just said, "Okay."

"I have to meet someone for lunch," Cate told Isabella.

"Snowy is going to kill you," Isabella said.

Cate considered this. Snowy had spent the better part of the morning screaming at Cate. "Three years!" she had yelled. "Three years you've worked here and you don't know how to do anything!" Yes, Snowy would probably kill her.

"I have to," Cate said. "I already promised."

"Is this the stalker?" Isabella asked. She squinted as if trying to understand.

"Yeah, but I just need to get it over with."

"It's your funeral," Isabella said. "We have a meeting at three, don't forget."

"I won't," Cate said. She grabbed her bag and headed toward the door. "I'll be back in an hour," she called over her shoulder.

Cate met Bridget the first day of college, when Bridget knocked on her door during orientation. "Hello," she called. "Caitlin or Maya, are you in there?" Cate was alone in her room, unpacking underwear into her dresser. Before she could answer the door, the knob turned and Bridget walked right in. "Hi," she said. "I'm just going up and down the hall introducing myself to people. All the names are on the doors, so it's totally easy. Are you Caitlin or Maya?"

"Caitlin," she said. "But everyone calls me Cate."

Bridget jumped on Cate's bed and sprawled out, leaning against her pillows and putting her arms above her head. "I love the name Caitlin," she said. "I'm totally going to call you Caitlin."

Bridget was short, with a big chest and a raspy voice that made it sound like she'd been at a great party the night before. She was bossy and happy. From the start, she was kind of annoying, but Cate was so lonely those first few days that she would have sold her soul for someone to walk to the dining hall with. They were inseparable for the first week of college, but as the year went on, they both met other friends, and their paths slowly went separate ways. Bridget was always there, of course. They'd get together every once in a while, and invite each other to parties they were having. Cate always said yes when Bridget invited her somewhere. She felt like she owed her something for her friendship during those first solitary days of college.

And Bridget wasn't an awful person. Not exactly. She was just, in her own way, exhausting. She never relaxed, never sat back calmly. She was always on the edge of her seat, laughing and cutting in on other people's stories to tell her own. When you asked Bridget how she was, things were always *amazing, wonderful, perfect!* When she lost her job, she was *thrilled to have the free time to explore other opportunities.* When she was in a relationship, she was *crazy in love,* and when she was dumped she was *excited to live the single-girl life and really get to know herself.*

It was infuriating to listen to her spout her happiness, her absolute joy at being herself. At first, you might think that she was putting on an act. But what was even more annoying was when you realized that she believed everything she was saying. In college, Bridget always assumed that she was invited everywhere. Overhearing talk of a party meant that she was, of course, going to go. It never occurred to her that people might not want her around. The thought just never crossed her mind.

When Bridget got back from her semester abroad in London, she developed a strange English affect in her voice. "This lift," she would say, waiting for the elevator, "is taking forever." It made you want to punch her.

But if Cate was being honest, there was a reason she kept in touch with Bridget, and it was this: Her lack of reality was fascinating. Listening to her tell stories was hilarious and horrifying at the same time. When her boyfriend cheated on her, Cate offered sympathy and Bridget just shook her head. "Can you believe," she said, "that he's so scared of being in love with me that he cheated?"

Cate logged these stories in her brain, saving them up to tell friends later. She had a whole catalog of Bridget stories to pull out at parties. They were unbelievable. The girl was a complete loon. It was comforting to Cate that no matter how messed up she was or how many mistakes she made, she wasn't nearly as crazy as Bridget.

ℬↄ

It was early October when Cate went to meet Bridget. It was one of those warm fall days in New York when everyone walks around without jackets and soaks up the last of the sun. There were no clouds in the sky and everyone seemed happy. As Cate walked among all of these smiling people, she felt anxious. She knew she should have stayed at work, but she told herself that Bridget would just have hounded her until she met her. Better to get it over with, she told herself.

From down the block, Cate could see Bridget sitting at an outside table at the restaurant, wearing sunglasses and a shawl. Cate could tell that she thought she looked like a movie star. Her face was tilted back toward the sun and she had the happy little smile of someone who is perfectly content. As Cate got closer, she saw that there were two glasses of white wine on the table and immediately she felt relieved. This lunch would be much easier to handle with alcohol.

Bridget shrieked as soon as she saw her, causing everyone to turn and stare, which embarrassed Cate to no end. "Caiiitliiin! Oh, how are you?" Bridget opened her arms wide for a hug, and then kissed both of Cate's cheeks. This would have been a little pretentious for anyone, but Bridget was from Pittsburgh, which just made the whole thing absurd.

Bridget pushed her sunglasses up on her head in a theatrical way and leaned back to laugh. "It is just so damn good to see you! I can't believe it. You look well! I ordered some wine for us. Now, I know it's a school day for you, but I thought we needed to celebrate. A little day drinking never hurt anyone, no?"

As always with Bridget, Cate barely said a word. Bridget rattled on about her job, and revealed that she was working on a memoir in her spare time. "I've always been a great writer," she said. "There's a lot of people interested to see it when I'm done. So we'll see! Maybe I'll have a fabulous book deal by the end of the year," she said and then laughed. "So, how are you?" she asked. But before Cate could answer, Bridget started describing how she'd redecorated her apartment, how she seemed to have a gift for choosing color palettes and antique pieces that just seemed to fit.

They ordered a second glass of wine and Cate drank while Bridget filled her in on the cooking class she was taking. Then she told her about the trip to Italy she was planning. "I just feel so lucky," she said. "To have a job I love that pays me enough that I can do other things that I love. Do you know how rare that is?" she asked.

"I do," Cate said.

Bridget sighed, and took a sip of her wine. "Caitlin," she said. "There was something else I wanted to tell you."

"Really?" Cate asked.

"Yes," she said. "I wanted to tell you that I'm dating Jim."

"Jim?"

"You know, Jim from college. Turns out he works near my building in Boston and we ran into each other at a happy hour. And you know, trouble!" Bridget raised and lowered her eyebrows and pursed her lips, then laughed out loud.

"Oh, now, don't look so shocked! Look, I wanted to tell you because I know you and Jim had that thing in college," Bridget said and took a sip of her wine. Her face suddenly grew serious. "But, I mean, college was about a million years ago! And I knew that you wouldn't really mind, but I still wanted to tell you myself. You know how funny girls can be about these things."

"Yeah," Cate said. "I do."

"Oh, I knew you wouldn't mind! I told him that you'd be fine with it. Boys are so silly, aren't they?"

"So, how long have you two been, um, together?"

"Almost a year. Well, about nine months. And I wanted to tell you earlier, but we've both been so busy that we've barely spoken!"

"I know," Cate said and raised her hand to the waiter for another glass of wine.

"Oh, you are so bad," Bridget giggled.

"So is it serious?" Cate asked. Her head felt light, and she struggled to keep her voice steady.

"Yes," she said. "It is."

"But it's only been nine months, right?"

"Well, yes. But he's already looking at rings."

"What?"

Bridget made a big show of clamping her hands over her mouth and making her eyes wide. "Look at me," she said. "I can't keep a secret to save my life! But between you and me? This is it."

Cate picked up her glass of water and drank the whole thing down in one swallow. She was afraid that if she stopped, she would throw the glass on the floor. Jim. Jim? Jim and Bridget? This didn't make sense. She was making it up in her head. Maybe Bridget was even crazier than Cate had ever known. The waiter brought over a new glass of wine, and Cate picked it up and started drinking it like it was water. She was so thirsty all of a sudden.

"We're going to Italy together, and I just know he's going to do it there," Bridget said.

"Really?"

"Yeah," she said. "Isn't that romantic?"

Jim was the person Cate still thought about, the person that her mind went to when things got bad. It was stupid and she knew that. It was obvious that they'd never get back together, but still she liked to think, "What if?" She knew that he would date other people, she'd even thought that maybe he'd be married soon. But to Bridget? No. Not to Bridget.

"Caitlin," she said. "Caitlin, does this bother you? Oh, that's not what I meant to do."

Cate shook her head. "No one calls me Caitlin. Did you know that? Not one other person on this earth calls me Caitlin."

"I know," she said. "That was always our thing. I love the name Caitlin!"

Cate left the restaurant in a hurry. All of a sudden, she needed to get out of there. "I have to get back to work," she said, throwing some money on the table. "My boss is on the warpath." Bridget was saying something but Cate wasn't listening. She stood up and her chair hit the table in back of them. "Sorry," Cate mumbled. "Sorry, sorry," as she wove in and out of the tables. She took a left on the street and walked quickly for a few blocks before she realized that she had no idea where the subway was.

Cate stopped for a second, just outside a little park, and leaned her head against the fence to gather her thoughts. There was a man in there feeding pigeons, and Cate watched him throw the seeds out at the dirty birds. They gathered all around him, pecking at the ground. How gross, she thought. How gross to let those disgusting creatures get close to you.

And then it happened. Cate hadn't noticed, but there was a net on the ground, and the man bent down and in one swoop had gathered all of the pigeons inside. He picked up the bag of pigeons, walked to a white van, got in the back, and drove away.

Cate looked around, waiting for someone else on the street to react so that they could stop this man. What was he doing? He was stealing pigeons! People walked past Cate on the sidewalk, and she tried to catch someone's eye, but they all kept walking. No one cared. No one had even noticed. "Didn't any of you see him?" Cate wanted to scream. "There's a thief in our midst!" But she didn't. No one would have listened anyway.

Cate went back to work, sweaty and disoriented. Isabella looked up as she ran to her desk. "What happened to you?" she asked. Cate shook her head and picked up a bottle of water she'd left on her desk. She unscrewed the top and held up one finger while she chugged most of it.

"You won't believe me," she said when she was done. "But you have to believe me."

"Are you drunk?" Isabella asked.

"No," Cate said. "I had some wine. But listen, I have to tell you something. And you have to believe me."

"Snowy is going to freak out if you aren't ready for the meeting. It's in twenty minutes, you know."

"I know, but just listen to me! Listen." Cate told her about the pigeons. She described the man who'd scooped them up and taken them away. Isabella listened, raising and lowering her eyebrows as the story went on.

"Why would anyone steal pigeons?" she asked when Cate was done.

"I don't know," Cate said. "It's crazy, right?"

"Yes," Isabella said. "It's crazy."

"You believe me though, right?"

"Cate, are you okay?"

"I'm fine. I'm just telling you, it was the weirdest thing. He just scooped them up, like it was his job. Like he was sent there to do that."

Isabella shrugged. "Maybe it was," she said. "Maybe he works for the city."

"No," Cate said. "I thought of that. The van wasn't marked."

Isabella sighed. "Okay, so it was just some crazy man. Why do you care?"

"It's not right," Cate said. "It's not right that people can just go stealing pigeons in broad daylight."

"They're disgusting," Isabella said. "I say, let anyone who wants to take them go ahead."

"But you believe me, right? You know I'm telling the truth?"

"Yes," Isabella said. "I believe you. Can we just go over the stuff for the meeting now?"

"Yeah," Cate said. "Okay, sure."

"Cate, are you sure you're okay? Did something else happen?" Isabella asked.

"No," she said. "I'm fine. Let's just get this over with, okay?"

⌘

Cate started to write an e-mail to her friends about Bridget, but she didn't get far. How embarrassing was it that her ex-boyfriend was dating Bridget Carlson? She looked at the sentence she'd typed and erased it. It was pretty embarrassing, she decided. She stared at her computer and tried to figure out how long it would be before everyone knew about Bridget and Jim. Knowing Bridget, she was probably posting it on Facebook right then. Her status would probably read, "Bridget Carlson is madly in love with Jim." Cate wondered if Bridget had a blog. She hadn't mentioned it, but if anyone was going to fill the world with pointless information about her life, it would be Bridget. This lunch was probably going to be in Bridget's memoir.

Isabella gave Cate suspicious looks all afternoon. Cate tried to ignore her. Once, she started to tell Isabella what had happened. Isabella didn't know Bridget, so she couldn't possibly know the extent of the awfulness. Cate tried, but she couldn't get the words out.

Isabella had saved Cate in the meeting. She'd talked for the both of them, acting as if Cate was involved in the work she'd done. "Thanks," Cate said to her when they got back to their desks.

Isabella just shrugged and shook her head. "Sure," she said. "No problem."

Isabella was always so serious. She constantly reminded Cate that she was older, and said things like "When I was your age" and "You'll understand in a few years." Whenever Cate told her to calm down, she said, "I don't have any time left to fool around." Isabella was only three years older than Cate, but she acted like she was a hundred. If Cate told her about Bridget and Jim, there was a good chance she would shake her head and say, "Oh, children these days."

Cate's phone wouldn't stop ringing the rest of the afternoon, but she refused to answer it. "What is going on?" Isabella demanded.

"I'm just trying to avoid a phone call."

"The stalker?" Isabella asked. "Why don't you just look at the caller ID?"

"No. You don't know this girl. She could be calling from any number."

"I guess," Isabella said. She chewed on her lip and looked concerned. "You know, I was thinking about the pigeons."

"Really?" Cate asked.

"Yeah, I mean, you're right. It could have been just some random man stealing them."

"I know," Cate said. "But why wouldn't anyone have stopped him?"

Isabella shrugged. "Sometimes I think that if you do something with enough confidence in New York, you can get away with anything. If you pretend to have authority, people never question you."

"I think you're right." Cate swallowed, looked back at her computer, and started typing.

Cate left work and stood on the corner waiting for the bus. A pigeon bobbed its head and walked toward her. She waited for it to stop and turn around, but it kept coming. Its beak was open, like it was going to bite her. She kicked her shoe at it and backed up, but it just flapped its wings at her. The people across the street watched her, giving her strange looks. The pigeon kept coming closer, and Cate wondered if it was a rabid pigeon. Was there such a thing? She kicked at it again and screamed, "Aughh!" Finally it turned to walk away. "Fuck you," Cate said to its back. She could have sworn it turned around to look at her. "You better watch it," she said. "There are people out there who can take you." The man next to her moved two steps away.

Cate stopped on the way home to get a bottle of wine, and opened it as soon as she got into her apartment. She poured some into a glass and took a sip before she even took off her jacket. No matter how many times she'd tried to make sense of it, she couldn't. "Bridget and Jim," she repeated aloud. "Bridget and Jim."

Finally, after a couple glasses of wine, she picked up the phone and called her friend Julia. "You won't believe this," Cate said. "I had lunch with Bridget today—I know, I know, she's a crazy person. But listen to what she told me. She's obsessed with Jim and totally stalking him. Yes, that Jim. I know, she's nuts." Cate took another sip of wine and smiled. "I think she's breaking him down," she said. "You know how she is. I know, I know. You almost feel sorry for him. Poor bastard."

The Showers

Riding backwards on a train makes me sick," Lauren said. Everyone ignored her. They were sitting in a four-person seat on the Long Island Rail Road, facing each other with their knees touching. "I'm serious, you guys, I might throw up. I always get motion sick when I ride backwards."

"You feel sick because you drank about forty-five vodka tonics last night," Mary said. She leaned forward and sniffed. "You smell like you just took a shot. I'm serious. I can smell liquor on your breath."

"Please stop it," Lauren said, closing her eyes and leaning her head back against the seat. "Could someone please just switch with me?"

"Fine, I will," Isabella said.

They stood up and grasped elbows, turning until they were on opposite sides. Lauren knocked Mary's coffee when she sat down and Mary swore at her. They were all annoyed. They were on their way to Long Island for a wedding shower and they were all annoyed.

"This isn't helping," Lauren said, and leaned forward to rest her head in her lap. "I hate Long Island."

"No kidding," Isabella said.

ॐ

Their friend Kristi was engaged. They were all happy for her. They were all bridesmaids. They were all sick of celebrating it.

Kristi was really embracing her role as a bride-to-be. She never said things like "Let's talk about something besides the wedding," or, "You don't have to buy me a present for every party." She wanted all of the attention and she wanted all of the presents. This was her time, she kept reminding them, like it was something she'd earned.

This was Kristi's sixth shower. First, her mother's side of the family had thrown her a "Time of Day" shower. They were all given a time of day, and had to buy a present that went along with it. Isabella got two a.m. "What am I supposed to get them for two a.m.?" Isabella asked everyone. She agonized over it, ignored Lauren's suggestion to buy them handcuffs, and finally bought sheets.

Kristi's second shower was thrown by her father's side of the family. (Her father's side had been excluded from the first shower, because of some family drama that none of the bridesmaids cared about.) They traveled to Rhode Island to sit in a tiny living room and listen to Kristi's aunt complain about not being invited to the other shower. "She could have had my invitation," Mary whispered to Isabella.

Kristi's third shower was thrown by her fiancé's grooms-men. It was a couples' shower to stock the bar, and everyone was supposed to bring a bottle of liquor and glasses. "What kind of groomsmen throw a shower?" Lauren asked. "Are they gay? I've never heard of such a thing. And you know what? I'm not going. I'm not in a couple, and I need the liquor more than she does." Lauren ended up going to the party and drinking almost the whole bottle of liquor she'd brought. "I need it more," she kept saying.

The fourth shower was thrown by Kristi's friends from work, and she insisted that they all go. "I need my bridesmaids there," she said. "Why?" Lauren asked. "To wipe her ass?" The fifth shower happened because Kristi kept saying, "No one can believe that my bridesmaids haven't thrown me a shower." They had a brunch at Mary's apartment to shut her up. "Is it just bagels?" she asked when she saw the food. When she opened up the present they got her, she said, "Who is this from? Oh, all of you. Is there another part? No, just this? Okay."

Now they were on their way to Long Island for Kristi's sixth shower and their patience was wearing thin. "My mother's bridge group wants to throw me a shower," Kristi said when she told them about this shower. "I just couldn't say no!"

The thing was, Kristi wasn't their first friend to get married. They had stood up in weddings of friends from home, friends from college, friends from work. Every time they were sure that they were done, someone else got engaged. And all that meant was that they would continue to spend their weekends at wedding showers.

They were good bridesmaids at the showers. They trekked

out to Long Island and the suburbs of New Jersey wearing pastel dresses and carrying presents. They cheered for stainless-steel pots and flowered serving trays. They gathered ribbons and crafted large bouquets out of paper plates, while taking notes on who gave the bride the toaster and who gave her *The Cupcake Cookbook*. They gasped in mock horror when ribbons were broken—"That's six babies now," they'd warn with smiles and raised eyebrows. When margarita glasses were unwrapped, one of them always said, "We'll be over to put those to good use," and the older women at the shower would laugh. They organized games to play, wound up timers, and put together quizzes titled "How Well Do You Know the Bride?"

As the weddings increased, it was harder to be pleasant. After they'd attended five showers, the novelty wore off. By the time it got to fifteen, they were tired of cleaning up wrapping paper. And when they had attended over twenty showers, they were flat-out exhausted. Who on earth needed an ice-cream maker? Why did anyone want a deep fryer? And where were the happy couples (who lived in tiny Manhattan apartments) going to store twenty-four wine glasses and a bread maker?

The train pulled into the station, and they all got up and left in silence. They stood in the sun for a moment. "It's really nice out today," Mary said. Lauren ran to a garbage can on the platform and threw up. "Yes," Isabella said. "It's beautiful out."

As Kristi unwrapped mixers and place mats, Lauren and Isabella snuck out to the patio to have a cigarette. "I bet she gets pregnant right away," Lauren said. She was sipping her third mimosa, and was in much better shape already.

"Why?" Isabella asked.

"Because then she'll have a reason for everyone to give her more presents. We'll have to throw her a baby shower too, and talk about her being pregnant, and then we'll have to babysit the little fucker."

"That's lovely," Isabella said. She peeked through the sliding glass doors to see if anyone missed them. Mary had been grabbed and chosen to write down all of the gifts, and she was looking around the room for them. She seemed pissed and Isabella felt bad, but better her than them. Their friend Abby was constructing a bouquet out of the ribbons Kristi threw at her as she tore into the packages. Abby worked with her head down, like a child in a sweatshop. Kristi had debated whether or not to even make Abby a bridesmaid in the first place. "I mean, I know she'd be honored," Kristi said. "But maybe it would be too much, since she just called off her own wedding not long ago. I don't want her to be a downer." Abby had shown up at every shower and party, and been a good sport. And now, here she was threading ribbons through a paper plate. She glanced up and saw Isabella through the glass door. Her eyes looked wounded, like she believed that Kristi was getting married just to punish her. Abby gave Isabella a small smile and kept her fingers moving, twisting and tying to make that stupid ribbon hat. Isabella tried to smile back and then had to turn away.

"This is getting ridiculous," Lauren said. She was cranky. "This is my fifth wedding this year. And I'm done with it. What

I don't get is why there have to be so many showers just for one person. And why do they have to have themes? Why? Just to make it more annoying than it already is?"

Isabella shushed her and then glanced inside to make sure no one had heard. The theme for this shower was "My Favorite Things." They had all received invitations that read: "Girls in white dresses with blue satin sashes, snowflakes that stay on my nose and eyelashes! Please come and celebrate with our bride-to-be, Kristi Kearney. Bring her one of your favorite things!"

"I should have brought her cigarettes," Lauren said thoughtfully. She took one more drag and then stamped her cigarette out on the ground. "They are one of my favorite things. Thank God I have them today. Kristi's being a nightmare, huh?"

Isabella didn't have anything to say. Kristi wasn't a bad person, she didn't think. But she was acting like one. "Maybe she's just stressed," Isabella said. They had been talking about Kristi for months now. If the wedding didn't come soon, they were going to have to stop being friends with her.

On the eve of Kristi's engagement party, Todd's great-aunt died. There was talk of rescheduling, and Kristi came to see them, crying. "I've just really been looking forward to this," she said. "How could they do this to me?"

"But someone died," Lauren said.

"I just think we still could have it. I mean, it's a party for me," Kristi said. She put her head in her hands and they all looked at each other. Then they all kept drinking.

The party ended up happening. And later, Kristi would say that it was a shame that the aunt's death had put such a damper on it. "I just felt like I couldn't really be as happy as I wanted to be, you know? Like I had to dial it back to be appropriate. It was really unfair."

"Do you think she needs to be on medication?" Mary asked later. No one laughed.

They kept waiting for it to stop, waiting for Kristi to realize that she was acting like a beast. But she never did. At her bachelorette party, she cried when one of their friends announced that she was pregnant. "I just really wanted this night to be about me," she wailed.

When Lauren hired a woman to come to the party and sell sex toys, Kristi turned to her and said, "This seems like something you would want more than I would. I mean, I have Todd now and we're getting married, so I don't really need a vibrator. But it's fun for the single girls, I guess."

"Last night I added up all the money I spent on weddings this year," Lauren said in a dreamy voice. "It was over five thousand dollars. I could have gone on a trip to Belize and then bought a new wardrobe."

"I realized yesterday that my credit card bill is never going to be paid in full. Never," Isabella said.

They weren't really talking to each other. It was the same conversation they'd been having since the weddings started. They finished their cigarettes in silence.

"We should go back in there before Mary never forgives us," Isabella said.

"Fine," Lauren said, and drank the rest of her mimosa in one gulp.

The food at the showers was always the same: ladylike salads, teeny sandwiches, cut-up fruit, white wine and mimosas, mini cakes for dessert. Lauren piled an alarming amount of mini sandwiches on her plate. "I would kill you for a cheeseburger," she whispered to Mary.

"I might just kill you for fun," Mary said. "How could you leave me in there alone? I had to write down all the presents by myself. And they kept asking me if I was dating anyone. Then, one woman who was hard of hearing said, 'What? Who are you dating?' And I had to yell loudly across the room, 'I'm not dating anyone!' "

"Shut up."

"Swear to God, it happened."

One of the bridge friends clinked her glass with a spoon until the room quieted down. "Welcome, everyone! I just wanted to say a few words about our lovely bride-to-be, Kristi!" Everyone in the room clapped.

"Why are they clapping for her?" Lauren asked. "She didn't do anything." Mary and Isabella both shushed her and she just rolled her eyes. The woman talked about Kristi and how she had watched her grow up. Lauren shoved a whole sandwich in her mouth and chewed while the bridge lady spoke. When Mary gave her a look, she swallowed and said, "What? I'm hungry."

"Our theme for today is 'My Favorite Things,' " the woman continued. "I hope that everyone is ready to explain the special meaning behind her gift for Kristi!" Then the woman started singing, "Girls in white dresses with blue satin sashes," and she raised her arms for everyone to join. All of the women in the room chimed in, "Snowflakes that stay on my nose and eye-lashes!" They kept singing and started swaying back and forth. Abby was standing unfortunately close to the woman who'd started the singing, and the woman wrapped her arm around Abby's shoulders, forced her to move in time with the music, and looked at her with an encouraging smile until Abby started to sing along with her. A few of the women were snapping their fingers. Lauren looked at Isabella and Mary and said, "You've got to be fucking kidding me, right?"

They struggled through the lunch and chatted with all of the women. They cleaned up balls of wrapping paper and stray ribbons, helped clear the plates and glasses, and then carried all of the presents to the car while Kristi thanked her guests. Abby told them that she had an appointment in the city that she had to get back for. "Go," they all told her. They almost pushed her out the door. "Get out while you can."

Mary arranged the presents in the back of the car. "It's almost over, right?" she muttered to herself. "Please tell me this is almost over."

Kristi asked them to help drive the presents back to her parents' house, so that they could unload. Then she insisted that they all come inside so that she could show them pictures of what the centerpieces were going to look like. They sat on the couch and tried to admire the pictures. Lauren leaned her head back and closed her eyes. Isabella was sure she was sleeping.

"So, we should probably try to get the next train," Mary said, as though it had just occurred to her.

"You guys aren't staying?" Kristi said. "I thought we could all have dinner and hang out."

"Oh, I guess we didn't realize that," Mary said. "We were planning to get back to the city tonight."

"It's just that it's my shower," Kristi said. She sounded wounded, like she had just told them it was her last day on this earth and they were leaving anyway. Isabella could see Lauren and Mary start to panic.

"I know you two have stuff to get back for, but I could stay," Isabella said. She hoped the other two appreciated her self-sacrifice. Mary perked up right away.

"We really do wish that we could stay, but it just doesn't seem like it will work out," Mary said. Isabella wondered if she was the only person who could hear the joy in Mary's voice.

"Could you stay over?" Kristi asked Isabella. "I have a fitting tomorrow and you could come along."

"Sure," Isabella said. "That would be fun."

Kristi showed Isabella a tape of the band they had chosen, and then they sorted through some of the shower presents, and discussed whether Kristi should have the band announce the wedding party or not. Finally, they got ready for bed in the room where Kristi had grown up. Isabella lay in one of the twin beds and looked at a picture of Fred Savage that was still taped to the bedside table.

"Iz, are you awake?"

"Uh-huh," Isabella said.

"Can I ask you something?"

"Sure."

"Do you think Lauren is acting weird to me?"

"Not really. Weird how?"

"It just doesn't seem like she's happy for me," Kristi said.

"She's happy for you," Isabella answered.

"I don't know. She seems a little distant. I guess maybe it's just hard for her to understand." Isabella didn't say anything. She didn't want to be in this conversation.

"I mean, Abby's not really into the whole bridesmaid thing, but she has her reasons," Kristi said. "But what I don't get is why Lauren's being a pain."

"Lauren seems fine to me," Isabella said.

"It's just, you know, sometimes I worry about her," Kristi said.

"Why?"

"I just feel like she's lonely, you know. Like she's not meeting any guys and it seems like the way she's going, she won't."

Isabella was quiet for a few moments. She didn't know how to answer.

"Well, the thing is that you don't meet someone until you do." Isabella started off talking slowly. "And the older we get, the harder it is. And maybe not all of us will meet someone."

"Well, you can't think like that," Kristi said. "Look at you and Harrison. You found each other."

"But who knows what will happen? And what if it ends and I don't meet anyone else? What if Lauren never meets anyone else? Is that the end of the world? People live, you know."

In college, Kristi's boyfriend cheated on her almost every week and Lauren was always the first one to comfort her. One time, she planned a bar crawl just to cheer Kristi up. Isabella could still remember the way they rode their bikes from bar to bar, with Lauren and Kristi leading the way, swerving and laughing. Isabella was always jealous of Kristi and Lauren in college. They were so close that sometimes they seemed like one person instead of two.

"Well, I'm just glad that you have someone," Kristi said. "It makes me happy when my friends can finally understand how great it is to have someone, you know?"

"Yeah," Isabella said. "I do."

When Kristi got married, she and her husband stood under a chuppah. "We're not having a traditional Jewish wedding," Kristi told them a million times. "We'll have a priest do the ceremony. But I don't want Todd to feel completely left out, so we're having a rabbi up there too."

The rabbi explained how the chuppah represented the new home the couple was starting. Then she had the family drape a cloth over their necks. "With this cloth, we are creating a chuppah within a chuppah," the rabbi said. "This is to symbolize that Kristi and Todd will be bound to each other in a way that is special only to them." Kristi and Todd stood with their shoulders touching, wrapped in the cloth. It reminded Isabella of the way that Lauren and Kristi used to huddle together, whispering and laughing at jokes that only they understood. "A chuppah within a chuppah," the rabbi said again. Lauren sighed and rolled her eyes at Isabella. Isabella tried to smile, but for the first time that day she felt like crying. She watched Lauren fidget in her bridesmaid dress, and watched Kristi and Todd smiling together, their faces almost touching. "A chuppah within a chuppah," she thought. Isabella felt tears come to her eyes, but just as she was about to cry, Todd smashed the glass with his foot and everyone yelled, "Mazel tov!"

Hope

Shannon knew the first time she saw him. His voice was soft and smooth and lulling, his build was fit and strong. As he spoke, her eyes went in and out of focus and she couldn't make herself look away. He was on TV, but it seemed like he was in the room, talking only to her.

Dan sat next to her on the couch, staring at the TV screen, his eyes still and his mouth open. He shushed her when she started to say something. "Do you know who that is?" he asked her. His voice sounded hushed, like he was speaking in a church. "That's our next president."

"Do you really think?" Shannon asked. She rubbed the back of Dan's neck. "It would take a lot for him to win."

Dan finally turned away from the TV. He looked disappointed as he shook his head. "You'll see, Shannon," he said. "Believe me, you'll see."

Later, Shannon would tell everyone this story. She would explain the way Dan's voice changed when he spoke, the way it made a little hop of worry enter her chest. Her friends would humor her. "I'm sure on some level you did know," they would say. "Hindsight's twenty-twenty," they would add. It didn't matter. Only Shannon knew how she felt that day when she first saw the Candidate. Only she knew that his voice made her start sweating, made her heart beat fast, the way an animal reacts right before it's attacked.

Dan had always loved politics. He was a cable news junkie who yelled along with the left-leaning political pundits as they got enraged about the state of the government, the failings of the current administration. He talked policy at parties and argued laws at bars. Shannon met him watching the 2004 presidential debates at a dive bar on the Lower East Side. Over Miller Lite drafts, he explained the details of the Swift-boating. Shannon nodded drunkenly and thought, "This guy is smart." They stood outside and smoked cigarettes and talked about the ridiculousness of the last election. "It turned this country's electoral system into a joke," Dan said. And then Shannon kissed him.

Her friends approved. "I get it," Lauren said. "He's hot, in a nerdy, political way."

"He's nice," Isabella said. "A little intense, maybe. But nice."

Shannon didn't care that he was intense. He was hers. Right after they met at the debates, they started dating and volunteering, urging people to get out and vote. For days before the election, they sat in the volunteer center and made phone calls until Shannon's fingers felt numb from dialing. "I think we can do this," Dan said. Shannon had never found someone so attractive in her life. They made out in a closet in the back of the volunteer center for ten minutes and then went back to their calls.

That night, they drank and watched as the Democratic candidate lost. "Four more years of this," Dan said. "I don't know if I can take it." Shannon took his hand and held it in her lap. She wasn't as upset as he was, but she tried to look like she was. "I'm so glad that I'm with someone who understands," Dan said. Shannon just nodded.

₿

Shannon and Dan moved in together and hosted dinner parties for their friends where political talk ruled the conversation and lively debate was encouraged. Dan sat at the head of the table and quoted articles he'd read, pulled out old *New Yorkers* to back up his point. He talked and lectured, raising his glass of wine when he made important points, as though he were their leader. Sometimes Dan almost crossed the line—like the time he called her friend Lauren ignorant, after she admitted that she'd voted for the Green Party candidate in 2000 because she'd felt bad for him—but most of the time, the dinners were free of fighting and full of wine, and Shannon was happy.

Dan worked in advertising, but his heart wasn't in it. He sat around all day, writing catchy copy to accompany ads. "I want to do something that matters," he always said. Shannon would nod in agreement. "I want a job I care about," he would say, and

Shannon would groan in sympathy. She thought it was just talk, just something people say to get through their day. But the more the young senator from Illinois showed up on TV, the more Dan talked about his discontent. He complained about his hours, his pay, his mindless duties. He slammed dresser drawers in the morning as he got ready for work, and drank a beer each night as he sulked in front of the news. And then one day he came home and announced that he was going to volunteer for the campaign.

"Do you have time to volunteer?" Shannon asked.

"The question is," Dan answered, "how do I not make the time?"

Dan organized rallies and trained volunteers. He went door-to-door making sure people were registered to vote. He skipped three days of work to attend a volunteer training camp in Chicago.

"I asked you last week if we could go on vacation, and you said you couldn't take any days off," Shannon said.

"This isn't vacation," Dan said. "This is our country."

He came home from the volunteer camp with a graduation certificate and newfound energy. "This is it," he kept saying. "This is the time."

"The time for what?" Shannon muttered.

"What?" Dan said.

"Nothing," she said.

At night, all they talked about was the election. Dan analyzed every word that came out of every candidate's mouth. He sat no more than two feet from the TV, so that he wouldn't miss a thing. "Did you hear that?" he asked, pointing at a face on

TV. "Did you hear the tone she used when she said his name? Unbelievable."

Shannon learned how to knit and sat on the couch twisting yarn into rows as Dan muttered to himself. "How can you knit at a time like this?" he asked her once. He looked at her like her yarn was the reason his Candidate was down in the polls.

Dan pored over newspapers, websites, and right-wing blogs to see what the opposition was saying. When Shannon asked him if he wanted to go out to dinner, he just shook his head no. They ate takeout in front of the TV almost every night. More and more often, she found him asleep on the couch in the morning, his computer propped up next to him and CNN chattering in the background. He'd wake up and rub his eyes, then immediately focus on the latest news. "I can't believe I missed this," he'd say. He'd turn up the volume. "Shannon, can you move?" he'd ask. "I can't see the TV."

Dan applied for every job the campaign had. "How much does this one pay?" Shannon asked once.

"Does it matter?" Dan asked. "You don't get this. I would do it for free."

"It would be kind of hard to pay rent then, wouldn't it?" Shannon asked.

Dan walked away from her and turned on the TV, to CNBC. Shannon followed him into the room, but he didn't look at her. "I was kidding," she said. "God, don't be so sensitive."

"This matters to me," Dan said.

"I know," she said. "It matters to me too." Dan raised his eyebrows but didn't say anything more. Shannon sat down on the couch next to him and watched the wild-eyed political commentator scream. It was the blond man, the one who interrupted his guests and got on her nerves. "He spits when he gets excited," she said. And then they watched the rest of the show in silence.

ॐ

When Dan quit his job, Shannon was supportive. "It will be hard," she said. "But if it's important to you, it's important to me." She was pretty sure she meant what she said.

"I'll be traveling a lot," Dan said. "But it's what I always wanted to do."

"Of course," Shannon said. She didn't really know what she was agreeing to, but her answer made Dan happy.

Later, Shannon explained it to her friends. "It's too good to pass up," she said. "It's the opportunity of a lifetime."

"Well, you knew this about him when you met him," Mary said. "I guess this doesn't come as a huge surprise."

"It just sucks for you," Lauren said.

"Yep," Shannon said. "Yep, it really does."

ॐ

At first, Shannon still saw Dan about once a week. Then his trips started to overlap with each other and he didn't seem to have time to come home in between. Soon, he was flying from stop to stop with barely enough time to call her and tell her where he was going. Shannon realized that if she wanted to see him, she'd have to go to him. And that's what she did.

Shannon shivered in New Hampshire while Dan arranged an outdoor rally. She attended a fund-raiser in Chicago and then took a bus to Iowa and painted campaign signs in a high school, while a snowstorm raged outside and Dan worried that the old people wouldn't be able to drive to the school. Shannon painted poster boards red, white, and blue. She painted the Candidate's name in fancy block letters, and made signs that said "Davenport for Change." She painted "Hope" over and over again, so many times that the letters started to look funny and the word lost its meaning.

Shannon went to Boston and followed Dan around to three different events in one day. She shook hands with the Candidate and nearly blacked out from excitement. She listened to him give the same speech over and over and she cried every time. He talked about the hardships people have to face, and he talked about wanting a better world for his children, and Shannon clapped and cried.

Shannon shouted that she was "fired up and ready to go" in seven different states. She passed out buttons and helped set up chairs. And sometimes, when she went to bed at night, she heard rally cries in her head, soft and far away. They sounded so real that she was sure there were people gathered outside her apartment, huddled together, chanting the Candidate's name as she tried to fall asleep.

Dan returned to New York for an event and Shannon recruited

all of her friends to come. They waited in line at Washington Square Park for three hours, getting crushed by the crowd. "Dan will be so happy that you came," Shannon told them.

"Where is he?" Lauren asked.

"Up there." Shannon pointed to the stage. Dan darted by.

"That's fun that you got to see him last night," Isabella said.

"Oh, well, I actually didn't," Shannon said. "He ended up working all night. He slept here."

"In the park?" Mary asked. "Gross."

"Tonight, maybe?" Isabella asked.

Shannon shook her head. "He's off to Pennsylvania," she said. The girls were quiet for a minute.

"Well," Lauren said. "It will be over soon, right?" Shannon started to agree, but the music came on and they all turned to the stage, and clapped and cheered.

As the primaries got closer, Dan traveled so much that Shannon didn't even have time to go see him. He'd be in a city for twenty hours and then on his way to the next one. Even phone calls became rare. Sometimes, though, she caught a glimpse of his head on the border of the TV, running from side to side in a gymnasium after the Candidate finished a speech. She watched for him closely, waiting for his blond head to flash on the screen. "There he is," she'd cry, although no one was there to hear her. And then as soon as she spotted him, he'd run off the other side, gone from her sight.

When the Candidate won Iowa, Dan called from the campaign center. He sounded muffled and far away. Shannon could hear screaming in the background and Dan had to yell to be heard. His voice was thick, as though he'd been crying or was just about to start.

ꝏ

When Dan did come home, he was exhausted and wrinkled. Sometimes, he'd been up for days. His hair stood up in clumps and his eyes were bloodshot. He'd come into the apartment, shower, and head straight for bed.

Shannon talked to him while he slept. She told him about her job while his eyes stayed closed. "Mmm-hmm," he'd murmur sometimes.

ꝏ

Dan wore two BlackBerrys, strapped to either side of his belt. "You look like a nerd," Shannon always told him. He didn't care. Once when Dan was home and lying in bed, Shanon saw a red mark on his hip. "What's that?" she asked. She touched it lightly.

"It's from the BlackBerry, I think," Dan said.

"You have a scar from your BlackBerry vibrating against you?" Shannon asked.

"I guess so," Dan said.

"And that doesn't strike you as strange? As not right?"

"Not really," Dan said. He rolled over and turned out his bedside light.

"You've been branded," Shannon said. But Dan was already asleep.

Every time Dan got ready to leave again, they fought.

"When will you be home?" Shannon would ask.

"You know I don't know that," he'd say.

"Do you even miss me?" she'd ask.

"Shannon," he'd say. "Don't start this now. You know I miss you. Don't fight with me right before I leave."

Sometimes she let it drop, but sometimes she didn't. Sometimes she'd poke and whine until they fought. It felt good to scream at him, to scream at someone. Once she asked him, "Let's say that you got to have dinner with one person and you had to choose: me or the Candidate. And you hadn't seen me in a month. Who would you pick?"

"You, of course," he said. He came over and kissed her good-bye. It was a lie. She knew deep inside that she was his second choice. Always. He'd fallen for someone new. And infatuation was winning.

Once after he left, the dog jumped onto the bed, lifted his leg, and peed. Shannon didn't even yell at him. "I understand," she said to the dog as she stripped the sheets. "It's a shitty situation."

As months went by, Shannon forgot what it was like to live with Dan. Some nights she convinced herself that he was gone for good. If he did leave, she decided, she would take his TV.

Her friends were worried about her. They took her to brunch and brought over wine. "How are you doing?" they asked.

"Good, good," Shannon always said. What was she supposed to say? That Dan would rather campaign in Texas than spend time with her? That she'd been abandoned? That the Candidate had stolen her boyfriend? It was easier to just say, "I'm doing great."

"You're such a good sport," they'd say.

Shannon drank the wine and agreed. "Yep, that's me." It was better, she thought, than the truth.

ᗺ

At the end of August, Dan got four days off from the campaign. Shannon thought they'd have all sorts of time together, but when he was in the apartment, all he did was e-mail with his campaign friends. He was constantly looking at his BlackBerry. They went to dinner, and Dan remained hunched over, his fingers clicking away. Sometimes he'd laugh at a response he got, or nod in agreement.

"Don't your fingers hurt?" Shannon asked him. He looked up, surprised.

"No," he said. "They're fine."

"Do you think you could put that away for twenty minutes while we eat, so that I could actually talk to you while we're in the same city for once?"

He whistled. "Whoa, Shannon. Calm down." He put his BlackBerry down next to his plate and held up his hands in a fake surrender. "It's away," he said. "Okay?"

"No," she said, holding out her hand. "Away, away. Give it to me. I'll keep it in my purse."

"Shannon, come on. Don't overreact."

She kept her hand out. "I'm not overreacting. You're not even e-mailing about work stuff, are you? You just miss your little campaign friends."

Dan handed over the BlackBerry, but looked at Shannon with narrowed eyes. "You've really got to figure out how to deal with your issues," he said.

"Yeah," she said. "That's totally the problem."

The last night Dan was home, he wanted to go on a double date with his campaign friend Charlotte and her boyfriend, Chet. "Why?" Shannon kept asking. "Why do we have to go out with them?"

"I want you to meet her," Dan said. "I think you'll really hit it off."

"I kind of doubt it," she said.

"Come on," Dan said, and finally she agreed.

On the way downtown, Dan told Shannon that Charlotte and Chet were having some problems. "Chet's not thrilled that Charlotte's traveling so much," he said. "He's not taking the campaign too well."

"Who is?" she asked.

"Shannon."

"What?"

He just shook his head.

They went to a tiny Mexican place in the West Village that served mango margaritas that tasted like candy. Dan and Shannon got there first, and stood at the bar drinking their margaritas. "Oh," Dan said, "there they are!" He waved his hand up in the air and a tall blonde waved back.

Charlotte was almost six feet tall and very thin. She was the kind of person you don't think is that pretty at first, but upon closer examination, you realize that she's gorgeous. Her angular nose was striking and her long limbs were graceful. She could have been a model. When Shannon stood next to her, her head came right up to her boobs.

"Shannon, hi!" she said, and she surprised Shannon with a hug. Shannon's face smooshed into Charlotte's chest and she could barely breathe. Finally she let Shannon go, but still held on to her shoulders. "It is so nice to finally meet you."

Shannon finished her margarita and shook the empty glass at Dan. "I'm ready for another one."

They waited a long time for a table and got two more rounds of margaritas. Chet and Shannon drank while Charlotte and Dan talked about the people they worked with.

"And Kelly," Charlotte said, rolling her eyes. "Can you believe the way she sets up the events? I mean, putting the chairs in a semicircle? Where does she think she is?"

Dan doubled over with laughter and Chet and Shannon looked at each other. Shannon licked the salt off her glass. "Semicircles, huh?" she asked. "Crazy." Dan stopped laughing and tilted his head at her. She smiled back.

By the time they sat down, Shannon could feel mango margaritas sloshing around in her stomach. The waiter put a basket of chips on the table and everyone grabbed for them. Charlotte took a handful and shoved them in her mouth. Then she started waving her hands around like, *Wait, don't talk! I've got a story to tell!* Chet looked at her from the sides of his eyes, and Shannon wondered if he hated his girlfriend too. Charlotte swallowed her chips and wiped the grease off her lips. She took a sip of her drink and smiled.

"I forgot to tell you guys," she said. "Last night, I had the most graphic, realistic, and extremely satisfying sex dream about the Candidate."

"Well, it looks like we know who the next Monica Lewinsky will be," Shannon said. She laughed and no one else did. Dan looked at her with his mouth open. "What?" she asked. "She can talk about the next president of the United States giving her an orgasm and I can't make a Lewinsky joke?"

Charlotte looked down in pretend embarrassment. "Oh my *God,*" Shannon said. "You brought it up. With your boyfriend sitting right there." Shannon meant to point at Chet, but he was closer than she thought and she ended up poking him on the cheek. He jumped in surprise. Shannon got the feeling he hadn't been listening to anything they'd been saying.

They finished their enchiladas quietly, with pleasant, bland conversation. On the way home, Dan reprimanded Shannon. "I can't believe you said that," he told her. "Charlotte was pretty upset."

"Oh, was she?" Shannon asked. "Do you think that Chet and I were upset that we went to dinner with our significant others that we never see and all they talked about was the random people they work with on the campaign? People that we don't know and have never met. It was so boring. And it was rude." Shannon's eyes started to tear up and she sniffled. Dan let his shoulders drop.

"I'm sorry, Shannon," he said. She shrugged and he grabbed her arm until she looked at him. "I mean it. I know this is hard for you and I really appreciate your support. You know that, right? You know how much that means to me." Shannon shrugged again and let him hug her.

"We shouldn't have gone to dinner with them," she said. "That's not fair. You're leaving tomorrow."

"You're right," Dan agreed. "It should have just been us. Charlotte suggested it and I didn't know what else to do. She's having a hard time with Chet. I'm not sure they're going to work it out. I feel really bad for them."

"Yeah," Shannon said. "How sad for them."

∂⟩

Shannon dreamt of the Candidate. She dreamt that they ran into each other at the grocery store and laughed about buying the same pasta sauce. "You like Ragú too?" Shannon said to him, and they laughed and clutched arms. She dreamt that he came over for dinner and she told him how he was making her life so hard. He smiled. He shook her hand. He talked about *hope* and *belief* and *getting fired up!* Shannon awoke from these dreams feeling exhausted and confused, until she noticed that she'd left the TV on CNN. They were showing a tape of the Candidate at some campaign stop. He was smiling and frowning, laughing and tilting his head to show concern. Shannon looked at him closely while he talked and gestured. Did he know? Did he know that he had stolen her boyfriend? Did he know that he was ruining her whole life plan? Did he know that he was making her miserable?

He finished the speech and a Stevie Wonder song came blaring out of the speakers. He clapped his hands toward the audience, gave a serious look, and then smiled and went to shake hands. He swayed his shoulders and hips to the song. She decided that the answer was no. He didn't know any of it.

☙

Everyone asked about Dan; people at work, friends, family, even the neighbors wanted to know what he was up to. "How's he doing?" they would ask. "How's the feeling on the campaign? Do we have this one wrapped up?"

Shannon knew they were all nervous. They were scared that they'd wind up with an old man and a crazy-booted gun lover in the White House. "It's going great," she would tell them. "Everyone's feeling positive."

"But what about this Muslim rumor?" they would insist. "Do you think we can shake this? What about the flag pin?" they asked. Shannon looked at their wrinkled eyebrows and tried to reassure them, but she barely had anything left.

☙

As the election went on, the rumors got nasty. People tried to paint the Candidate as anti-American, finding incriminating old footage of a reverend he knew, and playing it on what seemed like a twenty-four-hour loop. When this news broke, Shannon didn't talk to Dan for a week. He was jumping from event to event, trying to make people forget they'd ever heard the words "God damn America."

When Dan finally did call, it was in the middle of the night and Shannon wasn't sure if she was dreaming.

"I just wanted to say hi," he said. He didn't sound like he knew she'd almost put out an Amber Alert on him.

"Are you okay?" she asked.

"Yeah," he said. "Just tired. I keep thinking they can't do it again. They can't steal another election from us."

"That's good," Shannon said. She was still half caught in sleep.

"They can't take this away," he said. "The Candidate deserves this. We need him. The country needs him."

"Mmm-hmm," Shannon said. "They can't take it away," she repeated.

"That's right," he said. "And if they do, we're moving to Canada."

One evening in early fall, Shannon walked the dog up Broadway with her friend Lauren. The air was starting to turn and the wind made Shannon shiver just a little. The two of them were deciding where to get a drink, and Shannon was trying to hurry the dog along, pulling him past hydrants he wanted to sniff, when a smiling boy with a clipboard stepped in front of them. "Excuse me," he said. "Do you have a minute for the Democratic candidate?"

Lauren started to say something, but Shannon spoke first. "Do I have a minute for the Candidate?" she asked. The boy nodded and smiled and Shannon felt heat rush into her eyes. The dog sniffed the boy's leg and stood very still.

"Yes," he said. "If you have just a minute for me, I can tell you about how you can help—"

"Do I have a *minute* for the Candidate? Do I? Have a minute? For the Candidate?" The boy nodded again, but now he looked nervous. "Let me tell you something," Shannon said.

"I have given the Candidate weeks—no, months—of my life. No, I don't have a minute for him. You want to know why? My boyfriend has left to travel around with him. He quit his job to work for the campaign, and I haven't seen him in a month. A month! I'm not sure if he's ever coming back, and the thing is, he doesn't even care! He doesn't care because all he wants is to work on this godforsaken campaign that is just so important. More important than anything else, including me!"

The boy began to back away. "Okay, then," he said. "I didn't mean to—"

"You didn't mean to what? Interrupt my walk? Stop me on a cold night and make me listen to you tell me how amazing this Candidate is? Yes, you did. And I've heard it. I hear it all the time. From my boyfriend, from everyone. I get it. He's amazing."

"Yes, he is," the boy said quietly. Shannon narrowed her eyes. Lauren tried to pull her arm and make her walk away, but Shannon stayed right where she was.

"Why are you even here?" she asked.

"To inform people about the change we want to see in the world," he said.

"No," Shannon said. "Why are you *here?*" she pointed to the sidewalk. "Why are you in New York? You think you need to convince people here to vote for him? Let me give you a heads-up, buddy. He's got New York, okay? We got it. We're Democrats here. And you're on the Upper West Side, of all places. For God's sake. Don't waste your time. Go somewhere else! It doesn't even matter if I vote. I might not even bother. Did you hear that? I might not vote!"

The boy kept walking backward and then turned and ran

down the street, clutching his clipboard to his chest. He kept glancing back to see if Shannon was chasing after him. A few people stood on the sidewalk and stared, and Lauren took five steps to the right, trying to pretend that she didn't know Shannon.

"Every vote counts," an old lady said to Shannon. "Don't be stupid."

"Oh, fuck you," she said. The dog hung his head. He looked embarrassed. Shannon started to walk down the sidewalk toward her apartment. She walked quickly, and Lauren had to jog to keep up.

"Are you okay?" Lauren asked.

Shannon stopped. "Yeah. I guess maybe I'm not handling this whole thing as well as I thought."

"Really?" Lauren said. "Do you think?"

"Whatever," Shannon said.

"Hey, I get it," Lauren said. "If you want to go back and push down that old lady, I'm all for it."

"Maybe later," Shannon said. "Drinks first."

On Election Day, Shannon slept in. She got coffee and took her time walking to the public school where she would vote. Everyone at work would be late because of voting, and she might as well take advantage of it. She at least deserved that much.

Shannon had butterflies in her stomach as she walked, but they weren't from excitement. She'd been counting down to this day for months, and now that it was here she didn't quite know how she felt about it.

As Shannon turned on Ninetieth, she saw that the line

stretched all the way down the block. People were laughing and waving to their neighbors. Moms from the school were selling baked goods and hot chocolate. "All the proceeds are going to the school," they kept saying. The group at the front was rowdy and slaphappy from standing in line for so long, and they started cheering as people came out of the building. "Whoo!" they yelled. "You made a difference! Good for you!"

Everyone was acting like this was some strange election-themed street fair. Shannon debated going back to bed and not voting at all. She could just tell everyone she had. What was the difference? In the end, she stayed put, but she put on her sunglasses and refused to smile at anyone around her.

Shannon saw a guy she knew from work walking down the line. "Hey!" he said to her. He held up his hand for a high five and Shannon gave him a weak slap. "What a day, huh?" he asked. He turned his face to the sun and smiled. Like it was Christmas. Like there was a miracle to observe.

"Yep," Shannon said. "What a day. Where did you come from? Were you in the front of the line?"

"Yeah," he said. "But I gave my place to an elderly lady. I told her I'd go to the back of the line, you know? It's the least I can do."

This wasn't the New York that Shannon loved. These weren't the people who normally lived here. Everyone had gone crazy. Dan was gone and maybe he was never coming back. Shannon thought, as she waited in line, that she was crazy too, that she should have never waited for Dan in the first place. She should have made him choose: "Me or the Candidate," she should have said.

Shannon thought this as she stood in line and as she voted. What had she done? Why had she chosen to stand by and support Dan as he'd left her? When she came out of the building, the group of people waiting to get in smiled and waited for Shannon to smile back. She didn't. Finally, one of the women said, "I hope you made the right choice." Shannon just looked at her and said, "Me too."

That night, Shannon sat in a bar with her friends to watch the returns. Everyone was anxious, and they drank quickly. "So, our feeling is hopeful but cautious, right?" Mary said.

"Sure," Shannon said. She was drinking faster than any of them. Vodka went down like water. No one really noticed until she fell off her stool.

"Whoa," Isabella said. "Are you okay?"

"Maybe we need some chicken fingers," Lauren said. She held up her hand for the bartender.

"She's just really excited," Shannon heard Mary telling someone at the bar. "Her boyfriend's been working on the campaign and now he'll finally come home."

"He's not coming home," Shannon tried to say. But it didn't come out right and no one seemed to understand her.

When the Candidate gave his speech that night, Shannon cried, of course. Everyone did. The whole bar watched in tears because it was amazing and inspiring and they were all relieved. But Shannon didn't cry like the rest of them. She didn't have little tears dripping out. No, Shannon had flared nostrils and she heaved and hyperventilated and her face turned red. It was the way she used to cry when she was little, when her mom used to say, "You need to calm down" and would send her upstairs to do just that. Shannon sat in the middle of everyone and cried like a red hog.

All of her friends sat around her, taking turns patting her on the back. Finally, Lauren took her home and made sure she got into bed and took some Advil.

"Just go to bed," Lauren said. "You'll feel better tomorrow."

"Nothing will ever be the same," Shannon said.

"That's right," Lauren said, misunderstanding. "It's all different now."

Dan was offered a job in D.C. shortly after. Shannon cried and they fought, and he took the job and moved there. They tried to make it work for a while. She took the train to visit him, and he drove up to New York on free weekends. But it wasn't working. Shannon couldn't shake the feeling that she was his second choice, that Dan had chosen someone else over her. She couldn't forgive that.

One of the last times Shannon visited Dan, she ran into an old friend from college. He was sitting in a bar, drinking beers with a friend. He told her that his longtime girlfriend had joined the campaign and then gotten a job with the administration. She was in charge of finding hotels for the president and his staff and was currently in Germany. "I haven't seen her in two months," he said.

"Are you still together?" Shannon asked. He shrugged and took a long drink.

"How can you be with someone if you never see them?" he finally responded.

"That," Shannon said, "is a great question."

 ℬ

Dan and Shannon broke up over the phone about two weeks after that. She blamed the Candidate for their breakup. (She didn't call him the president, like everyone else. To her, he would always be the Candidate.) When Shannon thought about it, the Candidate was probably responsible for all sorts of breakups. She and Dan were just the tip of the iceberg. All over America, boyfriends and girlfriends had been ripped apart in the name of Hope.

Shannon was angry that no one was covering this news story. People were talking about health care, but no one was talking about the Relationship Misery Phenomenon that the Candidate had caused. She started writing an op-ed for the *New York Times* but she didn't get very far. She couldn't put into words what had happened.

Shannon stopped reading the newspapers. She stopped watching CNN and MSNBC. Every day that she woke up seemed to matter less. It was Tuesday or Monday or Friday or Wednesday. What difference did it make? She didn't care who the president was or what changes he was going to make to the country. She was alone and that was all she had room to think about.

Her friends tried to cheer her up. "Come on," they said. "Come out. Forget about Dan." But Shannon refused.

"You know," Lauren said, "you were too good for him anyway."

"That's just something people say," Shannon said.

"Shannon," Lauren said, "the guy wore two BlackBerrys on his belt. He wasn't perfect." But this only made Shannon cry.

In her darkest moments, Shannon wished it had gone another way. Lying in bed at night, with her head under the covers, she wished that the Candidate had lost. She never admitted this to anyone, and she wasn't sure that she really meant it. But maybe she did. She felt reckless when she had these late-night thoughts. She was a lifetime Democrat and here she was wishing that the Republicans had squeaked out another one. Sometimes she laughed by herself, feeling giddy, the same way she'd felt when she'd stolen a candy bar in the fourth grade. How ashamed her parents would have been if they'd known. How ashamed she was of herself when she looked in the mirror in the morning.

She thought of calling Dan just so she could say, "I wish he'd lost," and then hanging up. But she couldn't do it. She was afraid it would only reaffirm his belief that he was right to choose the Candidate over her, that it was the smartest thing he'd ever done.

Shannon wished that she were a stronger person, a more self-less soul that would be happy to put the needs of her country ahead of her own. But maybe she wasn't. Maybe she was nothing more than a weak and selfish brat who wanted what she wanted. Oh yes, she was ashamed.

She started watching a lot of reality TV. She watched it for hours at a time, surprised when she looked up at the clock and found that a whole day had slipped by. It soothed her to see people eat bugs and search for love in rose ceremonies. It gave her peace.

Shannon used to judge people who watched these shows,

this trash TV. Now it was all she could stand to do. She watched whatever was on—dysfunctional famous families, snotty teenagers at reform camp, even a couple with a litter of in vitro babies that squabbled and screamed. But her favorite one of all, the one she waited all week to watch, was a weight-loss show where morbidly obese people were sent to a ranch and forced to exercise and starve themselves to a healthy weight.

These people cried and fought. They fell down on the gym floor and begged not to be sent home. They tried to undo all of the bad choices they'd made. Shannon watched in her bed, curled up under the blankets, bawling at the big people as they struggled to break out of their giant bodies. She wept along with them as they ran on treadmills and lifted weights. She cried for their struggle and the goals they wanted to reach. She understood them, after all. All they wanted was a new beginning. All they wanted was some hope.

Little Pigs

Isabella and Harrison were going to Boston. Harrison wanted to get on the road early, and set the alarm clock for five a.m. "This isn't early," Isabella told him when the alarm clock started buzzing. "It's the middle of the night." All morning, Harrison told Isabella to hurry, which made her want to get back into bed. Finally, at eight-fifteen, they were in the car and heading out of the city. Isabella asked if they could stop for coffee at Dunkin' Donuts and Harrison wrinkled his nose and said, "Dunkin' Donuts? Really?" But he pulled over and went inside to get it for her.

"Here," he said, handing her the big Styrofoam cup. He sniffed.

"You don't want any?" she asked.

"I'll wait," he said.

They were going to Boston to see Harrison's friends Brinkley and Coco. Brinkley and Coco had had a baby a few months ago and kept insisting that they come visit. Isabella had heard the names Brinkley and Coco so much during the past week, she'd thought it was going to push her over the edge. All of Harrison's friends had names that reminded her of cartoon animals. These names used to be funny to Isabella. Now they were just annoying.

"What's the baby's name again?" she asked, even though she knew. "Bitsy?"

"Elizabeth."

"Right."

Isabella sipped her coffee and stared out the window. She was excited about going to Boston, even if she didn't care about seeing these people or meeting their baby. It was October and Isabella felt like she should be going somewhere. Fall always did that to her. It made her restless, like she was late getting back to school; like she should be registering for classes, and buying pencils and notebooks and folders that matched.

She'd bought a pink outfit for the child with little polka dots on the feet. She'd shown it to Harrison before she wrapped it. He nodded and said, "Nice." She also bought a little pink bunny to go with it, but at the last moment left it out of the package. It was soft and worried-looking and Isabella had a feeling that the baby wouldn't appreciate it. She pictured it lost among a shelf of bigger animals, and so she shoved it into a drawer in her bedside table and continued wrapping the present.

Harrison had gone to college in Boston too, and Isabella often wondered if they'd ever run into each other on the street or brushed shoulders at a bar. She'd asked him this once when they had just started dating and it seemed romantic to think that they might have been in the same place years ago.

"Probably not," he said.

"No," she agreed. "Probably not."

Harrison had gone to Tufts and was two years older, while she'd been at Boston College, on the other side of the city. It made her sad to think they'd never be back there again, never bounce from bar to bar drinking and dancing just because they could, just because they should. It wasn't that she wanted to be in college again, exactly. No, she just missed it sometimes, the aftermath of those nights out, inexplicable bruises and lost wallets, phone numbers being requested, make-outs with near strangers in crowded bars.

Harrison didn't seem to miss the past at all.

"But don't you wish you could go back, just for a week?" she asked.

"I guess maybe," he answered. She knew he didn't mean it.

Isabella could spend hours looking at pictures from college. She liked to set them next to the more recent pictures from weddings and reunions and compare the two. It wasn't that they looked old now—they weren't even thirty! It was just that they looked so young in the college pictures, so baby-faced and rubbery. Isabella studied the different shots of them, dressed up in ridiculous costumes or bundled up for a football game. It amazed her, how eager their expressions were, like they couldn't wait to get to the next party, like there was just so much fun waiting for them.

Isabella couldn't get over the way their skin looked in these pictures. It was dewy and pink and she couldn't imagine what they'd ever complained about. It looked as though they were smothered in highlighting cream. Now they were duller and more matte. And she was pretty sure they were going to stay that way.

Even Harrison's college pictures made her sad—him in a dirty house standing next to a keg, his arms around friends and a half-drunk smile on his face. It made her homesick that she would never know him there. They'd met after they both had jobs, and it broke her heart that she'd never know the college Harrison. She studied the pictures of him with his college girl-friend, trying to figure out what they were like, jealous that the girl in the picture knew Harrison in a way that she couldn't.

The ride to Boston took a while and they listened to NPR for most of the way. *Wait Wait . . . Don't Tell Me!* was on, which was Harrison's favorite show. He laughed at things that Isabella didn't find funny. She wanted to ask him what he was laugh-ing at, but knew that the answer would probably be a look that said, *You're not as smart as I am so you don't get it,* and so she stayed quiet.

Isabella fell asleep toward the end of the drive, and woke up confused and cranky as they pulled into the driveway. Her mouth was open and she had drool on her cheek. She wiped it away and looked at Harrison, annoyed.

"Why didn't you wake me up?" she asked.

"You're already up," he said and turned off the ignition.

Brinkley was outside the house with their golden retriever, and Isabella watched him wave and wished that they hadn't come. She wiped her mouth again to make sure she got all the drool off and ran her fingers through her hair.

"Ready?" Harrison asked. She opened the door and got out.

Brinkley walked over to greet her and kissed her on the cheek. All of Harrison's friends had impeccable manners. She resisted her impulse to curtsy.

"Coco's inside with the baby," he said.

ᕥ

The baby (Isabella had to admit) was gorgeous. There was none of the ruddy-faced pimply skin newborns sometimes have. This baby was pink and cream, with dark hair and deep blue eyes. Isabella didn't want to be in love with her but immediately was.

Coco was funnier than she remembered, which was maybe due to the fact that she'd gotten a little fat during her pregnancy. She had always been a tiny girl, but now on her short frame was the unmistakable blubber of leftover baby.

"All I want now is sausage," she told Isabella with wide eyes. "It's unreal. Red meat and sausage."

She offered Isabella a glass of wine and poured some red into two oversized glasses. "I'm not really supposed to drink if I'm breast-feeding, but fuck it. I just went nine months without a drink. Plus, I go crazy by the end of the day with just this little blob to keep me company," she said, smiling at the baby.

Isabella liked Fat Coco more than she'd ever liked the other one.

&

They drank until dinner and nibbled on cheese and crackers. They passed around the baby and Coco opened the present. Isabella held Elizabeth and wished that she'd brought her the bunny. By the time they sat down, they were all a little drunk.

Brinkley put the steaks on everyone's plates and gave Coco the largest one, which struck Isabella as incredibly kind. She'd always thought Brinkley would be the kind of husband who wouldn't want a chubby wife. But he didn't care! Coco had just had their baby and he was grateful. Isabella felt tears come to her eyes and made a mental note to stop drinking the wine.

&

Harrison and Isabella made a plan to go to Newbury Street to walk around and have lunch, but by the time Isabella was showered and dressed and got down to the kitchen the next morning, there was another plan all set. Coco was packing a picnic basket for them to bring to Boston Common. Who owned a picnic basket? Did everyone have one except for Isabella?

Isabella kept looking at Harrison to catch his eye. This was not the plan. But he didn't seem to notice. He poured himself a cup of coffee and talked to Brinkley about some guy they knew who'd been fired for stealing from clients. Isabella wasn't sure, but she thought the guy's name was Mortimer.

Harrison leaned over his coffee, stuffing his nose right over the top as he inhaled. "Now, this," he said, looking at Isabella, "this is real coffee."

Isabella hated him so much she almost spit. His nostrils looked huge when he smelled the coffee, and she felt nauseous. She smiled and asked for Advil.

ℬ

Isabella hadn't been on a picnic for as long as she could remember. Maybe even longer. And she knew why. It was uncomfortable to sit outside and awkward to pass around thermoses filled with soup, trying not to spill them on clothes, holding on to napkins as they blew away. She was smiling, though, so as not to be rude. Her head hurt from the wine and she wished that she were still in bed. It was cold when the wind blew—too cold, certainly, to be sitting outside for a meal.

Boston Common was pretty, especially with all of the leaves changing colors and the beautiful brownstones in the background. Everyone in Boston looked cleaner and more awake than people in New York. But Boston Common was not Central Park, and it looked small and eager to Isabella, like it was trying too hard.

The baby was bundled up to the point of insanity. All Isabella could see was a teeny nose sticking out of a pile of blankets. Coco leaned over and touched her nose to the baby. Isabella felt something that was certainly jealousy, although she wasn't sure why. She wished that she wanted to sit closer to Harrison and have his arm wrapped around her, but she didn't.

Harrison was explaining how the hedge fund he worked for

was adjusting to the economy and how their outlook was changing. Every time he said the word "derivatives," Isabella's temples throbbed. Coco and Brinkley listened intently, and not just to be polite. They were interested in what he was saying.

He was boring, Isabella realized. She watched him tell a story about work and it hit her: He was boring, and his friends were boring, and this picnic *right now* was boring. Harrison probably had a secret desire to get married and move to Boston and get a golden retriever and be boring all the time. She didn't know him at all.

And worse, what if he didn't want to marry her and move to Boston? She wasn't quite sure she wanted to be with him, but she was quite sure that she wanted him to want that. Her brain swirled inside her head, and she closed her eyes and tilted her head back to face the sun.

Sometimes Harrison seemed like an old man, crooked and worn out. He was cranky at the end of workdays, loosening his tie and watching the evening news. They probably shouldn't have moved in together so soon, but rent in New York was insane and both of their leases were up and they were spending almost every night together anyway. It seemed like a good idea. Now Isabella couldn't imagine how they would ever get out of it even if they wanted to.

"Do you ever hate Ken?" Isabella had asked her friend Mary a couple of weeks ago. They were getting manicures on a Wednesday night after work and the question just came out. Ken was Mary's new boyfriend, a nice guy who made all of their friends comment, "Oh, there he is. That's what she's been waiting for," as if finding your perfect match was a guarantee as long as you were patient enough.

Mary raised her eyebrows and looked closely at a nail she'd just smudged.

"Hate him?" she asked.

"Yeah. Hate him," Isabella said. "The other night I looked at Harrison and I just . . . I don't know."

"I don't know if I ever *hate* him," Mary said. "But he sure bugs the living fuck out of me sometimes."

&

That night they all went to the North End for Italian food. They ate pasta and drank less wine than they had the night before, and Brinkley, Coco, and Harrison all exchanged information about people they'd gone to school with.

"Cathleen's pregnant again," Coco said. "But she's not really telling anyone yet, so don't say anything."

Coco always knew the best gossip, and almost everything she said was followed by a disclaimer that she wasn't supposed to repeat it. The first time Isabella had met Coco was at a wedding of Brinkley and Harrison's friend Tom. Coco spent most of the reception sharing bits of information with Isabella. The bride had cheated on the groom in college with another friend, Dave, who hadn't been invited to the wedding, and also one of the bridesmaids had been in love with the groom since freshman year!

Isabella took these confidences to mean that Coco really liked her, that she wanted to be friends, and she was flattered by the attention. But after a few more encounters, Isabella realized there was nothing special about her. Coco just couldn't keep a secret.

Back at their house, Coco put out cookies and poured everyone some wine. The baby was wide awake, and lay on the floor on a pink blanket with a mobile of stuffed farm animals above her. She babbled at them like she was telling a story.

"You have a lot to say tonight, don't you?" Coco asked the baby.

"Just like her mother," Harrison said, and they all laughed.

For some reason this made Isabella feel left out, like she was crashing a reunion. She sat on the floor next to the baby, pretending to be so interested in Elizabeth that she didn't care about the conversation around her. The three of them were still trading information about people from college, but they had moved on to peripheral friends, people Isabella had never even met.

"Dorothea got laid off!" Coco almost yelled this one, so happy that she'd remembered it. She tucked her legs underneath her, gearing up to tell the whole story. "She was just about to be promoted too, or that's what she thought. And she was looking at places to buy in the city when they called her in. Can you believe it?" She took a sip of wine for dramatic effect. "She's pretty embarrassed about it, so don't broadcast it or anything. She had to move back in with her parents on Long Island. Can you imagine? Ugh," Coco shuddered.

Isabella actually could imagine it and she wondered if she was the only one. Her life, as it was, felt very thin, very transport-able. If she were to lose her job, moving back in with her parents might be exactly what she'd do. She wasn't married to Harri-son, and they didn't have a child. She could just sell her bed and couch and pack up and move home to her parents' house, easy as pie.

This wasn't normal, she didn't think. But was Coco more normal? They were almost the same age and Coco had started a whole other life with babies, and golden retrievers, and picnic baskets. It was a life that felt miles away for Isabella.

Isabella sat cross-legged in front of the baby and started tick-ling her toes. "This little piggy went to market, this little piggy stayed home . . . ," she began quietly. Elizabeth's eyes grew very round and she looked serious. "This little piggy ate roast beef, and this little piggy had none." Elizabeth was almost completely still, her eyes fixed on Isabella. "And this little piggy went weee weee weee, all the way home!" Isabella finished and tickled the baby up her legs onto her stomach. Elizabeth looked frightened for a moment and then started to laugh and snort.

"You're so good with her," Coco said. Isabella was offended that she sounded surprised.

"Isabella has a lot of nieces and nephews," Harrison said, not unkindly, though it made Isabella feel like an awkward teenager who they were trying to praise and include. She excused herself shortly after and went upstairs to bed. The three of them stayed up late talking and it felt lonely to listen to their voices from another room.

Isabella didn't sleep well that night and was up and dressed, sitting by her packed bag, before Harrison was even out of the shower. Coco had bagels and muffins and coffee ready, so they sat down to eat, and Isabella was sure that this weekend was never going to end. She sipped her coffee, wanting the good-byes and hugs and promises to visit soon to be over already. Harrison was slow to gather his things and lingered at the table. Isabella thought she might stand up and scream.

Finally they were on their way. Isabella wanted to drive by Boston College, maybe stop in the bookstore to buy a sweatshirt. The car windows were down and the wind blowing in was such perfect fall wind that it made Isabella happy. She put her hand outside and felt the crispness mixed with leftover summer.

"Did you have fun?" Harrison asked her, looking sideways and reaching over to put his hand on her thigh. "I'm sorry if it wasn't exactly what you wanted to do."

"Would you ever want to move to Boston?" she asked.

"No," he said. He looked over at her again. "Why? Is that something you think you want to do?"

She felt immediate relief and shook her head no. She smiled at him.

"It's a nice place to visit, a great city for college, but I can't picture living here again," he said. "It's like a fake city, you know?"

She laughed a little, thrilled that he'd said just what she was thinking. Isabella had flipped back and forth on Harrison so many times this weekend that she'd lost track of where she was. What did that mean, exactly? She thought it couldn't be good.

She took his hand and kissed it, then held it in her lap. "It was great," she said. "Really fun." He smiled and looked back out at the road.

"That baby's pretty cute, right?" she asked.

"Yeah," he said, and took back his hand to turn the wheel.

As they pulled up to the campus, Isabella felt the same way she had when she'd returned each fall. Her stomach dropped with excitement and her throat tingled. She started looking around as though she was going to see someone she knew. Groups of girls were walking to the dining hall in pajama pants and messy ponytails. They were laughing and screaming, and Isabella wanted to join them and eat bacon and eggs while they talked about the night before. What happened? Isabella wanted to know. Who made out? Were there any boys there you liked?

Isabella and Harrison walked around holding hands, and Isabella pointed out the dorms she'd lived in and different buildings to Harrison. He was bored, she knew, and she didn't care.

"Isn't it pretty here?" she asked. "Isn't it prettier than Tufts? It's really the prettiest campus I've ever seen."

Finally he laughed and put his arm around her shoulders. "You might be a little biased, don't you think?" he asked. He was talking to her in his *aren't you cute* voice, which he used to use a lot more at the beginning of their relationship. He hadn't used it much recently and Isabella wasn't sure if this was normal or not.

Isabella had realized a couple of weeks ago that this was the longest relationship she had ever had. She was now twenty-nine. She could no longer compare this to crazy Will from college or

Ben the Stoner. Now this had turned into her "real relationship," the one she would have to compare every other relationship to. Or not compare it to, if it was the one that would last.

In college, twenty-nine had seemed impossibly old. By now, she'd thought, she'd be married and have kids. But as each year went by, she didn't feel much different than she had before. Time kept going by and she was just here, the same.

It seemed like it all happened easier for everyone else. Look at Harrison's friends. They just got married and had kids and didn't seem to think about it too much. Maybe that was her problem. Maybe she was thinking about it too much. Or maybe the fact that she was thinking about it meant it wasn't right.

There was one morning recently when they were lounging in bed, which was unusual for Harrison. Sundays were his day to go running, and he was usually up and out the door before she woke up. But this Sunday he didn't go anywhere. They ordered breakfast in from the Bagelry and watched *Meet the Press* with the *New York Times* spread all over the bed.

It bothered her that he was such a go-getter on the weekend. It made her feel lazy to stay in bed when he was out running. That morning she was ready to pick a fight with him over leaving the apartment. And then, like he knew what she was thinking, he didn't go anywhere.

"No run today?" she asked.

He shrugged. "Don't really feel like it," he said.

Isabella had two tiny stuffed pigs that she kept on her nightstand, named Buster and Stinky. Harrison had always thought it was odd, the way she loved stuffed animals, the way she was drawn to little figurines and fuzzy things. "You're so weird," he said, laughing, when she made a stuffed frog ribbit at him. And she knew he meant it.

Boyfriends in her past had found this trait cute and charming. They had indulged her with little fuzzy animals as presents. Ben had even gone so far as to give them little voices (usually when he was stoned) and march them across the bed to make her laugh.

Harrison had largely ignored Buster and Stinky, except once when he had used Buster as a Hacky Sack during a long phone call. But that morning, Isabella came back from the bathroom to find the two pigs in the middle of the bed in a compromising pose. She stared at them for a minute before it registered that they were in the 69 position.

She stood at the end of the bed until Harrison finally looked up.

"Good Lord," he said. "Bunch of dirty pigs around here. They must have learned it from watching you."

"You know," she said, "that they are both boys, right?"

"Are you saying that two male pigs can't be in love? Did you learn nothing from the penguins at the zoo?"

Isabella laughed and climbed back into bed with him. For the rest of the day, anytime she left the room Harrison arranged the pigs in another dirty pose. Yes, she thought at the end of the day. Okay, I could be with him forever.

She worried that maybe they'd been dating too long to end up together. It was like when you tried to jump off the high dive and if you did it right away, you were fine. But if you stood there looking down, thinking of all the bad things that could happen, you were doomed. You would just climb back down the ladder to the safety of the ground.

Harrison was standing next to a dorm building, checking his BlackBerry. She watched him from behind. How was she supposed to be okay just hating him and then loving him on alternate days? What if that never stopped?

She went up behind him and stood on her toes until her nose was right next to his ear, and then she snorted softly and slowly. He tilted his head like she was tickling him, and he lowered his BlackBerry. She kept snorting until she heard him laugh and then she stopped and kissed the back of his neck.

"Hey, dirty pig," he said, turning around. "There you are."

"There you are," she said. She put her face next to his and snorted again until he smiled and kissed her.

Placenta

*E*veryone was talking about babies. It all started when someone suggested that Shannon was getting married because she was pregnant. "She just met the guy six months ago," their friend Annie said. "And here we are at their wedding. It's a little suspicious."

"You think there's a bun in that oven?" Lauren asked. "I don't think so."

"Maybe she just wanted to get married," Isabella said. Then, to change the subject, she asked their friend Katie how her pregnancy was going, and Katie launched into a speech about how hard it had been for her to get pregnant the second time. "You just always think it will be so easy," she said. "I already had Charles, and I just figured I'd be able to get pregnant whenever I wanted." Katie paused here to take a sip of her water, and Lauren looked hopeful that the conversation was over, but then Katie continued. "Anyway, I bought a book called *Taking Charge of Your Fertility,* and it really changed my life," she said.

Annie squealed, "I bought that book too! It's amazing." The two of them began discussing how they tested their cervical fluid to find out when they were ovulating.

"Cervical fluid?" Lauren whispered to Isabella.

"Discharge," Isabella whispered back. Lauren put down her cake and picked up her drink.

"That's really gross," she said.

"No kidding," Isabella answered.

When the two girls started comparing the difference between fluid that was like "egg whites" and fluid that was "fluffy," Lauren got up to get them new drinks. When she came back, they were talking about placenta. Isabella grabbed the drink from her and smiled.

"Remember when Michael Jackson said he grabbed the baby with the placenta still on it?" Lauren asked. Isabella laughed and shook her head.

"What?" Lauren asked. "That's really my only placenta story. I'm just trying to participate." The two of them snorted with laughter.

Everyone kept bringing up Michael Jackson. He had died earlier in the week, and every time Isabella turned on the TV, he was looking right back at her. It was impossible to forget about him. Even the band at the wedding was playing a lot of Michael Jackson. Shannon's wedding was turning into a Michael Jackson memorial concert. It was weird.

"You know what song has been in my head for like a week?"

Lauren asked. " 'Billie Jean.' It just keeps playing, and I don't know what to do about it. Do you think it will make me go insane? It's just always there in the background of my brain, 'Billie Jean is not my lover . . .' "

"You have the worst voice," Isabella said.

"It's really sad about Michael Jackson," Katie said.

"I don't think it is," Lauren said. "I don't know why, but I wasn't sad at all."

"Do you know what you're going to name the baby?" Isabella asked.

"Well, I like Jason but I'm not sure."

"Maybe you should name him Blanket," Lauren said.

Isabella wanted everyone to stop talking about babies before Mary came over to the table. Mary was pregnant two weeks ago, but no one knew that. She'd confessed to Isabella and Lauren one night when they were at her apartment. Lauren had brought champagne over to celebrate her new real estate job. "Come on," Lauren said when Mary said she didn't want any. "I'm finally gainfully employed. If you can't celebrate that, what can you celebrate?" She'd poured the glass anyway, and held it in front of Mary, right under her nose, until Mary turned her face away and said, "I'm pregnant." Just like that.

"Oh, fuck," Lauren said, lowering the glass. "Why didn't you say so?"

"I can't believe it," Mary kept saying. "I just can't believe it."

"Well, it's pretty good timing," Isabella said. "I mean, you'll be married soon."

"Yeah," Mary said slowly. "I just didn't plan it. I didn't think it was going to happen like this."

Then she called Isabella a week later to tell her that she wasn't pregnant anymore. "I'm not sure what happened," she said. "The doctor said it's normal."

"Well then, I'm sure it is," Isabella said.

"I feel so stupid," Mary said. "I know I didn't plan it, but then I wanted it. Now I feel like I wished it away."

"I don't think it works like that," Isabella said.

"I guess not." Mary didn't sound convinced.

Now they were at Shannon's wedding, and still all anyone could talk about was babies. "Do you know why Kristi said she couldn't come to the wedding?" Katie asked. "Because they only travel when her mother-in-law can come with and she was busy. They can't leave the baby even for a night, because Kristi *only* breast-feeds. She never even pumps. That is weird."

"Isn't the baby almost a year old?" Isabella asked. They both nodded.

"Gross," Lauren said.

Ken was worried about Mary. He told Isabella after the wedding. "I'm worried about her," he said. Isabella hugged him. He was a nice guy.

"I think she'll be okay," she told him. He nodded. Whenever he stood next to Mary, he had his hand on her arm.

⌭

Katie was talking about her birth plan for the second baby. Lauren looked at her with disgust and fear. This was nothing, Isabella thought. Harrison and Isabella had seen the actual video of Charles's birth. It happened quite by accident. Katie and Tim invited them over for dinner one night, and as they were drinking wine, admiring the baby, and eating mini quiches, Katie asked, "Do you want to see the birthing video?" Isabella was sure that neither she nor Harrison said yes, but they didn't say no either, and so they found themselves watching Katie writhing on the TV while a slimy Charles made his way into the world. When they walked out of the apartment that night, Harrison hit the elevator button and simply said, "Holy shit." Isabella loved him for that.

"They aren't that good of friends," she felt compelled to tell him. He just shook his head and put his eyes to the ceiling. "Holy shit," he said again. "Hooooly shit."

⌭

Lauren had pulled the first layer of her bridesmaid dress over her head and was dancing around to "Beat It." "I think maybe no more cocktails for Lauren," Isabella said to no one in particular.

"That's just really inappropriate," Katie said. Isabella made a mental note to tell Harrison this later. "Do you believe she thinks that's inappropriate?" she'll say. "How about showing your friends a video starring your vagina?" And he'd laugh.

⌭

Isabella hadn't seen Harrison in a while. He was probably avoiding being anywhere near Katie. Isabella was sure that he was afraid of Katie after the video. She didn't blame him.

She walked outside and saw Mary and Ken on the other side of the stone patio that overlooked the ocean. Mary leaned her head in the nook of Ken's arm and he kissed the top of her head. Isabella felt like she was spying, but she stood and watched them.

Harrison walked up behind Isabella and smiled when he saw that she was crying. "Are you crying?" he asked. She shook her head no. "You are the worst liar," he said. Isabella always cried at weddings. (Although normally she cried at the ceremony and not the reception.)

"Everything okay?" Harrison asked.

Isabella nodded. "I'm just happy."

"Clearly," he said. He pulled a handkerchief out of his pocket and handed it to her so that she could blow her nose. Harrison always brought handkerchiefs to weddings so that he could hand them to Isabella. He was the only person she knew besides her grandfather who carried actual handkerchiefs.

The first time he'd handed one to her, it was like finding a twenty-dollar bill in her winter jacket: unexpected and incredibly lucky. It thrilled her, the happiness that came with that gesture—and it never went away, it never even faded. Every time he gave her his handkerchief, she was dizzy with fortune.

"You missed a great conversation in there about childbirth," Isabella told him.

"I'm sorry I missed it," Harrison said. "Did Katie pull out some photos of Charles in the birth canal?"

"Not this time. There was just a lot of talk about placenta."

" 'Placenta' comes from a Latin word meaning 'flat cake,' " Harrison said.

"How do you know that? Why is that something that you know in your head?"

Harrison shrugged. "I heard it somewhere." He smiled.

"I think you watch too much Discovery Channel," Isabella said.

When Harrison gave her a dog for her thirtieth birthday, she was overwhelmed at the responsibility. "I think I'm going to kill it," she kept saying. He assured her that she would not. Isabella had wanted a dog for a long time, but once she had him she was sure she wasn't ready. She could step on him, forget to feed him, or leave something poisonous out for him to eat. The possibilities were endless.

The second night he was at the apartment, Winston cried so much that Isabella ended up lying on the floor next to him. She woke up to Harrison standing above her saying, "Who owns who?" Winston was curled in a tight ball by her stomach, and she looked closely to make sure he was still breathing. Then she looked at Harrison, rubbed her eyes, and said, "I think he might own us, but we'll see."

Harrison smiled. "You're a good mom," he said, and then he went to brush his teeth. Just like that, out of the blue, *You're a good mom.*

"Do you want to go back in?" Isabella asked him. "Katie is talking about her birthing plan."

Harrison considered. "No," he said. "I do not."

Isabella twisted the handkerchief in her hand and smiled.

Button

Ken's father had died, and so Mary couldn't be as honest about things as she wanted to. "I'm all my mom has," Ken said whenever Mary mentioned anything.

"She has three other kids," Mary said.

"None like me," he said, putting his arm around her shoulder.

Mary tried to be charitable. After all, she was Catholic. She could suffer in silence. She tried not to say anything when Ken spent whole weekends at his mom's house, doing her taxes or helping her pick out a door for the new garage. "My dad took care of all that stuff," he said whenever Mary complained that she didn't see him enough.

On Mary and Ken's first date, Ken took a call from his mom in the middle of dinner. "I'm sorry," he said when he got back. "My mom gets nervous when I don't answer. My dad passed a few years ago, and so she's all alone."

Mary could have cried from happiness. She was on a blind date with a truly nice guy who loved his mother and wasn't afraid to tell her. Three dates later it wasn't as charming.

Ken moved into Mary's apartment but warned her that he could never tell his mom what he'd done. "But we're thirty," Mary said. She'd never found him less attractive.

"My mom is just old-fashioned," he said. "And I don't want to upset her. She's been through so much with my dad and everything." And so Mary wasn't allowed to say much more.

"Some umbilical cords are stronger than others," Lauren told her. It sounded like the first line of a horror movie.

"Call me Button," Ken's mother said when they got engaged. "Or Mom."

Everyone called Ken's mother Button. They always had. Most people didn't even know that her real name was Virginia. "My dad just thought I was cute as a button," she explained once to Mary. "And the name stuck."

Mary couldn't imagine calling a grown woman Button. Calling her Mom was worse. Mary was certain the offer was insincere. She wanted to keep calling her Mrs. Walker, like she always had. But now that the subject had been broached, she knew she couldn't, so Mary just said, "Thank you," and stopped calling her anything.

"What am I supposed to do?" Mary asked Isabella. "His family is obviously crazy."

"So is Harrison's family," Isabella said. "They never hug. Did I tell you that? They literally just wave at each other from across the room when they haven't seen each other in months. It's bizarre."

"Well, Ken's mother hugs her children when they leave the room for more than five minutes."

"Really?"

"Yeah."

"That's kind of weird."

"I know."

"Harrison's family doesn't ever talk on the phone. Never. Except if they're going to meet somewhere and they want to confirm the time."

"Ken's family only goes out to eat at T.G.I. Friday's or Chili's," Mary said, and Isabella laughed.

"Harrison's brother eats with his hands and never says 'Excuse me' when he leaves the table. He just gets up to go."

"I don't think Button wants us to get married."

"Really?"

"Yeah. I think she wants Ken to pay attention only to her."

"Ew," Isabella said.

"I know."

Every summer, Ken's family went to Lake Minnetonka in Cable, Wisconsin. "Don't you guys ever want to go somewhere else?" Mary asked.

"That's where we go," Ken explained. "My dad started taking us there when I was just a baby."

Mary and Ken had been dating for two years, but Mary was never invited to "the lake." Ken came on vacation with her family, but never mentioned it when he went away. Now that they were engaged, Button called Ken to tell him to extend the invitation to Mary. He told her as though she should be thrilled. "You'll get to see the lake!" he said. She smiled. No lake could be worth a week with Button.

It took them all day to get there. They had to fly into Minneapolis–St. Paul International, and then drive three hours to the lake. When they arrived, Button was standing on the porch, waiting for them. "I'm so glad you could join us," she said to Mary with just a trace of a fake British accent. It sounded like she had been practicing the sentence.

Mary saw that Button was trying to smile but couldn't quite get her mouth to go the right way. Ken went in to change into his bathing suit and ran down the path to the lake before Mary had even gotten inside. She gave him a look that said, *Don't leave me alone here,* but he just called out, "Come meet me when you're ready!" Mary and Button stared at each other on the porch.

"Let me show you your room," Button said, and led Mary to a slim rectangular closet off the kitchen. There was a cot set up in there that took up most of the room. Mary put her bag down and tried to seem pleased to be sleeping in an old food pantry.

"Thanks so much for having me," Mary said. "I'm so excited to be here. Ken always talks about this place."

Button was flustered. "Well," she said. "Well, how nice."

"Do you need help with anything? Dinner or anything like that?"

"No, we're all set," Button said. "Dinner is at six." When Mary was finally alone in the pantry, she decided to lie down and take a nap.

"This is my family now," she thought to herself. "I am going to be legally bound to Button." She tried to tell herself not to be so overdramatic, but then she imagined spending holidays with these people and let a single tear slide out of her eye. She was allowed a single tear. She was going to have a mother-in-law named Button.

The lake was pretty but freezing. Ken took her out in one of the kayaks, assuring her that she wouldn't die. "Here," he said, tossing her a life jacket. "Put this on."

They paddled out to the middle of the murky lake. Mary was in the front because Ken said the heavier person should be in the back. She kept trying to turn around to ask him questions, but when she did the boat wobbled and so she remained looking straight ahead. The paddles were dripping into the boat and a pretty big puddle was gathering around their feet. The only nice thing about being in the boat was that Button was getting smaller and smaller on the shore. Mary was just starting to enjoy herself when she heard Ken say, "Uh-oh."

"What?" Mary whipped her head around and the boat tipped to the right. "What uh-oh? What?"

"No big deal," Ken said. "But we should start paddling back. I think there's some holes in the boat."

Mary grabbed her paddle and started slapping it in the water. She could hear Ken laughing. "It's okay," he said. "I promise, even if the boat sinks we aren't that far out. We can swim in."

When they got back, Button was standing on the shore with her hand pressed over her chest. "Oh, I was so worried!" she said. "What on earth made you think to take the kayak out? We haven't had those out in years." Mary thought Button was looking at her while she said this.

"Mom, we're fine," Ken said. He was taller than his mother, and when he put his arm around her, she looked tiny.

"Well," Button said. "Well, I was worried."

"I know, Mom, I know!" Ken and his mother walked ahead down the path to the cabin. Mary walked behind them, shivering, with wet feet.

It became clear to Mary that the Walkers had a routine at the lake and that just by being there, she was disrupting it. Sunday night they went to the Lodge for dinner and had walleye pike and cheese curds. Monday night was hot dogs on the grill. Tuesday night was taco night. When they went to the grocery store, Mary suggested that they get salmon to grill and the whole family looked at her like she was nuts.

"We only eat fish at the Lodge," Ken's sister said. Mary nodded like this made sense.

They went down to the Lodge on Wednesday night for bingo. "You know what this place reminds me of?" Mary asked. "The summer place they go to in *Dirty Dancing*, you know?" Ken's sister laughed.

"*Dirty Dancing*?" Button asked. "What kind of a movie is that?"

Mary felt as though she had just admitted to Button that she watched hard-core porn, and so she shut her mouth and focused on her bingo cards. Ken was in the other room getting his mother a gin and tonic. He walked in and looked around the bingo tables to see where they were sitting. Mary and Button waved their hands at him together. Ken saw Mary and smiled and then started walking over.

"Oh," Button said, "He saw you first. I guess you're his number one girl now."

For a moment, Mary thought she had heard wrong. And then for another she was just too creeped out to answer. Finally she said, "I'm wearing a pretty bright color. It was probably just easier to see me."

ᘒ

Ken's siblings didn't cater to Button the way that he did. They were perfectly nice to her, of course. They just didn't watch her every move to make sure she was okay at all times.

"Maybe it's because he's the oldest," Isabella said to her on the phone. Mary had driven into town and called Isabella from a pay phone. She had no cell service in Cable and she needed to talk to someone before she lost her mind.

"Maybe," Mary said.

ᘒ

Every year, Ken's family took a picture in front of the lake. This year, Mary volunteered to take it and Ken said, "No, you should be in it." Button straightened her shoulders and Mary said, "How about I take one of just you guys and then one with me?" Button smiled at her.

On the plane ride home, Mary counted the mosquito bites on her legs. "Twenty-three!" she announced to Ken. "No, wait—twenty-four!"

Ken laughed. "I told you that you shouldn't have gone running without bug spray on. You didn't believe me."

"I just thought I would be faster than the bugs," Mary said.

"I'm glad you got to see the lake," Ken said, and Mary smiled.

"Do you think we'll be able to go next year, with the honeymoon and everything?" Mary asked. "I'm not sure I have enough vacation time."

"We'll work it out. Even if you can't make it, I'll have to sneak away for a few days to get up there."

"It's a long trip for just a few days," Mary said. Ken patted her knee.

When they got married, Button cried. Mary was pretty sure that they were sad tears and not happy tears. "You're crazy," Ken said. "My mother adores you."

Ken danced with his mother and it was the happiest she looked all night. Mary stood near her for a little while at the reception, and when a waiter passed with a tray of shrimp, Button said, "You know that Ken can't eat shrimp, right? He breaks out in hives."

"Yes," Mary said. "I know."

"Oh, okay." Button seemed relieved. "I just wanted to make sure. I just didn't know why you would ever serve shrimp at your wedding if you knew your husband could break out in hives."

Mary went to the bathroom and locked herself in the handicapped stall. She stood in her dress and breathed deep breaths until she heard Isabella walk in.

"Mary?" Isabella called. "Are you in here?"

Mary unlocked the stall and stood there. "Button," she said.

Isabella nodded. "Harrison's mother told me last weekend that she thought polka dots were out of style."

"So?" Mary asked.

"I was wearing my pink-and-white polka dot dress," Isabella said.

"Okay," Mary said. "Okay." She and Isabella walked back out to the reception.

When Mary found out she was pregnant, Ken called his mother right away. "She's crying," he mouthed to Mary. Mary smiled.

They all went out to dinner to celebrate. "We should know the sex of the baby soon," Mary said.

"Oh no! You're going to find out?" Button looked horrified.

"Yeah, we thought it would be nice to prepare."

"But it's the greatest surprise of your life. Why would you ruin that?"

Mary didn't know what to say.

"You'll have to move out of that neighborhood," Button said. "You can't have a baby there. It's rather sketchy." The neighborhood they lived in hadn't been sketchy since the seventies. Now it was stuffed full of Starbucks and Baby Gap and no one in their right mind would call it sketchy.

"Maybe," Ken said. "We'll think about it."

"Have you thought of any names?" Button asked. Mary knew she was trying to be nice.

"We thought maybe Parker if it was a boy. And if it's a girl, we like Lola."

"Lola? You can't call a baby Lola! It sounds like a prostitute."

"Mom," Ken said, laughing. "It doesn't sound like a prostitute." Mary stayed silent.

"What about Brittany or Tiffany?" Button offered, looking at Mary. "Or Mandy or Christina?"

"Maybe," Mary said. "We've got some time to decide."

Button nodded. "Well, if you name her Lola, then maybe I'll call her something else." She looked pleased, like this solved the problem. Mary tried to catch Ken's eye, but he was looking at his cheeseburger.

℅

"She wants her grandchild to be a teenybopper!" Mary said. "Brittany and Tiffany? What kind of names are those? Those are pretend names that you gave your pretend children in second grade!"

"Really?" Isabella asked. "I always went with Brandy at that age."

"Isabella."

"Sorry, okay. So she has bad taste in names."

"Bad taste? She wants her granddaughter to be a teenage singer who wears leather pants and vows to stay a virgin before getting pregnant at seventeen."

Mary started to cry and Isabella patted her back. "Maybe it will be a boy," she offered.

℅

The baby was born with all of his fingers and toes, which made Mary happy. She hadn't been that worried, but there'd been one night before she knew she was pregnant when she and Isabella had drunk enough wine for a small country. And so, when she was able to count everything for herself, she was relieved.

He was a chunky little baby and they named him Henry, after Ken's dad. Mary knew it made Ken happy and also she liked the name Henry. Mary liked to hold his feet and put them in her mouth.

He had light blond hair and blue eyes, like Ken. Sometimes when he was concentrating on going to the bathroom, it looked just like Ken when he was working on a case he thought he was going to lose.

"He's the cutest baby you've ever seen, right?" she asked Ken.

"Yes," he said. "I think he is."

Button came over the day they got back from the hospital. "I just can't wait to see him!" she said to Mary when she walked in.

"You could have come to visit in the hospital," Mary said.

Button shook her head. "No," she said. "I remember how it is. You need some time alone to get it together. My mother-in-law stormed into the hospital right after I had Ken, and it was just too much! People didn't do that in those days." She leaned down to whisper to Mary. "Between you, me, and the lamppost, my mother-in-law was a little bit of a terror." She winked at Mary.

Henry waved his hands and feet in the air. "Oh!" Button cried. "Look at those feet! Don't you just want to eat them?"

"All the time," Mary said. She leaned over and smiled at Henry. "Look who it is," she cooed at him. "Look who came to see you! Grandma Button is here."

"I think he needs to be changed," Button said. "It's the kind of thing you should do right away."

Mary picked up the baby and brought him to the changing table. She started to wipe him, but Button came over and edged her out.

"No," Button said, grabbing the wipe from Mary's hand. "You want to do it like this. Here, let me show you. Go like this."

Jesus Is Coming

*J*esus is coming."

And then: "Jesus is coming, folks, you should be ready."

Isabella looked down the subway platform to see if she could find the man who was trying to tell her about Jesus. She couldn't see anyone, which made her nervous. His voice boomed around her: "Are you ready? Jesus will know if you aren't ready." It was Friday night and Isabella just wanted to get home. Lately, she'd had the feeling that someone was going to push her onto the track while she waited for the subway, and just because this man was talking about Jesus didn't mean he wouldn't be the one to do it.

"Will you be ready when he comes? Will you be ready?" the voice echoed down to her. Isabella shivered and hoped that the train would come soon.

The whole week, things had been off for Isabella. New York, it seemed, was out to get her. It started on Sunday, when a crazy bearded man spit at her on the street and called her a cunt. Monday, while she was watching TV, a giant roach the size of a small dog crawled out from behind the bookshelf and died in the middle of the room. It shook and gyrated and then finally stopped moving. Isabella thought it might have had a seizure.

Tuesday, there was the situation with her underwear. Her laundry was delivered to her door that night. Usually this made her feel wonderfully organized and put together—for only a dollar a pound, she could drop off all of her dirty laundry and have it delivered clean and folded the same day—but this time, as she unpacked the bag, she found a pair of underwear that didn't belong to her. It was a large, flesh-colored, silky pair of underwear with a rose on the waistband. She held it between her thumb and pointer finger like it was dirty, although she realized it must have been cleaned and washed with her things. Her dog, Winston, sat and stared at the underwear, his head cocked to one side, trying to figure out why Isabella was holding it in the air.

In the end, she threw it out. She thought of returning it but figured the cleaners wouldn't know who the owner was anyway. It was such a small thing, but it made Isabella feel sick, like someone had broken in and touched all of her underwear. It didn't make sense, she knew. After all, she paid these people to wash her underwear. She did it on purpose. But it still left her uneasy, the thought that people's personals could get mixed up so easily—that someone else's underwear could find its way into her drawers.

On Wednesday, Isabella found a whisker on her chin. She hadn't noticed anything strange that morning, but when she touched her face that night, there it was: a coarse black whisker. When had it had time to grow? "This is not right," Isabella said to the mirror as she plucked the whisker out. "This is not right!"

"What?" Harrison asked from the other side of the door.

"Nothing," Isabella said.

Thursday, Isabella found out that Beth White was getting a divorce. She couldn't believe it. It left her unsettled. Beth and Kyle had gotten married five years ago, in a perfectly bland New Jersey wedding where they'd had a DJ instead of a band and served chicken instead of steak. They weren't the kind of couple you looked at and thought, "Now, that's what love looks like" or "That's what I want to have someday." But they were a couple that was compatible in a very ordinary way, and Isabella had always thought they were a good fit.

Isabella had been one of Beth's bridesmaids, and she remembered how Beth was so bloated the day of the wedding that her dress wouldn't zip. Isabella had known Beth for twelve years, and for ten of those years, she'd been with Kyle.

"I'm moving into the city," Beth said when she called Isabella.

"Oh," Isabella said. "Great. What about the house?"

"We're selling it. Didn't Lauren tell you? I asked her for some real estate advice and she recommended someone to us. I'm getting out of this godforsaken suburb. We can hang out all the time!"

"Great," Isabella said. "Great."

Friday, Isabella's boss asked her to type up some notes. It was a job Isabella used to do when she was Snowy's assistant, but she'd been promoted to assistant editor over a year ago. So when Snowy walked by and dumped notes on Isabella's desk, she was thrown. Was she being demoted or had she imagined her promotion in the first place? Had time gone backward? She stared at the notes for a while, and then put them in a neat little pile in the corner of her desk.

"Did you know that Snowy asked me to type up her notes?" Isabella asked Cate.

"She does the same thing to me," Cate said.

"Doesn't she know that she has two new assistants?" Isabella asked, and Cate shrugged.

"Probably not," she said. "The woman is bat-shit crazy. Plus," she said lowering her voice, "I heard she's worried about her job."

"Isn't everybody?" Isabella asked.

Cave Publishing was in trouble. The CFO had been sending around e-mails that referenced the economy in vague terms. He used words like "cutbacks" and "accommodations," but no one knew what he was trying to say. Cate was convinced that they would all be fired soon.

"It's just a matter of time," she kept saying to Isabella. "Make sure you have money saved. This shitbox of a company probably won't even give us decent severance."

By the time Isabella made it to the subway station on Friday, she felt defeated. It was so hot that she was sure she was going to melt. "Jesus is coming," the voice said. Isabella wiped the sweat off her forehead. She thought she might faint.

Isabella went home, turned on the air conditioner, and lay down on the bed. Maybe, she thought, things just seemed worse because of the heat. It always made people agitated when it got this hot—the air seemed to stick in the middle of the buildings and that made it hard to breathe. There was no such thing as a breeze in New York, and the whole city started to smell like garbage. That's all it was, she decided. The weather. She tried to stay completely still. The air conditioner whirred in the window. Soon the sweat started to evaporate and she started to feel better. Harrison was away on a business trip for a few days. Isabella decided that she would order Thai food for dinner and stay in. She might feel better for now, but it was safer to stay in the apartment. No sense in going out.

Isabella's left side hurt. It started in her shoulder, then moved up to her jaw and down to her leg. She complained for a month, until Harrison told her she had to go to the doctor. "I mean, it's probably an advanced tumor," she said to Harrison. "What can they do for that?"

"I promise, it's not a tumor," Harrison told her. She knew he had no authority to make such a promise.

"Fine," she said. "I'll go to a chiropractor."

"You have a mean case of TMJ," the chiropractor told her. "You're carrying a lot of stress on this side. Your alignment is all off."

"So what can I do?" Isabella asked.

"I'll show you some stretching exercises. And you should get a mouth guard to stop clenching your jaw at night. You can come back and see me. But what you really need to do is lower your stress level."

"Oh," Isabella said. "That's all? Thanks."

〣

"You should take yoga," Mary told her. "It will relax you."

Isabella went to hot yoga, which turned out to be a horrible mistake. The room was a hundred degrees, and Isabella could barely breathe. "You may feel nauseous or faint during class," the instructor told everyone. "This is normal. This is a normal reaction. Just work through it."

"This is not normal," Isabella thought. During tree pose, her legs were so sweaty that she slipped and fell.

"Don't go to that yoga class," Lauren told her. "Oh my God, that's, like, the worst one. Go to hatha."

Isabella's new yoga class was better. It was a normal temperature, and kind of reminded her of church with all of the chanting and bowing and putting hands in prayer position. At the end of the class the teacher sprinkled them with lavender water as they lay still, which was nice. But her yoga mat smelled like feet, which got in the way of her transcendence.

〣

"Maybe we should move out of New York," Isabella said to Harrison. "Things aren't going well here."

"It's not like other cities are in great shape," Harrison said. "Plus, we both still have our jobs."

"For now," Isabella said.

"For now," he said.

"I pushed someone on the subway," Isabella admitted. "They were going too slow, and I just pushed a little bit."

Harrison laughed. "So you think you need to leave New York?"

"Yeah," Isabella said. "I always said when I push someone, it's time to go."

"Well, that's something to think about."

∂

Isabella went out for drinks with Lauren and Mary. All they wanted to do was talk about Beth White.

"The house is a piece of shit," Lauren told them. "They didn't take care of it, and in this market? They aren't going to get anything for it."

"Spoken like a wonderful real estate agent," Mary said.

"I told them not to sell," Lauren said. "Beth wouldn't hear of it. She said she wants it gone."

"Jesus," Isabella said. "What happened, exactly? Does anyone know?"

Lauren shrugged. "She said it was mutual."

"That sucks," Mary said.

"I was wondering why they weren't having kids, though, you know?" Lauren said. "I knew something was up."

"She told me that she's getting custody of the dog," Mary said.

"That's the saddest sentence I've ever heard," Isabella said. When she got home that night, she looked at Winston and said, "You would go with me, right? You love me more." The dog yawned, and looked away.

∂

"What's happening?" Isabella asked Cate. She'd gotten stuck on a subway with no air-conditioning and was twenty minutes late to work. When she walked onto her floor, the conference room was full of people and some of them were crying.

"They closed the whole YA division. They just told everyone today."

"So all those people are just fired?"

"Yeah," Cate said. "Crazy, right?"

"How can they just close a whole division?" Isabella asked. Her dress was stuck to her legs, and she tried to pull the material away without being obvious.

"The company is in some serious trouble," Cate whispered. "I say, we're lucky if we're still here in a couple of months."

ℬℭ

"There's nothing you can do about it," Harrison told her. "Just make sure your résumé is updated, and do your job. That's all."

Isabella felt sick to her stomach, and heard the yoga instructor in her head saying, "You may feel nauseous. This is a normal reaction."

"But that's all that I've worked for," Isabella said. "If I leave now, with the title I have, I won't be able to get a job anywhere."

"You still have your job for now," Harrison said. "You're very resourceful."

"*You're very resourceful?* What kind of a thing is that to say to someone?"

Harrison told her to calm down, and she started screaming. "I hate when people tell me to calm down! You calm down. Don't you call me resourceful, and then tell me to calm down."

Isabella packed a bag and left the apartment. "I'll be back

tomorrow," she said. Harrison stood in the door and looked confused.

Isabella went over to Mary and Ken's apartment. Ken took one look at her and carried Henry into the other room.

"I think you're just stressed from work," Mary told her.

"Maybe," Isabella said. "But I don't think that's it."

"It doesn't sound like Harrison was really out of line, though," Mary said.

"No," Isabella said. "I'm out of line." She thought about her left side, all gnarled and crooked. Then she sent Harrison a text message that said, "I'm sorry. I'm crazy." He wrote back, "That's okay."

Isabella and Mary drank a lot of wine, and Isabella ended up sleeping on the couch. She woke up to Henry dancing in front of her while he watched *Sesame Street*. "Hi!" he said to her. Isabella saw how full his diaper was before she smelled it. She sat up and smiled at him. "Hi," she said back, and this pleased him so much that he smiled and squatted.

"I think Henry needs a new diaper," she called to Mary. Then she stood up and ran to the bathroom to vomit. She heard Henry banging on the door. "Ummmbllll!" he screamed. Isabella knew he was saying, "Let me in! What are you doing?"

"Not now, Henry!" Isabella called.

"Bllll, baaa!"

"I know," Isabella said. "I'm a disgrace."

Every day at work, Isabella was sure she was going to be fired. And, as if that weren't stressful enough, Peggy, one of the copy editors, wouldn't leave Isabella alone. She asked her about every comma, every semicolon, until Isabella wanted to scream. Peggy was in her forties and wore odd-colored pantsuits with large shoulders and funky buttons. Whenever Isabella looked at her, she thought of her fifth-grade social studies textbook. Peggy looked like she should be in there, with a caption that said, "Someday you will work in an office and you will have coworkers. Women and men work together as equals."

Peggy alternately repulsed Isabella and made her sad. She complained about her almost every night to Harrison. Then one day she came into work and found out that Peggy had been fired.

"They got rid of half of the copy editors," Cate told her. "Crazy Pantsuits is gone."

Isabella went home that night and cried. "I feel so bad," she said to Harrison. He rubbed her back and said, "I know."

ॐ

Lauren had been trying to plan a trip for all of their college friends for the past year. She'd started out suggesting that they go to the Bahamas, but was met with too much resistance. Finally, she planned a weekend in the Hamptons. "This is pathetic," she kept saying. "This was supposed to be a trip for our thirtieth birthdays, and it's a whole year later. And all we're doing is going to the beach?"

"It will be fun," Mary told her. "The Hamptons will be perfect."

Beth White was excited about the weekend. She kept sending e-mails out to the whole group that said things like "Watch out for the divorced lady" and "It's like a reverse bachelorette party for me!" It was making everyone uncomfortable.

"I think she's lost it," Mary said.

"No kidding," Isabella said.

ℬↄ

Harrison lay on the couch and read the paper while Isabella packed for her trip. Winston was curled up on his chest. Every so often, Winston lifted his head and licked Harrison's chin. Winston was a little white fluff of a dog and when he sat still, he looked like a stuffed animal. Isabella loved him more than anything. As soon as she got her suitcase out, he wouldn't look at her. He turned his head away and only paid attention to Harrison.

"Harrison, if we break up, would you give me the dog?" Isabella asked.

Harrison lowered the paper and looked at her. "Excuse me?"

"Beth White is getting the dog, but she said that she had to fight Kyle for him."

"Oh," Harrison said. "I see."

"So would you give me the dog?"

"No," Harrison said. "If you broke up with me, I would kidnap Winston. Then I would take him around the country and photograph him in different states, so that I could send you the pictures and taunt you."

"Fair enough," Isabella said. She sat down on the bed and rested her head on Harrison's chest, right next to the dog.

"I love you," she said.

He took the end of her hair in his hand, twirled it around his finger, and said, "Good to know."

"You look tired," Isabella said to Mary. They were sitting on the top level of the double-decker train to the Hamptons. Mary stared out the window with dark circles under her eyes.

"I didn't sleep well last night," Mary said. "Can I tell you something weird?"

"Always," Isabella said.

"Okay, but you have to promise not to tell anyone else. It's really weird."

"I promise."

"I woke up from a nightmare and I was biting Ken on the arm," Mary said.

"Jesus, what was the dream?" Isabella asked.

"Well, I dreamt that Ken was marrying this big black woman. And he kept saying, 'Sorry, sorry, I'm so sorry. We can still be together, but I have to marry her.' And I was crying, and then the woman came over and started fighting me. I bit her ankle, and then I woke up to Ken screaming."

"That is really weird," Isabella said.

"I know. What if that's what I do now? What if I just keep biting Ken in my sleep?"

"I don't think that will happen," Isabella said.

"It might. Plus, I'm a bad mom."

"No, you aren't," Isabella told her. "Where did that come from?"

Mary sighed. "Henry was sick last week, and I didn't even notice. He was rubbing his ear on the floor and whining, *Niii, niii,* before I noticed anything."

"So? You took him to the doctor in time."

"I guess so. Now I feel bad for leaving him this weekend."

"I pushed someone on the subway last week," Isabella told her.

"Really?" Mary asked.

"Yeah, it just happened. Does that make you feel better?"

"Yeah, it kind of does."

Lauren bought about a million bottles of wine for the house, and when everyone walked in they said, "Oh, that is too much wine. We'll never get through that."

"I planned for five bottles a girl for the weekend," Lauren said. "Believe me, we'll go through it."

"No," everyone said. "No, that's too much." By the second night, more than half of it was gone and everyone stopped talking about it.

Beth White talked the whole weekend. From the moment she got there, she went on about her divorce. "Such a hard decision," she said. "But I'm in a much better place now."

Isabella tried to avoid getting caught alone with her. "I know she needs to talk about this," she said to Lauren, "but she has a therapist, right?"

Lauren shrugged. "God, I hope so. I know way too much about their bedroom life now. Way too much."

"I'm not changing my name back," Beth told them. "I thought about it, but I'm going to stay Beth White." Isabella didn't think this was a wise decision.

"Why wouldn't she go back to Beth Bauer?" she asked Lauren. "She doesn't have any kids. It's so weird."

"I don't know," Lauren said. "Maybe she's afraid no one will remember who she is."

"Maybe," Isabella said. The thought left her uneasy.

∂

The last night, they went out to a seafood restaurant. They returned to the house stuffed and tired. Everyone was drinking wine and talking when they noticed that Beth White was crying in the corner.

Her head was down and her shoulders were shaking. She was crying so hard that no one could understand what she was saying. "What happened?" Mary whispered to Isabella. She just shook her head. "I have no idea," she said. They sat and listened to Beth gasping for breath. "She's choking," Isabella thought. She tried to remember the proper steps for CPR in case they needed to use it. They all stood around and watched until Isabella stepped forward and knelt in front of her. She touched Beth's leg and said, "This is a normal reaction." Lauren was standing to her right and shook her head at Isabella. Finally, their friend Sallie took Beth by the arm and walked her upstairs. The rest of them dispersed in silence. No one wanted to talk about what they had just seen.

Mary and Isabella sat on the porch, and Isabella smoked a cigarette. "I thought you quit," Mary said.

"I did," Isabella said. "This is an emergency."

"I don't really miss smoking as much as I used to," Mary said.

"You sound disappointed," Isabella said. Mary shrugged.

"Where's your wine?" Isabella asked her.

"Oh, I left it inside, I guess."

"Are you pregnant?"

"What?"

"Oh, my God, you are! You're pregnant, you fucker."

"Most people say congratulations."

"I can't believe you're pregnant!"

Mary smiled and looked embarrassed but pleased. "It's really early. I haven't even told my mom. I'm like, three days pregnant."

"Wow," Isabella said, "you're going to have two kids. You're going to have two kids before I'm married."

"I wish you were pregnant too," Mary said to her.

"So you would have someone to be sober with?"

Mary nodded. "Yeah. I'd be happy. If you got knocked up right now, I wouldn't even feel bad. I'd just be happy for me."

"You," Isabella said, "are a good friend."

Mary laughed. "Don't tell anyone, okay? It's so early. Anything could happen."

"Okay," Isabella said. "And I'll make you a deal. If you wait for me, I'll time my first pregnancy with your third. Then we can be pregnant together. Deal?"

"Deal."

They all woke up on Sunday morning with headaches. Mary had to take an early train and was gone by the time Isabella got up. The house was a mess, and they all walked around in silence, throwing out cans and bottles. Lauren attempted to sweep the floor, but there was so much sand that she gave up after a few minutes.

Beth White came downstairs with her packed bag. Her hair was wet and slicked back in a ponytail. She looked young standing there, like a high school girl who'd just finished swim practice. Abby and Shannon stood a little behind her on either side, like they were her jailers or her bodyguards, ready to step in if needed. "I'm sorry," Beth said. "I'm sorry I caused such a scene."

"Don't apologize," they all said. "Don't be silly."

Isabella left to catch her train. "Fun weekend," she said to Lauren.

"Yeah," Lauren said. "That's one word for it. What a way to celebrate our thirties."

"Everyone says it's the best decade," Isabella said.

"I know," added Lauren. "But I think it's just to make you feel better, like when people say it's good luck that a bird poos on you, or it rains on your wedding day."

"Maybe," Isabella said.

"Maybe not, though."

"Yeah, maybe not."

ꞵꝺ

Isabella fell asleep on the train ride back, and woke up cranky and thirsty as they pulled into Penn Station. Everyone on the train jostled one another to get out first. Normally, Isabella elbowed her way out with the best of them, but now she just let everyone go past. She climbed up the steps to exit Penn Station, and then noticed that the man in front of her had stopped and was taking his pants off.

"Excuse me," she said and ran past him.

The sun was bright as Isabella waited for a taxi. She stood

and watched all of the people returning to the city. They popped out of Penn Station, one by one, in their wrinkled clothes. Sun-burned and sweaty, they raced to get cabs. Girls carried bright paisley-covered bags stuffed full of wet bathing suits and sandy shirts, and walked quickly in their flip-flops as they typed on their cell phones. Everyone was tired from too much sun and too many drinks, and they all just wanted to get back to their apartments.

They were all scrambling, Isabella thought. Scrambling, scrambling.

She got in a cab and rolled down the window. Harrison sent her a message that he was making dinner. Harrison knew how to make exactly two things: Manwiches and fajitas. Her phone buzzed again and she looked down. "It's fajitas," Harrison wrote. Isabella smiled.

The air blew through the window, and she watched all of the people moving like ants outside. She was happy to be sitting still in a cab, happy to be on her way home. She imagined Har-rison and Winston sitting on the couch waiting for her. The cab stopped at the corner of Fifty-ninth and Eighth, and she saw a man standing there wearing all white. He was a tiny man, with a perfectly round face. "Jesus is coming," she heard him say, and she laughed out loud. The cabdriver looked at her in the rear-view mirror. "I know him," she said. It felt lucky to her. What were the odds? She couldn't explain it, but she was so happy to see him. She smiled at the man and waved her hand out the window. He looked up and waved back to her as the cab pulled away, and she leaned her head back and closed her eyes and let the breeze blow over her face.

Flushing Willard

On their second date, Mark brought Lauren a goldfish, which made her nervous. Lauren knew that the normal life span of a goldfish was about five days, but growing up she'd had one that lived for five years. And so, it seemed a big commitment when Mark gave her the plastic bag with the fish in it.

"Here," he said, "I got you this." He held out the baggie like he had just found it in the hallway before he came into her apartment, like it was a normal thing to do to hand a goldfish to a girl you barely knew.

"Oh," Lauren said. "Thank you. I guess I should put these in some water." Mark didn't laugh. Either he didn't get the joke or he didn't think she was funny. She couldn't decide which was worse.

Mark stood by the door while Lauren looked in her cabinets for an appropriate fish bowl. She finally settled on a glass mixing bowl she never used. Was the water supposed to be lukewarm or cold? She didn't know. She settled on lukewarm so that the fish wouldn't be chilled, and dumped him into the water. It smelled.

Lauren had won her other fish at the Pumpkin Festival when she was seven, and named her Rudy, after Rudy Huxtable from *The Cosby Show.* Her parents were annoyed. "You won a fish?" they asked when she came home. They rolled their eyes and warned her that it would probably die soon. They dug up an old fishbowl from the basement and bought fish food. "Don't get too attached," they told her. But little Rudy raged on. She swam fiercely year after year. When they finally found Rudy floating belly-up at the top of the bowl, the whole family was shocked. It was as though they'd expected her to live forever; as though they'd forgotten that her dying was even a possibility.

Lauren watched the new fish swim around. He looked weak. Not like Rudy at all. "I guess I'll need to stop and get fish food," she said.

"Just give it some bread crumbs," Mark said. He sounded like he wasn't the one who'd brought her the fish in the first place.

"I'm not sure that fish can eat bread," Lauren said. Mark just shrugged.

"What are you going to name him?" he asked.

Lauren considered this. Should she name the fish Rudy as a good-luck gesture? Maybe it would help strengthen the little guy.

"Willard," she finally said. "After Willard from *Footloose.*"

"Where?"

"*Footloose.* The movie?"

"Never heard of it," Mark said. He looked at his watch and then back at Lauren.

"Well then, we'll have to watch it," Lauren said. "It's amazing."

"You ready?" Mark asked. Lauren nodded and put her coat on.

"Good night, Willard," she said to the bowl. She left the light on in the kitchen so that he wouldn't be disoriented.

Mark was odd. Lauren knew that. She knew from the time that he approached her in the deli that he was not normal. He interrupted her while she was putting Equal in her coffee. "Hello," he said, and she jumped in mid-stir.

"Hi," she said. She was running late to meet a client and didn't have time for pleasantries with a stranger.

"I've seen you here before," he said. "Every morning around this time, I see you here getting your coffee and sometimes a bagel."

Lauren stared at him. She had never noticed him before. "Really?" she asked. It didn't occur to her until later that she should be nervous.

"Here's my card," he said. "Call me. I'd like to take you out."

Lauren took the card, but didn't look down at it. "Okay."

"I look forward to hearing from you," he said. Then he turned and walked out.

Lauren thought that was sort of cocky. He was very handsome. She could give him that. But still, people didn't just approach other people in the middle of their morning coffee to ask them out. Did they? No, they did not.

Lauren thought about him all during her appointments that day. She was escorting a young Kansas City couple around. They were relocating to the city and wanted to find a place immediately. The wife had blond hair and wore a pastel minidress. She complained about every place they saw.

"I don't know," she kept saying. "It's so small. It's just so small."

"This is pretty standard for a one-bedroom in New York," Lauren said. The wife glared at her.

"We want to have children soon. Babies," the wife said. Lauren nodded.

"Right. Well, a lot of people in this building put up a wall for a second bedroom. It's a pretty nice size, so you wouldn't feel so tight for space."

The wife looked at Lauren's hand. "Are you married?" she asked.

Lauren shook her head. She reminded herself to be nice so that she wouldn't lose a good commission. This couple had to move soon. They were against renting. They were a guarantee buy.

"I'm not married," Lauren said. "But one of my best friends lives in a building very similar to this one, and they put up a wall to make a bedroom for their little boy. It might be hard to imagine what it would look like, but if you picture it over there you might get a better idea."

"I think that would work nicely," the husband said. "Don't you?" He put his arm around his wife and squeezed her shoulder. He had been chipper all day. He felt guilty for making them move and was trying to make it up to his miserable pastel wife.

"If you want to see some bigger places, we could look in Brooklyn or maybe Hoboken," Lauren offered.

The wife shook her head. "No," she said. "We want to be in Manhattan. We told you that. Didn't you listen?" She walked away and stood facing the wall with her arms crossed. Her husband gave Lauren a little smile and went to stand next to his wife. Lauren waited quietly while the couple stared at their imaginary baby's imaginary room. Sometimes, she knew, people just needed a little time to be able to picture themselves in a new place, to see possibility in a blank space. And so she waited.

Lauren called Mark that night. She didn't even mean to. Not really. She was eating take-out sushi and saw his card in her purse. She dialed before she could really think about it.

"Hi," she said when he answered. "Mark?"

"Yes," he said.

"It's . . . hi, it's Lauren? From the deli?" She realized after she introduced herself that she had never told him her name.

"Hi, Lauren." He sounded not one bit surprised. He sounded like he'd been waiting for her call.

"So," she said. "So, I decided to give you a call."

"So you did." He was silent and Lauren waited. She decided not to say one more word and just when she was about to give in, he asked her to dinner.

"Sure," she said. "That would be fun."

"It's nice," Mark said on their third date, "that you eat." Lauren had just ordered steak. His comment made Lauren sure that he had only dated anorexic girls in the past, thin, waify people who only ordered salad. The whole idea made her tired.

They went back to his apartment that night. It was clean. No, not clean. It was OCD. There was almost nothing on the shelves. No magazines lying around the coffee table. No pictures or knickknacks. Nothing. It looked like an apartment after she'd staged it to be sold, wiped clean of all traces that a human lived there.

"It's nice," she said.

"I know," Mark said.

His bed was low to the ground, with a plain, dark blue cover. He stood in the bedroom and started taking off his shirt, unself-consciously, as though they had been together for years. He hung it up in his closet and then took off his pants. Lauren stood there, trying not to watch but also trying not to have it be obvious that she wasn't watching.

"Do you need a shirt to sleep in, or are you okay in your underwear?"

"A shirt would be nice," Lauren said. Who the hell was this guy? He went over to his drawer and took out a perfectly folded T-shirt that said "Colgate" on it.

"Did you go to Colgate?" she asked.

"No, I went to Princeton."

"Right."

Lauren went into the bathroom to change, and for the first time that night got very nervous. She didn't know this guy at all. She had never met any of his friends, had no idea if he was telling the truth about where he worked, or even what his name was. Lauren had just watched *American Psycho* on TV the other night, which was a mistake. She was short of breath. Had she even agreed to stay over? All he'd said was "Do you want to come back to my place?" This was pretty presumptuous of him, wasn't it?

She took her phone out of her purse and sent Isabella a text message that she was at Mark's apartment, and then she sent the address. At least someone would know where she was. Although, if she was dead, it wouldn't help much, would it?

When she got out of the bathroom, Mark was sitting up in bed reading a thick book. "You are crazy," Lauren told herself. "You are nuts. You have just been single for too long." Lauren imagined that with each year she lived alone, she would get crazier and crazier. She would be stuck in her weird way of living and would never be able to meld together with someone.

Mark smiled at her when she came out of the bathroom, and waited for her to climb into bed before he turned off the light. She felt his lips on her neck, and then he positioned himself over her while he softly sucked on her clavicle. No, she decided. He is not a killer.

Lauren waited for Mark to get less weird, but it didn't happen. He changed his pillowcases every other night and left porn magazines in plain view in his bathroom. He had certain ties that he wore only to meetings, and he wouldn't let Lauren sit on his bed when she was wearing clothes she had worn outside. But hands down, the weirdest thing about Mark was this: His favorite food was macaroni and cheese.

He didn't like the fancy kind of macaroni and cheese that was retro-trendy and served in pricey restaurants, with Gruyère and lobster. He didn't even like the homemade kind that was gooey and comforting. No, Mark favored the fluorescent noodles that were created from powder, milk, and butter—the kind that came in a box for $1.79.

At least once a week, Mark made a box of macaroni and sat down in front of the TV to shovel it into his mouth. He didn't share. He ate straight from the pot. He ate the whole thing.

If he were a different person, maybe this wouldn't have been so shocking. But he wasn't. He was Mark. He wore suits that Lauren was pretty sure cost more than the rent for her apartment. He sent back bottles of wine at restaurants after he'd tasted them and declared them "off." She'd never met his family, but she was sure that they would be horrified to learn what Mark did with his macaroni. Could she date someone who attacked pasta like this? She watched him closely each time he did it, sure that she was witnessing something deeply personal and telling. It was like watching him masturbate, but Lauren couldn't turn away. It was fascinating, disgusting, and delightful all at once.

ℬ

"Do you like him?" her friend Mary asked after their seventh date. Lauren shrugged. She didn't feel like talking about whether or not she liked a boy with her friends. It made her feel like a child they were all entertaining.

When they were younger, Lauren and her friends talked about boys constantly. They told each other every detail and dissected each sentence. But as the years went by and they moved into separate apartments, it changed. These weren't just random boys they were going to date and then break up with. These were boys they might end up marrying. And so, they stopped sharing so many details without even realizing it. Well, most of them did. Their friend Annie was slow to catch on, got drunk on red wine, and told all of them that her boyfriend Mitchell had a tiny penis. At their wedding, it was all Lauren could think about.

Lauren wanted to tell Mary about the macaroni and cheese, and how when Mark had met her one-year-old niece, Lily, he had taken her hand without smiling and said, "Hello. Hello, Lily." She wanted to ask Mary if it was bizarre to like a guy who'd brought you a fish. She wanted Mary to help her decide if Mark was a sociopath or just a little strange.

Mary looked at her expectantly, rubbing her stomach and groaning at fake contractions. Her little boy, Henry, bopped around the room, and Lauren knew she couldn't do it. It was too odd to sit there and tell Mary these things, too strange to talk about Mark bringing her a fish, while Mary toddled after her toddler. So Lauren just said, "Yeah, I do. I do like him." It was the truth, she thought. Just not all of it.

☙

The day that Rudy died, Lauren went to feed her before school and found her belly-up and completely white. She let out a little scream and her parents came running. Her dad looked shocked, and her mom looked as though she had opened a Tupperware full of mold.

"We'll have to flush him," her dad said.

"Rudy's a she," Lauren said.

"Of course she is." Her dad put a hand on her shoulder.

Her mom had left them to it, let them carry the bowl to the upstairs bathroom and dump Rudy in the toilet. Her dad had started to carry the bowl to the downstairs bathroom, but her mom yelled at him, "That's the guest bathroom." She said it like he was crazy, like everyone knew you weren't supposed to flush fish in guest bathrooms. She shook her head and said, "Take him upstairs."

"Do you want to do it?" her dad asked, and Lauren shook her head. He looked relieved and pressed the flusher. They stood next to each other and watched little Rudy go round and round.

Lauren didn't cry during the flushing, and she was embarrassed when her dad hugged her good-bye. But that day in school, during a spelling test, tears began to fall out of her eyes. She was mortified. You didn't cry in sixth grade. Lauren especially didn't cry in sixth grade. She was tough. But as the teacher read the words "Submarine, crystallized, immigrant," Lauren's tears dropped onto the page and made a mess of her test. She felt awful that Rudy had died. She couldn't even remember if she had checked on her the night before or not. What if Rudy had been dying all night? The tears came faster, sliding in one motion down her cheeks and falling with a plop on her paper. Finally she raised her hand and didn't wait for her teacher to say anything before getting up and going to the bathroom, where she locked herself in a stall and cried until her friend Lizbeth was sent to check on her.

She told the whole class that she'd had an allergic reaction to the kind of cereal she'd eaten for breakfast that morning. It was a reaction, she said, that gave her a sudden pain so bad that she cried. When Tina Bloom suggested that Lauren's story was a lie, because her dad was an allergist and she'd never heard of such a thing, Lauren told her she was stupid and, above all, mean for not having more sympathy, and none of the girls in the class talked to Tina for a week.

On their tenth date, Mark told Lauren he never wanted to live with someone else.

"Never?" Lauren asked.

"Never," he said. He didn't sound sorry about it. Lauren wasn't sure that she ever wanted to live with anyone else either, but it wasn't the kind of thing you said aloud. It was something that you kept to yourself, knowing that if you ever found yourself seriously dating someone or getting married, that you would just do it. Because that's what people did.

"So, what's your plan?" Lauren asked.

"My plan for what?"

"I mean, let's say you meet someone one day and get married. Separate residences?"

"Maybe," Mark said. "One uptown and one downtown? Or maybe just two separate apartments that join together somehow?" He was lost in thought and Lauren was horrified for him.

It was like on their fifth date, when he'd tied a windbreaker around his waist and had no idea that he should be embarrassed as they walked around the Central Park Zoo.

"Maybe you'll change your mind someday," Lauren said finally. She wanted him to stop thinking about it.

"Maybe," Mark said. "But I doubt it. I don't like other people touching my stuff."

&

Lauren met the Kansas City couple on their closing day. The wife was wearing a plaid dress and a headband. "Congratulations!" Lauren said. "You're going to love New York."

The couple walked around the empty apartment and Lauren recommended a cleaning service they could use if they wanted to get it scrubbed down before they moved their furniture in. She found the wife standing in front of the new wall that had been put up to make the second bedroom.

"Is everything okay?" Lauren asked.

The wife smiled at her. "I just never pictured myself here, you know?"

"Yes," Lauren said. "I know how that goes."

&

On their fourteenth date, Lauren brought Mark over to Mary's apartment for dinner. Mary and Isabella had been hounding her. "It's really weird that we haven't met him yet," they'd kept telling her. "Fine," she'd said. "Fine, we'll come to dinner."

Henry took an immediate liking to Mark. Henry always chose the person who paid him the least attention and then spent the night trying to win him over. This worried Mary. She was sure he was going to end up in some sort of abusive relationship. "It's just so odd," she always said. "It's like he can sense who doesn't like children and then he won't leave them alone."

This night was no different. Henry sat on the floor at Mark's shoes and played with his shoelaces. Every once in a while, he patted Mark's leg affectionately. Mary gave Lauren a look like she was sorry, and Isabella laughed and tried to distract Henry. "No!" Henry yelled at Isabella. "Go away." He grabbed tight fistfuls of Mark's pants and held on to them for dear life.

"So, he hates babies," Lauren thought. She had kind of suspected it, but now Henry confirmed it. She watched Henry climb onto Mark's lap and rest his head on his chest. "Mark," he said in a perfectly clear voice. He'd never been able to say Lauren's name right. He called her "Peg" for reasons that no one could figure out.

"I think the little guy might need a diaper change," Mark said at one point. When Mary came to take Henry away, he screamed like she was a stranger ripping him out of the arms of his parents.

"I'm really sorry about this," Mary said to Mark.

"Not a problem." Mark brushed the legs of his pants where Henry had been sitting.

"I just don't know what has gotten into him," Mary said as Henry kicked and cried. She locked eyes with Lauren. *Your boyfriend hates babies,* her face seemed to say. "So what?" Lauren thought. She wasn't so fond of them herself. But she didn't actually hate them. You weren't supposed to hate them, were you? Even if you didn't know if you wanted them, you were supposed to like them a little bit. Lauren had never thought she would date a baby lover, but she'd certainly never thought she would date a baby hater. She searched Mark's face for a sign that he was baby neutral, but she couldn't decipher anything.

ℬ

The day that Lauren's sister had her baby, Lauren drove to Boston to see it in the hospital. She hadn't been planning on it, but as the due date neared it was clear that it was expected of her. She was tired and a little hungover as she entered the hospital room. Her mom and Betsy's mother-in-law were hovering over the bed, holding the baby like they were going to steal it. When Lauren walked in, they excused themselves to get some coffee.

Before Lauren could even say, "The baby is cute," Betsy started talking.

"I ripped," she said.

"Excuse me?" Lauren said.

"I ripped during the birth. The doctor I had doesn't like to do episiotomies anymore, and he didn't do one."

"Epeeze-whats?"

Her sister sighed. "Episiotomies. You know, where they cut the vagina to make it easier to give birth."

"No," Lauren said. "I did not know." She sat down, suddenly feeling light-headed.

"Well, the birth took forever and the numbness started to wear off down there and I could feel the tearing, and I said, 'We should do something,' but no one would listen."

"Mmm-hmm," Lauren said. She wondered if her sister was still drugged up. She must be, Lauren thought, otherwise she would never be discussing such things. Her sister was so embarrassed of everything that once, when they were teenagers, and Lauren asked her if she could borrow a tampon, Betsy turned bright red and called Lauren a pervert.

"They had to stitch me up, which I felt all of," her sister went on. "I bet it's a mess down there. I can't even imagine. And now we have to be careful of infection."

Lauren looked at her niece, who was red and sort of busted-looking. Her head was pointy and she looked like she had some pretty bad acne.

"It will go back to its normal shape," her sister said.

"Excuse me?"

"Her head. It's just in a cone because it took her so long to make it out of the vaginal passage."

"Right," Lauren said.

"Listen, Lauren, can you do something for me?"

"What?"

"Can you take a look down there and tell me what it looks like? I'm imagining Freddy Krueger's face right now, and it would really help if you could tell me that it's not that bad."

"You want me to look at your stitched-up vagina and describe it to you?"

"Don't make it sound gross," her sister said. "Come on."

Lauren pressed her lips together. She and Betsy had shared a room for fifteen years, and every single night, Betsy had turned to the wall when she changed into her pajamas. Lauren used to wonder if Betsy would ever let a boy see her naked. She'd honestly been surprised when Betsy had announced that she was pregnant.

"Please, Lauren? Please? Before Mom and Mrs. King get

back? Please? I don't want to ask Jerry to do it. It's too humiliating."

Betsy started to cry a little bit, her nose running and dripping down to her mouth. It made Lauren want to vomit.

"Oh my God, fine," Lauren said. "Let's just do this."

Months afterward, when Lauren's niece had turned cute and roundheaded, and Betsy had gone back to her prudish ways, Lauren teased Betsy about this moment.

"My vagina feels dry today," she would say out of nowhere.

"You're disgusting," Betsy would say.

"Oh, I'm sorry. Are we not allowed to talk about our vagina's moods? I was under the impression that this was a safe space," she said, gesturing to the car. Lily babbled in the backseat.

"You know what, Lauren? Don't be a bitch. I had just gone through thirty hours of labor and they should have done a C-section and they didn't, and I hadn't been alone with anyone I could talk to about it."

"It's fine," Lauren said. "I'm totally cool with it."

Once when they were walking down the street and saw a dead pinkish slug on the ground, Lauren hit Betsy on the arm and pointed to it. "Look at that. Did that fall out of your vagina?"

Betsy narrowed her eyes. "I hope when you have a baby, your vagina tears into a million pieces," she said.

"Well, thanks to you, dear sister, I'm not sure I will ever have a baby."

"Oh, you will." Betsy laughed like she knew something. "Believe me, you will."

Lauren was scared by Betsy's knowing voice. Betsy was two

years older and Lauren sometimes had to remind herself that Betsy didn't know everything. Still, it scared her to think that labor had turned Betsy into a person who talked out loud about her vagina ripping. If that's what it did to Betsy, what would it do to her? For a while, she stopped teasing Betsy about it. If karma existed, then it wasn't a good idea, Lauren decided. Then, last Thanksgiving, when the turkey was all done and stuffed, little dried cranberries and hunks of corn-bread stuffing falling out of the open cavity, Lauren put her arm around her sister and motioned to the turkey.

"You know what that reminds me of?" she asked.

"Go to hell," Betsy said, and Lauren laughed and laughed. Karma be damned.

On their twenty-seventh date, Mark made macaroni and cheese at Lauren's apartment. They had planned to order Chinese food, but Lauren had had a late lunch and wasn't hungry, so Mark decided to make a box of Kraft. They sat on the couch and watched sitcoms, and he ate the neon orange noodles as he always did, in huge, heaping spoonfuls. He ate the whole pot and then leaned back and rubbed his stomach. He let out a giant belch and then a happy sigh.

"Lovely," Lauren said. He smiled.

The two of them sat and watched TV in silence. Then they got into bed and read. In the quiet, Lauren thought about her pastel client from Kansas City staring at the empty place where the baby's wall would go. She looked over at Mark.

"That's the first time you've ever eaten macaroni and cheese at my apartment," she said.

Mark put his finger in the magazine to keep his place and moved his eyebrows together. "Huh," he said. "I guess it is." Then they both went back to reading.

⁊⊃

Willard died on a cold November morning. Lauren found him tilted to the side. He was turning white and only one fin was paddling. She was sure he'd had a stroke. She sat in the kitchen with him for a while, and then (believing it to be the humane thing) she took him to the bathroom and flushed him. She did it quickly.

Lauren washed out the bowl, then threw it out. She should have gotten him a real fishbowl. He'd deserved that much. The kitchen looked empty without him there, and Lauren felt alone in her apartment. "This is so stupid," she said aloud. "It was just a fish." Then she laid her head on her arms and cried.

⁊⊃

"The fish died," Lauren said, "which can't be a good sign."

"Well," Isabella said, "fish die a lot. I think we had, like, four hundred different goldfish at my house growing up. A couple of them committed suicide by jumping out of the bowl."

"What's that supposed to mean?" Lauren asked.

"I'm just saying, it could have been worse."

"I don't know," Lauren said. "It just feels like a bad omen."

⁊⊃

They were out to breakfast, eating blueberry pancakes on their forty-ninth date, when Mark said, "I would like to hire you."

"Hire me?" Lauren asked. "You know, I'm already doing it for free. If you started paying me now, it would change the nature of our relationship."

Mark smiled just a little. "I would like to hire you as a Realtor. I want to buy a new place."

"Oh," Lauren said. "Okay."

᠀

Lauren had shown Mark only three apartments before he found one he liked. He went to see it seven times. On the eighth visit, Lauren didn't even bother talking about it. They just stood and stared at the bedrooms. Finally, Mark said, "I think I'm going to buy it. I like it here."

"Me too. Let's look at the closets one more time."

Mark nodded and went over to the front hall closet. He bent forward so that half of his body was inside. "I think you should live here," he said. His voice was muffled.

"It smells like liver?" Lauren asked. She didn't even know what liver would smell like.

"No," Mark said straightening up. "I think you should live. Here."

"Oh," Lauren said. "That might be a good idea."

"There's enough closet space."

"Definitely." And the two of them stood and looked at all of the space in the empty liver closet.

᠀

The day they moved into the apartment, Mark brought Lauren a turtle. "Here," he said, like he had just found it in the hall. "A turtle to replace the fish."

Lauren took the plastic container and looked at the little turtle. She had always wanted one.

"I'll have to go to the pet store," Lauren said. "I don't even know what a turtle needs."

"What are you going to name it?" Mark asked.

"I'm not sure," Lauren said. She put the box on the table and they stared at it. "Maybe Rudy?" she said. She considered it. It was definitely a possibility. A possibility now, where it hadn't been before.

Until the Worm Turns

Isabella," her mom said. "There's no need to be so down. Things seem bad, and they will until the worm turns. And then, you will look back on this time and laugh."

"Until the what?" Isabella asked. "Until what turns?"

"The worm," her mom said. "It's an expression." She sounded tired of Isabella. Isabella didn't blame her. She was tired of herself.

"Okay, Mom. I should go. I need to update my résumé." This was sort of a lie and sort of not. Isabella did need to update her résumé. But she wasn't going to do it when she got off the phone. She just needed to stop talking to her mother. They said good-bye and hung up. Isabella sat in the apartment and stared at the dog. Should she go to the gym? It was two-thirty p.m. on a Tuesday. Did people go to the gym at that time? The dog stared back at Isabella. He seemed to know she was lying about her résumé.

"What?" Isabella asked him. He sighed and lay down on the floor.

ॐ

"Sometimes," Mary said, "when people get fired, they end up getting amazing new jobs. It forces people to get out there and find what they want to do."

"But I already found what I want to do," Isabella said. "And it just so happens that I picked a failing industry. I'm never going to get another job like I had. They won't even exist anymore."

"Yeah," Mary said. "I guess that's true." She shifted on the couch, leaning back and then swaying from side to side.

"Are you all right?" Isabella asked.

"Yeah," Mary said. "It's just if I don't have this freaking baby soon, I'm going to rip open my stomach."

"Oh," Isabella said. "Well, if that's all."

ॐ

"Maybe you should take a shower," Harrison suggested after he touched the top of her head. She had been in bed for three days. "It's kind of starting to smell in here."

"That's so mean," she said. "That is so mean, Harrison."

"I know." He hugged her, and when she reached up to wipe her tears away, she touched her greasy hair. It felt like wax. A shower, she decided, wasn't such a bad idea.

"Okay," she said. "I'll take a shower." She went and stood

underneath the hot water with her arms crossed over her chest and her eyes closed. She stood there until there was so much steam in the bathroom that she couldn't see. Afterward, she put on clean sweatpants and brushed her newly washed hair.

"Don't you feel better?" Harrison asked.

"Yes," Isabella said. "I do." And she did. But she still slept for most of the day. She just hid it from Harrison better than she had before. When his alarm clock went off, she got up and poured herself a cup of coffee and then sat on the couch and watched the *Today* show. After he kissed her good-bye, she would wait a few minutes before putting the chain lock on the door and getting back into bed. Around five-thirty, she would get up and wash her face and put on clothes. She'd sit in front of her laptop on the couch until he got home.

"Just job searching," she would say when he got home.

Cos

"You look queer," Isabella said to Harrison when he walked in the door. She had never used that word to describe anyone before, but when she saw him that night, it was the only word that was right. "You look queer," she said again.

Harrison looked at her out of the sides of his eyes and went to get a beer from the fridge. He opened it and leaned his hands against the counter but still didn't speak. Isabella began to get scared. He was going to leave her. Or tell her that he was having an affair. Or that he had a baby. He took a sip of his beer and then said, "They're downsizing my division."

It took Isabella a moment to realize that he was talking about his job. She had been so ready to hear that he had a secret baby that she was almost relieved. Then she realized what he'd said.

"Wait. Are you being downsized? You, yourself?"

Harrison shrugged. "They aren't really saying. They're being really shady about the whole thing. But my boss did pull me into his office to tell me that there are opportunities for me in the Boston office."

"What does that mean?"

"It sounded like he was telling me that I could work there or be fired."

"In Boston?"

"In Boston."

They were both quiet for a couple of minutes. Isabella wasn't sure where the conversation was going to go next. They weren't married. It wasn't automatic that she had to go with him wherever he went. In fact, it was the opposite of automatic, whatever that was.

"So, are you thinking about it?" she asked.

"I guess so. I'm not sure I have a choice."

"Right," Isabella said. "I guess you don't." Isabella started to cry and Harrison watched her.

∂

"Do you want to go with me?" Harrison asked. It was later, almost the middle of the night. Neither of them was sleeping.

"Go with you where?" Isabella asked.

"Isabella. To Boston."

"Oh," Isabella said. "I don't know. Do you want me to go with you?"

"Yeah, I do. I know it might be unfair to ask, but I do want you to come."

"Okay," Isabella said.

"Okay, you'll go?" Harrison asked.

"No. Just okay."

"What does that mean?"

"I'm not sure. What if you just stayed?"

"I can't," Harrison said.

"Well, you could," Isabella said. "You could do anything you wanted to."

"I'm not going to, though," Harrison said. And then they both lay there until it was morning.

ᛒ

"Isabella," her mom said. "The important thing to do is to stay calm and make a rational decision."

"You say that like it's easy," Isabella said.

"I'm just saying that it's no help to wallow in your misery. People have ups and downs, but I'm telling you, when the worm turns, you will be stronger for having gone through this."

"You know," Isabella said, "I've never heard you use that expression before in my life until the last couple of weeks. Not ever."

"Of course you have. Now you're just being ridiculous."

"You're the one who keeps talking about worms."

ᛒ

"The baby is really cute," Isabella said to Mary at the hospital. "Any closer to a name?"

"No," Mary said. She squinted at the baby. "I really thought I would go with Ava, but look at her. She's too big to be an Ava, don't you think?"

"Um, I think whatever you think," Isabella said.

"What I think, is that I never thought I would have a nine-pound baby, and it's throwing me off. I pictured Ava being a tiny baby, and now it just doesn't fit. If I don't think of a name soon, I think Ken is going to kill me. He still likes Ava."

"Henry and Ava do sound good together," Isabella said. "Also, I think that Harrison is being transferred to Boston."

"No!" Mary said. "I don't believe it." She immediately started crying.

"Mary? Are you okay?" Isabella asked.

"Yeah," Mary said. "It's just the hormones. Start at the beginning."

"Do you want to concentrate on naming the baby before Ken gets back?"

Mary sighed. "That could take days. Why don't you go first?"

☙

"That sucks," Lauren said.

"I know," Isabella said.

"I was wondering why you wanted to meet me in a bar in the afternoon," Lauren said. "Not that I mind."

"It seemed like the only place to be," Isabella said. She took a sip of her grapefruit and vodka. "Plus, this has juice in it, so it's completely appropriate to drink it during the day."

"Totally," Lauren said. "So, do you know what you're going to do?"

"I have no idea." Isabella started crying. "Except apparently, I'm going to cry about it every day."

"Good," Lauren said. "You should cry about it every day. It's a good release. Crying helps you live longer."

"Really?" Isabella asked. "I've never heard that before."

"Well, I sort of made it up. It's a theory that I have. But it makes sense, doesn't it?"

"Maybe," Isabella said.

"Listen, whatever you decide to do will be the right thing," Lauren said.

"How do you know?"

"Because if it wasn't the right thing, then you wouldn't choose to do it."

"That doesn't make any sense," Isabella said.

"Or does it make perfect sense?" Lauren asked.

"Are you drunk?"

"Yeah, I think I am."

"Good," Isabella said. "Me too. Let's order grilled cheese."

ℬ

"Did you think any more about it?" Harrison asked.

"Yeah," Isabella said.

"I really want you to come with me. I don't want to be there alone." He took her hand and waited for her to talk. "Don't you want to be with me?"

"You're the one that's leaving in the first place," Isabella said.

ℬ

"Isabella, I don't think you should move to Boston with Harrison unless you two are engaged," her sister, Molly, said. She'd called Isabella just to tell her this. "Mom thinks it too."

"You know what else Mom thinks?" Isabella asked. "She thinks your haircut was a mistake. I do too. I don't think you should get a lesbian haircut unless you are really ready to make the leap into that lifestyle."

"I'm trying to help you," her sister said.

"I'm really trying to help you too," Isabella said. "Do not cut your hair again. I know it will take years to get it to an acceptable length, but you need to do it. In the meantime, clip a bow in it or something."

ℬ

Mary was trying to tell Isabella a story, but she kept crying. "I'm sorry. I don't know what's wrong with me."

"It's okay," Isabella said.

"This didn't happen with Henry," Mary said. "I think my hormones are permanently damaged. I can't stop crying."

"I'm sure you'll be back to normal soon," Isabella said. "Now, what happened next?"

"Okay." Mary took a deep breath. "So I'm at Target, and I'm trying to return the bottles, and the woman at the counter told me that they had a policy that you could only return three things in a month. And so I couldn't return the baby bottles even though someone gave them to me as a gift and I didn't need them." Mary stopped here to blow her nose.

"Okay," Isabella said. "Okay. Try not to get too upset."

"I know, I know. I just told that bitch that we got duplicate presents and she acted like I was trying to shoplift. She kept saying, 'Ma'am, you need to calm down.' Like it was my fault."

"She sounds awful," Isabella said.

"She really was," Mary said. Her voice wiggled just a little. "Okay, I'm done. Now we need to talk about you and Boston. Do you think you're going to go?"

"I'm not sure yet. What do you think?"

"Sometimes I wish Ken would be transferred to another state," Mary said.

"Really?" Isabella asked. "You want to move?"

"No, not move. But if Ken was transferred to Boston or something and then he traveled all during the week. That would be nice."

"Really?" Isabella said.

"Yeah, I mean, I could have the remote every night and we'd still see each other on the weekends. It would just be nice to have some alone time."

"Well, you'd still have the kids," Isabella said. "You wouldn't really be alone."

"Right. Yeah, I guess it wouldn't work."

"Is everything okay?"

"Yeah, it's fine. Sometimes I'm just tired of having people all around me. Sometimes Ken asks as many questions as Henry. He offered to go to the store yesterday and then he called me three times while he was there. If he doesn't know what kind of American cheese we buy now, will he ever?"

"Probably not," Isabella said.

"No," Mary said. "Probably not. It's exhausting. I'd rather just do it myself. He came home with fat-free American cheese and pepper-smoked turkey. I mean, what is wrong with him?"

"Maybe he just needs practice?" Isabella said.

Mary shook her head. "No. He's had practice. He just doesn't know how to do it. I can already tell in ten years he'll still be calling me from the store to ask if we get pulp-free orange juice or not. He drinks it every morning and he still doesn't know!"

"Was he always like that?" Isabella asked.

"Yeah," Mary said. "He was. I just never really thought about the fact that he was going to be like this for the rest of my life."

"So what are you going to do?" Isabella asked.

"What do you mean?"

"Well, are you happy?" Isabella asked. She didn't know if this was the right thing to ask, or if she was even allowed to.

"Yeah," Mary said. "When I think about it, he might really bug me but I like having him around more than I don't like having him around."

"So if he took a job in Boston?"

"Yeah, I know. I was just talking. I wouldn't really like it, I know. Sometimes it's nice to dream. But I know it's not what I really want. I like the bastard."

"That's good." Isabella let out a breath. She had been worried that Mary was going to tell her she was leaving Ken.

"I guess that's how you decide about Harrison and Boston," Mary said. "If you like him enough not to be away from him."

"Yeah," Isabella said. "I guess so."

"But you know what?" Mary asked.

"What?"

"I'm going to start writing out the most detailed grocery lists ever for Ken. And if he comes home with the wrong stuff, I'm going to send him back out."

"That sounds like a plan," Isabella said.

"It really does."

☙

"Sometimes things in life aren't easy," her mom said. "Sometimes you have to make really hard choices."

"I know," Isabella said. "But some people don't. Some people don't have to make decisions like this at all."

"And some people in this world are starving, Isabella. Life isn't fair."

"I know," Isabella said. "But that seems unfair."

☙

"You can't move," Lauren said. "You're my last babyless friend. If you go, I'm going to have to start going to Mommy and Me just to see people."

"I don't think you would like that class," Isabella said.

"Yeah," Lauren said. "Not to mention it might raise red flags if I go without a baby."

"Probably."

"So, you're really going?"

"Yeah," Isabella said. "I guess I am."

"I feel like that's a really adult decision to make," Lauren said.

"Really?" Isabella said. "Because I feel like I'm fourteen."

"Join the club."

᪥

"What about the second apartment we saw?" Harrison asked. "The one that was in the Cleveland Circle area. It had the really big closets."

"I'm not sure I really liked that one," Isabella said.

"Why?"

"It's in Boston."

"Right," Harrison said. "I forgot about that."

᪥

"I think you need to network more," Harrison told her. She still didn't have a job in Boston. It didn't bother her that much. If she didn't have a job, she could pretend that she wasn't really moving there.

"I think *you* need to network more," Isabella said. Harrison sighed.

"I'm serious, Isabella. It's not a good time to get a job. You really need to get out there and pound the pavement."

"Pound the pavement? Could you sound more like my seventy-year-old father if you tried?"

"I'm just trying to help."

"Well, you aren't."

"It seems like you don't really want to find a job," Harrison said.

"What are you worried about? That I'm not going to be able to pay rent? Calm down, I got it covered."

"It's not that," Harrison said.

"Then what? What?"

"Nothing," Harrison said. "Forget it."

"I'm not going to forget it. You know, I'm only moving there because of you."

"I know," Harrison said. He walked out of the room and left Isabella lying on the bed. Two hours later he came back. "I'm sorry," he said.

"Good," Isabella said.

"I don't care if you have a job or not," Harrison said. "I just want you to be happy and find something there that you like."

"I know," Isabella said. "I know."

"Are you sure you want to go?"

"Yeah," Isabella said. "I'm sure."

"How do you know?"

"Because I'd rather have you here than not here," Isabella said.

"That sounds pretty simple," Harrison said.

"I think it is."

"The only pill in the pot," her mom said, "is that you've never driven a U-Haul before."

"The pill in the pot?" Isabella asked.

"Isabella," her mom said. "Don't be difficult."

"Well, anyway, I'm not driving it. Harrison's going to. He's the pill in the pot."

"No," her mom said. "I meant that the rest of your moving plan sounds good, but that the drive will be difficult."

"Maybe the worm should take the pill," Isabella said. "Then there won't be a pill in the pot."

Her mom sighed. "Isabella, I think you're the pill in the pot."

ॐ

"People on the subway that stand too close," Harrison said. "Put it on the list." He threw the boxes on the floor and the dog jumped.

Isabella got up and went to the refrigerator, where they had hung a running list of things that they hated about New York. It was supposed to make them feel better about leaving. So far, they had rats, cockroaches, huge puddles that you have to leap over, people walking with umbrellas that hit you, Duane Reade pharmacy workers, and now people on the subway that stand too close.

"Oh, and how about people on the subway that let their leg rest against yours and then when you move over, they move closer?" Isabella asked.

"Isn't that the same thing?" Harrison asked.

"No way," Isabella said. Harrison nodded.

"Put it on the list," he said.

ॐ

"I can really have your couch?" Lauren asked. She was holding Mary's new baby. She and Isabella had been passing her back and forth all night and drinking wine. Mary just sat on the couch and watched. She didn't even seem worried that every time they passed her to one another, they said, "Don't drop her."

"Yeah," Isabella said. "You can have it. I don't think it will look right in the new apartment."

"Why didn't you offer me the couch?" Mary asked.

"You have a baby," Lauren said. "You don't need a couch."

"Yeah," Isabella said. "That's why."

☙

"Why is there so much crap in this apartment?" Isabella asked. "Do we never throw anything away?"

Every drawer they opened was full of garbage. Every shelf was crammed full of clothes they never wore.

"We're pigs," Isabella said. "We are pig people." She held up an old sweater of Harrison's that had a neon sort of print on it. "Harrison?" she asked. "What is this?"

Harrison shrugged. "A sweater."

"Yes," Isabella said. "I realize that. But why do you have one of Bill Cosby's sweaters?" Harrison grabbed it away from her and put it in a garbage bag of give-away clothes.

"It's old," he said.

"Please put it on," Isabella said. Harrison sighed and took it out of the bag and pulled it over his head. He was very willing to appease her these days. It was cropped and boxy, with a pattern that resembled a lightning bolt. Isabella bent over laughing until her knees buckled and she sat right down on the floor.

"Oh, you like that?" Harrison asked. He took it off and started swinging it at her. She gasped for air. "Don't mess with the sweater, Isabella!" He swung it around and around, hitting her on her butt while she laughed.

"You know what?" Harrison said. "Just for that, I'm keeping it." He folded it and put it on top of a pile on the couch. Isabella lay on her back and wiped her eyes.

"No," she said. "Don't punish yourself just to get back at me."

"Punish myself?" he asked. "I'm only going to wear it when we're together. And then I'm going to hold your hand, so everyone knows we are a couple."

"That should help us make a lot of new friends in Boston."

"That's my plan," Harrison said.

ॐ

"I'm worried that Winston isn't going to adjust well to the move," Isabella said. When she said his name, the dog tilted his head and looked at her.

"I'm sure he'll be fine," Harrison said. "You worry too much about that dog."

"He has his friends at the dog park here, and he's comfortable here. He might hate Boston."

"Do you think you're projecting just a little bit?" Harrison asked.

"No," Isabella said. "That's the stupidest thing I've ever heard."

ॐ

"Why do you still have this?" Mary asked. She held an unopened bottle of tequila that Isabella had gotten in Mexico during spring break of their junior year.

"I just never threw it out," Isabella said. "I kept moving it from place to place, but it seems ridiculous to bring it to Boston."

"Your apartment is really depressing with all of the stuff gone," Lauren said, looking around. "I can't believe you guys are sleeping on air mattresses tonight."

"Me neither," Isabella said. They all sat in a circle on the floor of the empty apartment, with the bottle of tequila in the middle of them.

Mary looked closely at the bottle. "Do you think the worm is fake? Wouldn't it have decomposed by now?"

"Alcohol keeps things fresh," Lauren said.

"Is that why you're still so young-looking?" Isabella asked her. Lauren swatted her butt and Isabella shrieked and scooted forward. "Come on, you guys," she said. "I think we should drink it. I'm not packing it. It will be fun."

"I'm pretty sure if we drink that, we'll die," Mary said.

"Oh my God. Is that your plan? Do you want to kill us all so that you don't have to move to Boston?" Lauren asked.

"You clever little bitch," Mary said. "It will look like a mass suicide."

"You two are complete freaks," Isabella said. "You know that?"

"Look who's talking," Lauren said.

"Here," said Isabella. "I saved some random shot glasses just for the tequila. Come on, you guys, I'm moving tomorrow. Let's just drink a little of it. Here, I'll put the phone right here so that we can call 911 if it's poison."

"Fine, fine," Lauren said. "Let's do this."

They took the first shot, and Mary held the empty glass and sniffed it. "Can you imagine," she said, "if my children had to go motherless because I died of bad tequila?"

"I think what would be more disturbing is if Ava found out

that you named her Gertrude for three days before changing it," Lauren said.

"She didn't look like an Ava until we got her home," Mary said. "I told you that."

"Right," Isabella said. "Little Gertie will totally understand that."

"Let's do another shot to little Gertie," Lauren said. She poured more of the tequila into the glasses.

"Fine," Mary said. "But stop calling her Gertie. It really freaks me out that I named her that."

Lauren picked up the bottle and swirled it around so that the worm swam in the tequila. "You know," she said, "this was really my bottle of tequila."

"I know," Isabella said. "I remember."

Their third night in Mexico, the three of them had fallen asleep on the beach and woke up with uneven streaks of sunburn and sand in their mouths. For two days, Mary lay on the hotel bed, moaning and covered in aloe. Isabella stayed with her, burned and nauseous, refusing to go out until her streaks had faded just a little bit. Lauren's burn turned quickly to a tan, and she resumed her spring break the next night, winning a bikini contest at the hotel bar. She came into the room that night wearing several strands of beads and carrying the tequila with the worm on the bottom.

"Look what I won!" she yelled and jumped up and down on the bed until Isabella threw up. Lauren apologized and gave her the tequila to make up for it.

"I can't believe you entered a bikini contest," Mary said from her spot on the bed. Her face was covered with a wet washcloth and her skin was tinted green from the aloe.

Lauren stood up and put her hands on her hips. "I'm an adult," she said. "I can do whatever I want. I'm a grown woman."

Slowly, Mary removed the washcloth from her face and whipped it at Lauren. "You are the drunkest grown woman I've ever seen," she said.

For years, whenever one of them went on a rant about anything, one of the others would say, "You tell them. You are a grown woman!"

Isabella poured three more shots. "To grown women," she said, holding up her glass. She realized that it wasn't as funny anymore. Maybe it didn't always seem true, but they were no longer sunburned in Mexico. Somehow, in the past ten years they'd gotten from there to here.

They all took the shot. Mary stretched out her legs in front of her, and Lauren leaned back on her palms. "I think that Mark and I might get married," Lauren said. "We were talking about it the other day. We might go down to city hall and just do it."

"Are you pregnant?" Isabella asked her.

"Yes, Isabella. I'm pregnant. I'm pregnant, and so I decided to come drink a bottle of poisoned tequila with you and announce it."

"What?" Mary asked.

"Oh, for God's sake!" Lauren said. "I'm not pregnant, you morons."

"Oh," Isabella said. She shook the bottle and watched the worm swirl around. "That's good news for baby."

"So you really think you'll get married?" Mary asked. "Are you going to have a wedding or what?"

Lauren shook her head. "No. No wedding. We were just talking about how we like living together and he suggested getting married, and I thought it sounded like a good idea."

"What the hell?" Mary said. She looked at Lauren and then she looked at the bottle. Her eyes were pointing in different directions. "I think the worm just moved." Mary hiccupped and laughed, then gagged.

"Sweet Jesus," Isabella said, looking at the bottle. "You're right. The worm turned."

Acknowledgments

This book is dedicated to my parents, Pat and Jack Close, who deserve a million thanks for their support and encouragement over the last few decades. M&D, you are the best.

I am also forever thankful to:

Kevin Close, for always wanting to read what I wrote and for thinking I'm funny.

Chris and Susan Close, for so many things but especially for giving me Ava Jane Close, the most adorable niece and goddaughter ever.

Carol and Scott Hartz for opening their home to me, offering me legal advice, and most important, for welcoming me into their family.

Sam Hiyate, a wonderful agent and friend, for taking a chance on me and my writing.

Moriah Cleveland, for answering late-night e-mails about story ideas, editing at a moment's notice, and just generally keeping me sane.

Lee Goldberg, one of the first people to see this, who helped shape it early on and gave me reassurance that it was, indeed, a book.

Steve Almond, a teacher that every writer should be lucky enough to have.

Helen Schulman, who always told me to take a deep breath and start over.

Acknowledgments

Margaret Kearney Hoerster, for eighteen years of best friendship.

Mairead McGurrin Garry, Erin Murphy Claydon, and Erin Foley Bradley, for making me laugh all through college, and ever since.

Wrigley, the Yorkie, who sat on my lap as I wrote most of this book. A more loyal writing partner will never be found.

Megan Angelo and Jessica Liebman, who offered early insights and edits for this book and were just as excited as I was every step of the way.

Jon Claydon, for helping me to understand the life of a first-year lawyer.

Jacob Lewis, the best boss ever and a good friend.

Joanne Lipman, for hiring me at *Portfolio,* even though I said I wanted to be a fiction writer.

My friends at Politics and Prose, who taught me more about bookselling than I ever knew there was to know.

Everyone at Knopf who has championed my book and made it better with each step: Sonny Mehta, Chris Gillespie, Pat Johnson, Paul Bogaards, Ruth Liebmann, Julie Kurland, Abby Weintraub, Molly Erman, and Andrea Robinson. I am so lucky that my book found a home with all of you.

My incredible editor, Jenny Jackson, who understood the Girls immediately, got this book into shape, and was able to see what I wanted to do before I even knew. I am so thankful to have you as an editor and friend!

And finally, all my thanks and love to Tim Hartz, who cheered me on and calmed me down in all the right places, listened to me read sentences out loud with a great amount of patience, and always believed. You are truly my favorite.